# THE DEADLY OMENS

BOOK THREE

# THE DEADLY OMENS

## THE UNCOMMONERS

BY JENNIFER BELL

ILLUSTRATED BY
KARL JAMES MOUNTFORD

CROWN BOOKS
FOR YOUNG READERS
NEW YORK

Text copyright © 2018 by Jennifer Rose Bell
Jacket art copyright © 2020 by Kirbi Fagan
Interior illustrations copyright © 2018 by Karl James Mountford

All rights reserved. Published in the United States by Crown Books for Young Readers, an imprint of Random House Children's Books, a division of Penguin Random House LLC, New York. Originally published as *The Frozen Telescope* by Penguin Random House U.K., London, in 2018.

Crown and the colophon are registered trademarks of Penguin Random House LLC.

Visit us on the Web! rhcbooks.com

Educators and librarians, for a variety of teaching tools, visit us at RHTeachersLibrarians.com

*Library of Congress Cataloging-in-Publication Data*
Names: Bell, Jennifer, 1985– author. | Mountford, Karl James, illustrator.
Title: The deadly omens / Jennifer Bell; illustrated by Karl James Mountford.
Description: First edition. | New York: Crown Books for Young Readers, [2020]
Series: [The Uncommoners; #3] | Summary: "Ivy and her friends travel to Nubrook, the magical trading city under New York to look for Valian's long-lost sister Rosie and put an end to the Dirge once and for all"—Provided by publisher.
Identifiers: LCCN 2019019482 (print) | LCCN 2019021558 (ebook)
ISBN 978-0-553-49851-6 (hardcover) | ISBN 978-0-553-49853-0 (ebook)
Subjects: CYAC: Fantasy. | Magic—Fiction. | Brothers and sisters—Fiction. |
Families—Fiction. | Secrets—Fiction.
Classification: LCC PZ7.1.B452 De 2020 (print) | LCC PZ7.1.B452 (ebook)
DDC [Fic]—dc23

Printed in the United States of America
10 9 8 7 6 5 4 3 2 1
First Edition

Random House Children's Books
supports the First Amendment and celebrates the right to read.

For Peter: with love

# CHAPTER ONE

The new babysitter was a stout woman with a moss-green head scarf, long trench coat and round spectacles.

She was also *dead*.

"You must be Ivy," the babysitter said curtly, dropping her bag on the welcome mat by the front door. The corners of her mouth lifted clumsily, as if she was unaccustomed to smiling. "Your mum and dad have told me all about you. You can call me Curtis."

Ivy took a step back. Although she could sense the races of the dead, she'd never come across one on common land before. "My parents have just left to catch their train. . . . I'll get my brother." She dashed up the stairs two at a time and slammed her hand against his bedroom door. *"Seb!"*

Dressed in a warm hoodie, jeans and sneakers, Seb appeared slouched against the doorframe, scowling at Ivy from under his wavy blond hair. On any ordinary evening he would have answered the door in his pajamas, but at midnight tonight they had planned to sneak away. They were going to Nubrook, an uncommon market hidden under New York City, to help their friend Valian search for his missing sister. "You're interrupting my favorite Ripz video," Seb snapped. "What is it?"

"Our babysitter is *dead*," Ivy told him.

"What?" He straightened. "Are you sure?"

Ivy peered over the banister. Down in the hallway Curtis was hanging up her coat. A brooch in the shape of a forked arrow glittered on the lapel. Curtis might *seem* normal, but Ivy knew the tricky thing about most races of the dead was that you couldn't tell them apart from the living until they did something impossible—like float through a wall or transform into a giant stick bug.

"Positive," she replied. "I can feel it." As a whisperer, Ivy could detect the fragments of human souls trapped inside the dead. She widened her field of sense slowly, just as she'd practiced. The fleeting voice of Curtis's broken soul brushed at the edge of her hearing. "Her name's Curtis. If she's dead, then she must be an uncommoner. What's she doing here?"

A line appeared between Seb's thick brows. "Dad was complaining yesterday that all the local babysitters are fully booked because so many schools are closed for repairs, not just ours. Look—" He grabbed his TV remote and flicked through the channels until he found the one he wanted. A weather map on one half of the screen showed the isobars of a huge storm moving across the English Channel from Paris to London. The reporter was shouting at the camera, his coat flapping madly in the wind.

"*. . . Meteorologists are still struggling to explain Storm Sarah's sudden appearance in Paris three days ago. The category two storm has caused widespread damage and disruption, with school and road closures throughout London and the Southeast. . . .*"

"I *tried* to convince Dad that we could look after ourselves," Seb continued, "and that we wouldn't need a babysitter for the few nights he and Mum are away at the wedding. But then Mum came home announcing she'd had a stroke of luck and had 'bumped into' an available sitter. . . . It must have been Curtis."

Ivy's skin prickled. It couldn't have been a coincidence. She snatched the TV remote and turned up the volume to mask the sound of their voices. "What if Curtis is working for the Dirge? They employ the dead all the time. She could have been planted here to spy on us—or worse." *The Dirge . . .* Ivy wished she didn't have to bring them up, but it was difficult to forget the organization that kept trying to kill them.

Seb stiffened. "I've been checking the uncommon newspapers that Valian sends us; the Dirge have been linked to all kinds of incidents since the spring. Surely they're too busy to bother with us?"

Ivy could tell by the tremor in his voice that he didn't believe that last bit, although he was right about one thing: the nefarious guild's activity *had* been prolific. Their calling card—a crooked sixpence—had been found at multiple scenes of crime around the uncommon world. In the Russian undermart, Mosvok, the Dirge had been connected to several cases of blackmail and kidnapping; in China, to widespread fraud. A series of shop raids in the Egyptian undermart of Cryp bore signs of their handiwork, as did the mysterious disappearances of key officials from Ausmark in Germany. Ivy was astonished that, with so much criminal activity linked to the guild, its six members still managed to keep their identities secret.

"Now that I think about it," Seb said, his pupils flicking, "I suppose Curtis turning up might be connected to a message Valian sent me earlier. He wanted to let us know that we can't use an uncommon bag to travel to Nubrook anymore—he didn't say why—but he's given us new instructions instead."

"He has? Why didn't you tell me before?"

"I couldn't risk it, not with Mum and Dad around. Don't worry; I'm sure it's nothing."

Ivy gritted her teeth. Her brother had a frustrating habit of taking everything at face value. "Seb," she said reproachfully, "Valian's been looking for Rosie on his own for seven years. . . . He's not used to asking for help. Something could have happened—" Ivy got a hollow feeling in the pit of her stomach when she thought of the repeated disappointments Valian had endured in his search for his little sister. She was determined to do everything she could to help him now. "This trip is his best chance yet to find her," she said, "so we've got to be there every step of the way."

Seb's cheeks flushed guiltily. "All right then, let's leave now for Nubrook. I don't fancy sticking around here to learn whether Zombie Poppins is planning to kill us or not." He dragged his prepacked backpack out from under his bed and switched off the TV. Ivy collected her things from her bedroom, stuffing an extra sweater into her satchel. A thick, leather-bound book poked out the top. The front cover was embossed with a symbol: a smoking hourglass. Seb glanced at it warily.

"You're bringing Amos Stirling's journal?" he asked. Ivy understood his concern. The journal was a notebook containing many dangerous secrets about the Great Uncommon Good—the five most powerful uncommon objects in history—and it attracted all kinds of trouble.

"I've only been able to translate a bit of it," she told him. "Amos wrote in languages not even Google understands. He'd discovered all sorts of things about the Great Uncommon Good, and he was trying to prevent the Dirge from getting hold of them. If I leave the book here and Curtis finds it . . ."

". . . the Dirge will learn all Amos's secrets," Seb finished. "I get it." He led her into the bathroom, shutting the door behind them. Ivy closed the blinds at the window.

"Did Valian tell you there was a secret entrance to Nubrook hidden somewhere in *here*?" she asked, thinking of the time she and Seb had entered Lundinor via a shed in a garden. There were many different ways of accessing London's undermart; perhaps entering Nubrook was the same.

"No," Seb replied, "his instructions were weirder than that." He plugged the sink and ran the taps. " 'Wash your hands and find the man in red.' That's what he wrote."

Ivy wondered why Valian had been so obscure. She tapped her satchel. "Scratch, are you listening to this? Do you have any idea what Valian means?"

The bag vibrated against her hip. She unfastened it and pulled out a damaged steel bicycle bell. Like all uncommon objects, the bell felt strangely warm against her skin, as if it had been resting in the sun.

"Finally goings!" exclaimed a childlike voice coming from the bell. "Never journeys to Nubrook has Scratch before." Ivy could hear the fragment of soul whispering inside Scratch—the very thing that made him uncommon. "Hmm. Unsure Valian why wantings hands clean," he added.

Ivy's shoulders slumped. Even with Scratch's back-to-front way of speaking, she understood his meaning.

A door slammed shut downstairs: Curtis was moving around.

With renewed urgency, Ivy steadied Scratch on the edge of the basin, pumped some liquid soap into her palm and lathered it up. Perhaps everything would become clear if she followed Valian's advice exactly. As she rinsed her hands she became aware of a broken soul somewhere nearby. She could tell by the clanging sound of its voice that it was trapped inside an uncommon object—

But this one wasn't coming from inside Scratch. Ivy opened the cabinet above the sink and saw, sitting on one of the shelves, a silver soap dish with two dolphin-shaped handles. "Seb," she said, "*this* is uncommon."

"Is it?" He eyed the soap dish nervously as Ivy removed it from the cabinet. "I've never seen it before. What's it doing here?"

Ivy turned the dish over to examine it from all sides. "Maybe Valian sent it? That could be why he told us to wash our hands—because he wanted us to find it. What do you think it does?" She deliberated the possibilities. Every object gained a special ability when it turned uncommon.

"Experimentings should Ivy," Scratch suggested helpfully, knocking against the taps. "Good way of discoverings uncommon uses."

Taking his advice, Ivy tried floating the soap dish on the surface of the water. A strange green froth appeared, churning around the dish and quickly swallowing it under. Before Ivy had time to decide whether that was a good thing or not, a shout erupted up the stairs.

"Do you need me to COME UP?" Curtis boomed. There was an unmistakable edge of suspicion in her voice.

"We won't be a moment!" Ivy called back, trying to sound as casual as possible.

Seb rattled the door, checking it was locked. "We need to be quick," he hissed. "Curtis might already have an inkling that we're planning to leave. She must have noticed you look more prepared for mountain-climbing than bed."

Ivy studied her reflection in the bathroom mirror. Her messy auburn curls contrasted sharply with the navy blue of her duffle coat. In her thick cargo trousers and clean hiking boots, she was dressed exactly as Valian had advised: she was ready for anything.

"We'd better try something else," Seb said, combing his fingers through the soapy water to locate the dish.

There was a sharp grating sound—

—and then Seb disappeared.

"Seb!" Ivy leaned over the basin, still careful not to make contact with the water. The soap dish had vanished along with Seb.

A distinct *creak* sounded in the hallway: Curtis was climbing the stairs. Ivy projected her thoughts inside Scratch: *Help! Do you know what's happened to Seb? Should I touch the water?*

*Thinkings is Scratch,* she heard him reply in her head. *Ivy must being carefuls.*

The ability to communicate with him like this was a recent development. To begin with, Ivy had only been able to hear vague murmurings coming from the fragment of soul inside Scratch, but now she could distinguish full sentences and send her own conversation back. She was learning that the more she used her whispering, the stronger her talents became.

The landing groaned.

*Curtis outside!* Scratch warned her.

With no other option, Ivy quickly shoved the bell back into her satchel. She splashed her hand in the basin, just as Seb had done, causing tickly bubbles to immediately rush up her nose. "Ah-*choo!*" she sneezed. In the split second her eyelids were shut, she heard another sound, shrill and scraping—

And the next moment she was standing in the shaky hull of an underwater vessel. Seb stood beside her, his nose scrunched up, as if flies had just flown up both his nostrils.

"What just happened?" he asked, rubbing his face. "Where are we?"

The metal craft was the size of a tugboat; it was round at both ends with a transparent hood of bubbles that sealed it off on all sides like a wobbly sunroof. Beyond it, the craggy forms of rocks were just visible in the murky water, and, closer to the vessel, Ivy spotted the elegant curves of a silvery dolphin.

"We're *in* the soap dish!" Ivy realized. Judging by the strong current, they were submerged in a stream or river. The air reeked of chlorine mixed with perfumed soap, like the changing rooms at the swimming pool.

"*Welcome aboard this aqua-transport vessel number 2895,*" said a machine-like voice. Ivy didn't know where it was coming

from; there were no speakers or controls visible inside. *"What is your desired destination?"*

"Nubrook," Ivy said.

The grating sound came again, like metal grinding over stone. The soap dish began rocking, knocking them to their knees. Seb clutched his stomach. *"Ugh* . . . I feel sick. . . ."

"We'd better stay down until it's over," Ivy advised. She

didn't know how long it was going to last or how turbulent it would be.

Then the dolphin at the rear of the craft flicked its tail, sending them speeding forward. Ivy held on to the sides for support. Their surroundings were full-sized, so she presumed the dish had enlarged after moving to its present location; but she still wasn't sure how she and Seb had been transported inside.

They swept through tendrils of muddy pondweed before moving into clearer water and diving deeper. As they zoomed along, Ivy gazed through the swirling rainbows in the hood at slow-swimming fish and barnacle-encrusted pipes. They were soon skimming over a dark and sandy plateau. *The seabed.*

In no time at all, the dish began to ascend. It rose to the surface of the water and, with a heavy shunt, beached itself on a platform. The bubble hood burst, and Ivy jolted as a wall of noise hit her in the chest.

"Welcome to Nubrook," declared a jolly voice, "the deepest undermart in the world!"

# CHAPTER TWO

The happy voice belonged to a red-cheeked man in a paisley shirt, who offered Ivy his hand as she stepped out of the soap dish onto a short jetty. "Mind your step, please," he cautioned.

"Thanks," she mumbled. Other soap dishes were moored in the same long canal; it cut across the limestone floor of a vast arrivals hall teeming with people. Iron lampposts shaped like dancers posed around the edge of the chamber, each holding a glowing uncommon lemon squeezer.

"Land! *Finally*—" Seb staggered out behind her, his face pale.

Something hit Ivy on the arm and she looked down to find a tatty paper pamphlet at her feet. She picked it up and read the front cover: *Nubrook: Farrow's Guide for the Traveling Tradesman.*

"Free guide to Nubrook!" called a boy with an American

accent as he walked along the jetty. He tossed a few pamphlets at another soap dish. "Discover the secrets of the undermart that built *down* while commoners were building *up*."

*Farrow's Guide* . . . Ivy had been given one about Lundinor too. The guidebooks were written in a strange back-to-front code that Scratch was able to decipher; others needed uncommon binoculars to read them.

"Exit's that way," the man in the paisley shirt said, pointing to the end of the jetty. He handed Ivy the dolphin-handled soap dish, which—somehow—had returned to its original size.

She shook the dish dry and stuffed it and the leaflet into her satchel for safekeeping before grabbing Seb's jacket sleeve to steer him in the right direction. The color soon returned to Seb's cheeks as they began walking. A horde of aqua-transport travelers jostled past them; Ivy had to swerve to avoid a girl wearing a gold-fringed sari and deerstalker hat, while Seb almost got sandwiched between two bald men dressed in flares and Roman sandals. "Hobsmatch," Seb murmured, side-stepping a lady in an evening gown and cowhide waistcoat. "Uncommon style must be the same no matter where in the world you are."

Ivy thought fondly of her Hobsmatch outfits hidden in her wardrobe at home. The fashion was to wear as many different styles of clothing at once, but, in keeping with Valian's advice, she and Seb had decided not to bring theirs along. Hobsmatch might be dizzyingly spectacular, but it certainly wasn't practical.

Standing at the end of the dock was a woman in a navy-blue uniform. She had a white sash draped over one shoulder and a smart peaked cap. Seb nudged Ivy's shoulder as they approached her. "She's got to be a Nubrook underguard," he said under his breath. "They're the only uncommoners I've ever seen in uniform."

The woman looked different from the underguards who policed Lundinor, although she carried the same weapon tucked into her belt: an uncommon toilet brush, capable of electrocuting anyone who didn't abide by the Great Uncommon Trade laws.

"Afternoon, folks," the officer said solemnly, blocking their path. "I must ask you both to shake my hand before proceeding. Security's been heightened as a result of this morning's news: we're monitoring everyone traveling on the waterways."

*This morning's news?* Wondering what had transpired, Ivy produced her white uncommon dress gloves from her satchel. Unique to each trader, they recorded every deal the wearer made. Ivy's pair looked remarkably clean considering she had to wear them *all* the time in undermarts. Seb's uncommon drummer's gloves, she noticed, were decidedly grubbier.

"Sorry, we didn't catch the headlines," Seb said, extending his hand. "What's happened?"

The officer's voice hardened. "Thieves broke into the private vault of a quartermaster in Montroquer three days ago. The investigators only released their findings this morning."

Ivy knew that Montroquer was a famous undermart in Paris. Like all undermarts, it was presided over by four quartermasters. She hadn't heard anything about a break-in, but then Valian hadn't sent any uncommon newspapers for over a week.

"Evidence revealed that the thieves spent two weeks

tunneling under Montroquer to gain access to the vault," the officer continued. "A crooked sixpence was discovered at the scene: it's the Fallen Guild who are responsible again."

Ivy swallowed. The Fallen Guild was meant to be a less shiver-inducing name for the Dirge.

The officer stepped aside to let them pass. "They must have wanted something important," Seb commented as he and Ivy walked away, "if they went to so much effort to steal it. I wonder what it was. . . ."

Ivy tried to push the Dirge to the back of her mind as they crossed the floor, surveying the crowd. They had to focus on helping Valian find Rosie, not become distracted by other problems.

"This is going to take ages," she moaned. "We don't even know what this 'man in red' is. It could be a symbol on a wall or the name of a shop inside Nubrook—"

"Or someone wearing red Hobsmatch," Seb added, scouring the floor for anyone who might be him. "Trouble is, there are so many uncommoners here, I can already see three people dressed in red. Why couldn't Valian have told us to look for a man in a banana costume? Now, *that* we could spot easily."

Ivy wondered whether they were meant to have arrived later, because it would have been quieter then. As New York was five hours behind London, it was currently only two in the afternoon in Nubrook. "We'll just have to keep searching. Maybe we should look for a man in red doing something out of the ordinary?"

"Sure," Seb muttered, ducking to avoid a boy surfing overhead on a flying doormat, "because we're surrounded by ordinary right now."

Everywhere Ivy looked, people were arriving on the back of airborne uncommon objects. Mops, vacuum cleaners and carpets, all carrying several passengers, were shooting out of giant holes in the ceiling, swooping low over the crowd, then settling on landing strips that ran parallel to the aqua-transport canals.

Finally, after a good ten minutes, Ivy's attention was drawn to a lone man in all-crimson attire. He was leaning against an old wooden chest of drawers in the shadow of the cavern wall, fiddling with the chain of a pocket watch. "What about him?" she suggested. "He's not hurrying off anywhere."

Crossing the floor to investigate, they noticed the man in red kept checking the time, over and over like he was waiting for something to happen. Suddenly he dropped the watch into his pocket and pulled open the bottom drawer of the chest.

The ground rumbled. . . .

With a loud crackle, a fountain of tiny gold lights erupted from the open drawer like the sparks of a Roman candle. Where they landed, regular-sized uncommoners appeared out of thin air, stretching their arms and rolling their shoulders as if they were all about to do a yoga class. Then, after smoothing out their Hobsmatch, they all strolled off into the swelling crowd.

"Valian!" Seb yelled, jumping and waving at the same time. "Over here!"

With a blink of surprise, Ivy picked out Valian's scrawny figure weaving toward them through the throng. His straggly dark hair shone with sweat, but he brightened when he saw them. "What are you two doing here? I wasn't expecting you for a few hours yet; I was going to wait around."

"Is everything all right?" Ivy asked urgently.

Valian's mouth drew into a grimace as he wiped his forehead with the back of his fingerless glove. "Yeah, fine. I just hate traveling in those impossibly cramped drawers. I've had my face pressed into a stranger's back for the last twenty minutes." He threw a scowl over his shoulder as if it might hit the person in question. "Unfortunately, it's the fastest way to move long-distance at the moment. The International Uncommon Council banned bag travel this morning so as not to worsen Storm Sarah."

"*That's* why you changed the arrangements . . . ," Ivy said with a sigh of relief. For some reason, bag travel affected the earth's geothermal gradient. She knew of at least one occasion when an increase in uncommon bag journeys had caused a snowstorm in London, so perhaps the IUC's decision was for the best.

"I had to send the soap dish last minute by ghost-courier," Valian explained. "I take it you found it all right? Sorry about the vague instructions—there was a phantom in the line behind me at the featherlight mail tower and I didn't like the look of him one bit."

"We figured it out," Ivy told him, gathering that there had probably been a ghost in their bathroom earlier. "How does drawer travel work?"

"Stationmasters in red operate the chests," he said. "A different drawer is opened every few minutes. Each one leads to another drawer in another part of the world." He signaled toward the far end of the hall, where a monumental arch decorated with elaborate Art Deco carvings was cut into the stone wall. "That's the entrance to Nubrook," Valian said. "Let's go."

They zigzagged across the arrivals chamber, doing their best to avoid the swinging legs of riders dismounting from vacuum cleaners, then squeezed through the giant vaulted passage along with everyone else. Valian marched ahead, cutting a path through the masses. Ivy understood his urgency: like most undermarts, Nubrook only opened at certain times of the year, and Valian had been waiting for this visit for six months.

She realized that he wasn't wearing his trademark red basketball shoes as part of his Hobsmatch, which was very odd. Instead, he had on a pair of brown leather boots, so worn at the heel that she could see his socks poking through. "I know they look awful," he admitted, catching her gaze. "But they're uncommon: they allow me to step through most walls, like the dead do. I bought them with the winnings you gave me from the Grivens tournament. You never know when they might be useful, and I wanted to be as prepared as possible for this trip."

The heat and noise turned stifling as they reached the other side. "It's always busy around here," Valian shouted. "This way."

As Ivy stumbled after him, her eyes darted around like she was watching an aerial display. Nubrook's buildings were covered in dazzling neon signs and flashing lights, all demanding her attention. Mounted on the walls, giant tablecloths played advertisements like the screens in Times Square, while music blared from conch shells on either side. She thought of the uncommon bedsheets used to stream live video in Lundinor; uncommoners called those devices materializers.

"*Whoa,*" Seb breathed, looking at the illuminated billboards on the rooftops. "This is insane."

Thanksgiving decorations adorned almost every building. Glittering chains of acorns were draped around window frames, and star-shaped wreaths of wheat and cornhusks hung from doors. Valian guided them to an area of pavement dotted with pushcarts selling coffee and hotdogs. The tempting aroma of fried onions filled the air.

Ivy stared up at the distant concrete ceiling festooned with crystal chandeliers the size of hot-air balloons. She could sense Scratch inside her satchel, giddy with excitement. "I assumed Nubrook would be in a huge cave like Lundinor, but it feels more like we're inside a massive shopping mall," she said.

Valian laughed. "Nubrook's famous for being entirely man-made. The best thing about it are the basements. Some shops have fifty floors below street level—each one with a different theme."

*The deepest undermart in the world* . . . Now Ivy understood why.

"Nubrook has four different quarters, like other undermarts," Valian continued, "but here they're one on top of each other. We're in First Quarter now. Second, Third and Fourth are below us." He removed three white table tennis balls from his jacket pocket. "Here, take one of these. Throw it at every blank surface you can find—walls, storefronts, doorways, drain covers. . . . We need as many people as possible to see them."

Seb arched an eyebrow. "How is playing ping-pong going to help us find Rosie?"

Valian dropped a ball to the floor. It gave a low *ping* as it sprang off the pavement and returned to his hand. Where it

had fallen, a colorful poster appeared printed on the concrete. In bubble writing at the top were the words MISSING PLEASE HELP and below them was a photo of a little girl dressed in Hobsmatch.

*Rosie.*

"Uncommoners use table tennis balls to copy things," Valian clarified. "You load them up by repeatedly bouncing them on the image you want copied. Then, when you next throw them against something, they leave behind an exact duplicate stamped on the surface."

"It's faster than using a photocopier," Seb remarked, "I'll give you that."

Ivy noticed Valian's baffled expression and shook her head. "Never mind," she reassured him. (It was easy to forget how little Valian knew about the common world, having lived all his life in undermarts.) She tucked her ping-pong ball in her pocket and took a closer look at the poster. Ivy had only seen a picture of Valian's sister once before, but the family resemblance was clear: Rosie shared Valian's sloping cheekbones and fierce brown eyes. Her ice-blond hair was tied in bunches, and a silver necklace hung over the top of her polka-dot blouse.

"That picture was taken on the morning she disappeared," Valian said, "when she was six. She'll look different now . . . she'll be twelve—thirteen next month."

Ivy committed the details of Rosie's image to memory. "Her hair color's really striking. People should remember if they've spotted her."

"That was my hope at first too," Valian said, his voice hardening. "The trouble is, no one ever *has* seen her. I've used all kinds of uncommon objects to search, but nothing works. The only thing I've learned is that she's definitely alive."

Ivy saw the determined expression on Valian's face. His parents had died not long before Rosie had gone missing, so he'd shouldered the responsibility of finding her all on his own. She admired him; it must have taken a great deal of courage to take on the task by himself.

"Something uncommon must be hiding her," Seb concluded. "It's the only explanation."

"Yeah, but without knowing what object that is, I can't undo its effects." Valian shook his head. "It's got something to do with what happened when I tracked her using the Sack of Stars. You remember—before it got destroyed, it brought me to where Rosie was, only it couldn't settle on one location, as if she was in several different places at the same time."

It was a frustrating puzzle. The Sack of Stars, one of the five Great Uncommon Good, had taken Valian tantalizingly close to his sister, but with no results. Ivy had gone over the facts all summer, trying to find a solution. "At least that invitation Mr. Punch gave you has provided you with another clue," she said.

Valian put his hand in his pocket and removed the card with the gold border that Mr. Punch had given him in Lundinor. He reread it carefully.

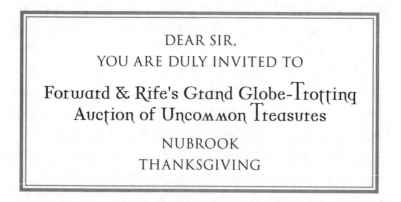

DEAR SIR,
YOU ARE DULY INVITED TO

Forward & Rife's Grand Globe-Trotting
Auction of Uncommon Treasures

NUBROOK
THANKSGIVING

"Mr. Punch might be the smartest man in Lundinor, but he's also the most secretive," Seb warned. "We still don't know why he gave you that invitation in the first place—or why he gave Ivy Amos's journal."

Ivy thought about Mr. Punch, one of Lundinor's quartermasters. She considered him mysterious, it was true, but he'd also demonstrated he was brave and selfless, defending Lundinor from the Dirge's evil schemes.

"All I know," Valian said, tapping his thumb against the card, "is that, according to the Sack of Stars, wherever Forward & Rife's auction has traveled to, Rosie has been there too. There's got to be a connection between them." He lifted his chin as he continued walking. "So this is my plan to find her: investigate the auction house, distribute the posters, ask as many traders as we can if they've seen her. If Forward & Rife are here over the next few days, there's a strong chance she will be too." He squinted along an adjoining road. "Come on, the auction house is this way."

As they set off, the clamor of a thousand fragmented souls—both those trapped inside uncommon objects and those that had formed races of the dead—invaded Ivy's ears. Although most murmured wordlessly, Ivy limited her senses to Scratch, aware she'd get a headache if she tried to listen to all the others. Bustling through the crowded streets, she scanned the faces of passersby, seeking brown eyes and blond hair. It was silly to think that Rosie might walk by, but Ivy felt they should be searching all the time. She noticed several somber-faced dead traders hovering about, each with a cardboard sign hanging around their neck. All the signs displayed a drawing of a different object with the caption HAVE YOU SEEN THIS? followed by a list of identifiable details. Ivy had never spotted one of the dead with such a sign before. She wondered if maybe the practice was unique to Nubrook.

After a short while, they arrived at their destination. Forward

& Rife's auction house was situated in the lush rooftop garden of a tall marble building. A burly-looking security woman in a tartan kilt and chain-mail tabard stood outside the entrance to the building on the ground floor. "It's invite only," she informed them, peering doubtfully at Valian's scruffy boat shoes.

"Right—yeah," Valian muttered, fumbling with his gold-edged invitation before handing it over. Ivy realized he was probably more accustomed to sneaking in to such events.

The security woman read the card, and then flashed them an admiring glance. "Oh, you're guests of Mr. Punch? Please, come in."

They were ushered through a courtyard and onto an intricately patterned Chinese rug, which ascended to the roof as gently as a napkin floating in the wind. The air turned thick with flowery perfume as they stepped into the garden. Narrow stone pathways ran between the exotic plantings, labeled according to species. Dotted among the ornamental bonsais and potted cacti stood glass cabinets exhibiting the objects due to be auctioned in two days' time. A catalog was attached to the side of each. Uncommoners in elaborate Hobsmatch milled around, clinking champagne glasses and scrutinizing the articles for sale. Security guards shuffled between them.

Ivy took a look inside the closest display case. It contained two objects: item number 235—a decorative ceramic music box once owned by Queen Victoria; and item number 236—a solid-gold magnifying glass, which, according to the catalog, could magnify a person's talents. A hastily scribbled note in the corner of the case explained, however, that it had been withdrawn from sale.

"Do you think that music box really belonged to Queen Victoria?" Seb asked.

"It's doubtful," Valian said. "I've done loads of research on Forward & Rife, and there were several reports of them getting into trouble for false claims. Mr. Rife owns the company. I got the impression he was a bit of a charlatan."

"What do you mean 'was'?" Ivy questioned, her curiosity spiked. "Did you find out anything else about him?"

Valian shrugged. "For the last five years there haven't been any accusations of dodgy deals at all. It seems Mr. Rife must have cleaned up his act." He shook his head slowly from side to side. "Although . . . ," he went on, "for a man with nothing to hide, he is impossible to get hold of. I sent him several featherlight messages, hoping he might be able to explain the connection between Rosie and his company, but they were all returned unread."

They moved on to the next case. Inside was a long-stemmed pipe turned from cherry wood. Its bowl was engraved with an elaborate pattern.

"I don't believe it." Valian gasped, pressing his nose to the glass.

" 'Item number 245—tobacco pipe, *circa* 1565,' " Seb read in the catalog. " 'Allows the user to speak any language on Earth. Scouted in Bolivia by Cherry and Florian Kaye'—" He looked up. "*Kaye*—isn't that *your* surname, Valian?"

Valian's voice faltered. "Cherry and Florian Kaye are my mum and dad."

# CHAPTER THREE

Ivy hadn't often heard Valian talk about his parents. All she knew was that they had been scouts, like him: people who hunted for uncommon objects in the common world before selling them.

"I didn't know that my parents had traded with Forward & Rife," he said in a small voice.

"Do you remember them going to Bolivia?" she asked.

He nodded. "They were always away on business. They'd only just gotten back from their last trip when they were—"

Ivy lowered her gaze. On some occasions he managed to say "murdered" straightaway; at other times the word got stuck in his throat. She couldn't imagine how painful it was to say aloud that your parents had been killed by the Dirge.

A burst of applause interrupted their conversation. Valian shook his head clear and walked around a wall of bamboo to see what was going on; Ivy and Seb hurried after him. Standing beside another display case was a suave-looking gentleman with a quiff of silver hair and deep wrinkles around his twinkly blue eyes. A spotted handkerchief peeped out of the breast pocket of his crushed velvet jacket, which he wore with matching cape and moccasin boots. An ostrich feather in his blue buccaneer's hat quivered as he spoke.

"Ladies and gentlemen!" he announced in a smooth voice that told Ivy he was used to charming a large crowd. "My name is Mr. Rife, and it is my honor this afternoon to introduce to you some of the extraordinary treasures in the Forward & Rife collection. First, we have this paper knife from London, England." He held up in his gloved hand a small gold dagger with an enamel handle.

Valian's face widened. "That's *him*! According to my research, he's attended every single auction Forward & Rife have ever held. He's the person most likely to have noticed Rosie. We have to talk to him."

"As I'm sure you all know," Mr. Rife was continuing, "uncommon blades give the user complete control over one or more variables. You may find swords that adjust speed, daggers that modify direction or knives that can manipulate weight. The higher the grade of the uncommon blade, the greater the number of forces it can control, and this delightful paper knife can control the energy between molecules, allowing it to alter states of matter." He stepped aside flamboyantly to reveal a large vase of water. The audience murmured in anticipation. "For this demonstration, I will require the assistance of an absolute beginner: someone who's never used an uncommon blade before." His gaze moved through the audience and came to a stop above Ivy's shoulder. "Sir, what about *you?*"

Seb looked left and right before pointing to his own chest. *"Me?"*

"Now, don't be shy," Mr. Rife chided, "this is going to be fun."

Seb's blank face said it all.

Valian elbowed him in the ribs. "Go on—we might learn something useful about the auction."

Seb groaned as he trudged up to the front. Ivy felt a twinge of sympathy. She'd seen her brother with that same sweaty, pale-faced look whenever he went onstage to play a gig with his band. He always got nervous in front of large numbers of people.

Mr. Rife whispered something into Seb's ear, and he mumbled a response. "Thank you, Seb Sparrow from London," Mr. Rife said, holding the uncommon paper knife out toward him. "If you'll just take this, please."

Seb cradled the knife in his hands, staring helplessly out into the audience.

"Today," Mr. Rife declared, holding up his finger in the air, "I shall prove that even a novice can operate this remarkable object. First, I will ask Seb to attempt to use the knife to turn this liquid"—at this his hand swept over the vase of water—"into gas."

"Er, how am I supposed to do that?" Seb mumbled.

"Just try it," Mr. Rife insisted.

With a sigh, Seb swished the paper knife over the vase like he was using a magic wand. Nothing happened. A few people sniggered.

"Good effort, Seb, but not quite enough," Mr. Rife said. "The key is to think of uncommon knives as dials that you can turn up or down. Now, imagine this knife has invisible threads attached to it and, by moving your hands on either side, you can manipulate those threads in order to operate the dial inside the knife."

"OK . . ." Adjusting his stance, Seb stared at the paper knife, his face straining with effort. Very slowly, he moved his hands apart.

The knife remained floating in midair. The crowd gasped. Mr. Rife pressed the tips of his fingers together. "Excellent. Now point the knife at the vase."

Seb shifted his palms, tilting the handle so that the blade was directed toward the water.

"And finally," ordered Mr. Rife, "to operate that dial inside the knife, send it spinning clockwise."

Heeding Mr. Rife's instruction, Seb pulled his hands wider to set the knife in motion. As the blade rotated, tiny bubbles appeared in the water.

"That's it, keep going!" Mr. Rife encouraged as steam rose from up out of the vase.

Concentrating hard, Seb thrashed his hands back and forth as if he was playing air guitar.

The vase steadily filled with steam. "And there we have it!" Mr. Rife announced. "The liquid is now—"

But someone clapped too soon, making Seb jolt. His hands flew wider; there was a high-pitched whistle and then, with a crack, the glass shattered, sending a spray of icy shards over the audience.

Quicker than lightning, Mr. Rife whipped his cape from

his shoulders and threw it over the vase, containing the explosion. The audience ducked; some people shielded their faces with their hands.

"Is everyone all right?" he called. "I think our young volunteer may have turned the gas into a solid by mistake."

Seb mumbled an apology, but it was lost in the subsequent cheering.

"Bravo, Mr. Rife! Well saved!"

The audience straightened themselves back up again and applauded, while Mr. Rife beckoned a cleaner to come and tidy up the mess. Seb handed back the paper knife and hastily returned to his place, drying his face on the end of his sleeve. Amid the commotion, a loud *bang* suddenly resonated from the other side of the garden, and several people turned their heads to see where it was coming from. A few flinched and pulled displeased faces.

Mr. Rife's neat gray brows lowered. "Ladies and gentlemen, I'm afraid you'll have to excuse me. In an hour's time I will be demonstrating the so-called Frozen Telescope of the North—recovered from a shipwreck in the Arctic Bay. Please help yourself to another glass of champagne while you wait." His smile withered as he hastened away.

"Come on," Valian said. "Now's our chance to talk to him."

The ostrich feather in Mr. Rife's hat bobbed above the trees as he strode along, making him easy to spot. Ivy, Seb and Valian trailed him to the edge of the roof, where he turned into a stairwell leading down through the building. They paused at the top when they heard voices.

". . . yes, my assistant's a little deaf, so she probably didn't hear you knock." (*Mr. Rife*—though he sounded frailer than before.) "Is there a problem, officer?"

"I've been sent by the master of Second Quarter," said a cheerless voice. "You still haven't paid your trading taxes for last spring: objects to the value of thirty-two and a half grade."

There was a shuffle. "The thing is, grade-flow's a little slow at the moment. I'm sure you understand—because we travel so much, it can take weeks to collect all the payments." He continued hastily, "I *am* delivering a gold magnifying glass after the auction in two days' time. The buyer is a gold obsessive and will pay generously. I'll have more than enough grade to settle the debt then."

"I see. . . ." The other speaker paused. "Can't you visit this buyer earlier? Or perhaps I could collect the payment from them on your behalf?"

"Afraid not," Mr. Rife said. "The buyer insists on concealing their identity, so goes by the alias Midas. Only *I* am allowed to collect the grade myself."

"In that case, I'll visit you again on Friday to recover what is outstanding. Good day, sir."

Ivy, Seb and Valian stumbled backward as a broad-shouldered underguard appeared at the top of the stairwell. He eyed them suspiciously from under the peak of his cap before walking away. When Mr. Rife didn't emerge, Valian took a few steps down. "He's gone inside. Let's talk to him now—he might reveal more if he's distracted."

At the bottom of the stairs they found an old wooden door covered in peeling green paint. Hanging from the knocker was a chalkboard scrawled with the words *Offices of Forward & Rife*.

"That conversation doesn't make sense," Seb observed. "If Forward & Rife can afford this fancy rooftop garden and all that champagne, why can't they pay their debts?"

"Perhaps the firm's in more trouble than Valian's research made us all think," Ivy speculated.

She knocked twice on the door. After a moment they heard Mr. Rife answer soberly, "Come in, it's open." The hinges creaked as they entered a dimly lit living room. Cardboard boxes bursting with polystyrene nuggets filled the spaces between the furniture. Half-hidden under a silvery blanket, a celestial globe and antique pram stood in one corner of the room, while a doorway at the back appeared to lead into a small kitchen. Mr. Rife sat in one of the two leather armchairs, his buccaneer's hat resting in his lap. He squinted at them. "Oh—Seb, wasn't it? What can I do for you?"

Before Seb could answer, there came a rattle from the kitchen and an elderly woman carrying a tray of teacups hobbled out. She had dark hair and a round belly. A flowery apron partially covered her Hobsmatch: a high-necked blouse and glittery Capri pants. "Tea's made for your guests, Mr. Rife," she said in a husky southern drawl. "I'd just boiled the water when I heard them come in."

Mr. Rife looked at the ceiling. "And yet somehow, Mrs. Bees, you failed to hear the underguard knocking at the door. Thank you anyway." He smiled apologetically at Ivy, Seb and Valian. "My housekeeper is uncommonly fast at making tea. Don't feel obliged to drink it if you don't want to."

"Thank you, tea would be lovely," Ivy said, smiling at Mrs. Bees as she took a mug filled with the pale-yellow liquid. From its floral perfume, she guessed it was chamomile—Ivy's

32

mum's favorite. She thought of her parents at the wedding and hoped they were having a good time.

"You'll have to be careful with that cup; it leaks," Mrs. Bees warned. She hurled Mr. Rife an accusing stare before offering the tray to Valian and Seb. "I would buy a new set, but *we can't afford it*." She rested the final cup on the arm of Mr. Rife's chair before scowling at him again and marching back into the kitchen.

Mr. Rife sighed. "You might as well sit down. You'll have to stay until you've finished your tea or else I'll never hear the end of it."

Ivy perched on the edge of a cardboard box, Seb on a moth-eaten footstool.

"I'd prefer to stand," Valian said, placing his teacup on the mantel above the fireplace. Then he said, "We're here because we need your help, Mr. Rife." He cleared an area of the floor and dropped his ping-pong ball onto it. Rosie's poster appeared immediately. "We're looking for this girl, and we've reason to believe she's in Nubrook. Do you recognize her?"

Mr. Rife leaned forward. "Hmm . . ." He looked at the poster, then at Valian, and then back again. "You're related?" he asked.

"She's my sister."

"Yes, you look alike. I'm very sorry she's missing. But I'm afraid I've never seen her before."

Valian's face tightened. "We think she might have visited several of your auctions. Are you positive you haven't noticed her hanging around?"

"Certain," Mr. Rife said, checking the poster again. "I'm excellent with faces. I'm sorry, I can't help you."

Ivy's stomach dropped. She thought of what they'd over-heard on the stairs and said, "We can pay you for any informa-tion. Please try to think harder. You must have seen her—we discovered that she's been following your auction company around the world."

"I assure you, it would be quite impossible for anyone to do that," Mr. Rife declared. "Mrs. Bees and I travel using—" He stopped himself. "Look, I'm sorry I can't be more useful, but I really must get back to my guests, which means you need to leave." He pushed his buccaneer's hat onto his head and rose from his seat. "Good day."

*So much for "stay until you've finished your tea,"* Ivy thought, putting down her mug.

Valian looked empty and bewildered. Ivy knew he'd

pinned all his hopes on finding Rosie here. She couldn't bear it if they left with nothing. "We understand," she said. "We'll get going." She turned to the door that led out up to the roof garden, hoping Seb and Valian would trust her enough to play along. The shuffle of footsteps told her they did. Quickly, before they left the room, she extended her senses to the walls, trying not to wince as her ears were bombarded with the gabble of broken souls. With a little focus, she identified the fleeting whisper of one of the dead among them: it was Mr. Rife. She scanned the uncommon objects in the room: the vintage pram in the corner immediately drew her attention. She'd never sensed a soul so restless or fidgety before, like a spider trapped in a jar. She listened carefully, trying to focus on what it was saying, but it was speaking too quickly for her to understand, and—before she knew it— Mr. Rife had ushered them out of the door. He slammed it shut behind them, breaking Ivy's concentration. She pursed her lips in frustration.

"Did I miss something?" Seb asked as they trudged back into the garden. "What was that all about?"

"I was using my whispering to examine the room," she said, "but I hadn't really finished—and my senses don't stretch far enough to continue doing it from here." As they wound their way back through the trees and flowerbeds she told them about the pram and Mr. Rife being dead. "Do you think Mr. Rife was telling the truth about Rosie?" she asked.

"Hard to tell," Valian said in a suspicious tone, "but if he does know something, it seems he's not going to tell us willingly. We need to do more digging."

"How could he be so certain that Rosie hadn't followed

him?" Seb asked. "I know the dead travel super-fast, but Mr. Rife said that he and Mrs. Bees traveled *together*—and she is living."

Ivy's head jerked around. She hadn't extended her senses as far as the kitchen to where Mrs. Bees was, so she hadn't been able to check. "How can you be sure?"

"She was bleeding from a cut on her finger," he replied. "There are only two races of the dead who can bleed: Sasspirits and the Eyre Folk, and Mrs. Bees can't be either of those."

"Since when did you know what a Sasspirit is?" Ivy had never heard of that race of the dead before.

"Sasspirits look human but they have superior hearing and brilliant memories," he explained. "Mrs. Bees didn't hear the underguard knocking, so she can't be a Sasspirit. And she didn't have swirly black holes for eyes like the Eyre Folk . . . so she must be living." Seb shrugged, adding, "Scratch has been giving me a few lessons about the dead. You know . . . just in case."

Ivy got the feeling there was more to it than that, but before she could delve deeper Valian said, "Mr. Rife must be using that uncommon pram to get around. They're super rare. I've never seen one before, but I've heard stories about them. If you sit inside one, you can travel short distances faster than the speed of light."

"No wonder Mr. Rife didn't want to tell us about it," Seb quipped. "What grown man is going to admit that he rides in a baby's pram?"

"If Rosie was traveling faster than light, it would explain why the Sack of Stars sent you to several different undermarts in such a short space of time to find her," Ivy said to Valian. "Perhaps she has a pram too?"

Valian kicked a plant pot in frustration. "But where would Rosie have gotten an uncommon object that powerful? And why would she be trailing an auction company in the first place?"

Ivy shook her head, lost for an answer. "I wish I knew."

# CHAPTER FOUR

Ivy and Valian followed Seb across a wooden bridge into a small Zen garden covered in patterned dove-gray shingle. The place was quiet and empty, although the rumble of applause could be heard coming from somewhere on the roof. Valian took out his ping-pong ball and set about replicating Rosie's missing poster every few meters along the decking.

"I'm sorry we didn't learn more," Ivy said gently. "At least this whole 'traveling by pram' thing seems to confirm the link between Rosie and Forward & Rife. And we've still got another day to look for her before the auction on Thursday."

"Yeah." Valian squeezed the ball. "I don't know . . . sometimes it bothers me that Rosie's never come looking for me. It might be that she can't for some reason, or maybe it's that she doesn't want to. She could have a great new life somewhere else."

Ivy understood that seven years was a long time for doubts to fester. "Valian," she said gently, "Rosie's your sister. Wherever she is, and whatever has happened to her, I guarantee that she misses you." Then she added, in a more mischievous tone, "Even I don't like it when Seb goes away for long periods of time, and he's an idiot."

Valian smiled, but it didn't reach his eyes.

"Hey, guys, look at this!" Up ahead Seb stood beside an empty display cabinet. Resting on top was a gleaming silver telescope, the length of his forearm. The metal was engraved with tiny stars joined by straight lines—*constellations*. "'The Frozen Telescope of the North,'" he read from the catalog. "Mr. Rife said he was giving a demonstration with this item next."

Ivy wondered if Mr. Rife had taken the object out to practice for the demonstration and had forgotten to lock it away afterward. Curious, she probed it with her senses. The broken soul within it chattered furiously, as if it was trying to stay warm. Perhaps a whisperer had given it its nickname.

"It says here that uncommon telescopes gaze back in time to allow us to discover something new about our past," Seb told them. "They're like the opposite of uncommon clocks."

"Except that clocks are useful," Valian remarked bitterly. "They predict the future so that you can stop bad things from happening. It doesn't matter what a telescope shows you: you can't change the past."

Peering at the freshly printed trail of posters they were leaving in their wake, Ivy replied, "No, but you can learn from it. If we aimed the telescope back to the time when Rosie disappeared, it's possible we could unearth a fresh clue."

Valian looked left and right, checking they were alone. With a shrug, he picked up the telescope. "Anything's worth a try."

"I'll keep a lookout around the corner in case people start arriving for the demonstration," Seb offered, passing Ivy the catalog.

"The instructions aren't that detailed," she said, running her finger across the page. "To direct the telescope's gaze, you must 'first recall a moment you wish to look back to'; then to focus, 'concentrate on an image of someone who was present.'" Her insides went heavy, realizing that all of Valian's memories around the time of Rosie's disappearance were probably painful to recall. "You can do this," she encouraged.

Valian nodded gravely and lifted the telescope to his eye. "Does it say anything else?"

"It warns about paying attention to what you find," Ivy replied. "You can't revisit the same period again, and everything will go dark once the vision is over."

"Something's happening," Valian said suddenly. "I can see my parents arguing in our kitchen. Rosie and I are hiding under the table. I remember this! It's the night they were murdered."

Ivy could hear the panic rising in his voice. Perhaps if she helped direct his thoughts, he'd be able to concentrate. "Try to relax," she told him. "What other details do you notice?"

"On the table is a collection of objects with numbered labels," he said, describing the scene breathlessly. "Twenty-five of them. My parents must have brought them back from their latest scouting trip. It looks like they've used a fork to grade them, and a feather has automatically written the results on a piece of paper—I think that's what my parents are arguing about."

Ivy had witnessed the use of an uncommon fork before— one tap of its prongs against an uncommon object and a number between one and ten rings out. The higher the grade, the more powerful the object. "Can you read what it says?"

"Almost . . ." Valian adjusted his grip on the telescope, then gave an exasperated sigh. "No, it's gone. Rosie and I have just jumped out, surprising our parents. Something fell off the table and Rosie put it in her pocket. The only object missing is number seventeen—it must have been that one . . ." He flinched. "Wait, I can see the paper now. . . ."

After a short pause he lowered the telescope. His face was pale.

"Is that the end of the vision?" Ivy asked.

He nodded slowly. "I saw the list. It only went up to number seventeen—the object Rosie got hold of." He took a couple of deep breaths, as if he was trying to calm down.

"Why did your parents stop there?"

"Because object seventeen was a Grade *Ten*."

Ivy went rigid. The only objects believed to be Grade Ten were the Great Uncommon Good.

"Security guards," Seb called, jogging toward them. "Two of them, coming this way." Then he read their expressions. "What happened?"

Taking the Frozen Telescope from Valian's hands, Ivy placed it back where they had found it. "I'll tell you, but first Valian needs to sit down."

A safe distance away, they found a stone bench nestled

under an arbor of drooping wisteria. Valian slumped on the edge of the seat; Ivy and Seb perched on either side.

Ivy briefed Seb about their discovery. "Back then, the Great Uncommon Good were still a myth," she said, keeping her voice low. "Valian's parents must have scouted one of them by accident and only realized what it was when they graded it at home. Rosie can't have understood what it was either."

"That's got to be what's hiding her," Seb said. "Perhaps she picked it up and started playing with it. It could even be the whole reason she disappeared. Who knows what powers the object has."

"It must also be the reason my parents were killed," Valian said in a hollow voice. "I've always known the Dirge did it and how it was done, just never why." He stared at his feet, saying nothing more.

Ivy recalled the details of his parents' murder. They had been poisoned with a mixture of toxins including tongueweed—a foul uncommon substance that makes you tell the truth before you die. "The Dirge must have realized that your parents had one of the Great Uncommon Good and came looking for it," she said softly. "That could be why they used the tongueweed—it would have forced them to reveal the object's location."

Valian gave a slow nod. "Except, when the underguard examined our house afterward, it looked like someone had raided the place—smashing furniture and tearing through walls. If my parents had revealed the object's location, then the Dirge wouldn't have needed to search like that." His shoulders slumped. "I think Mum and Dad had no idea that Rosie had accidentally taken the object. They couldn't tell the Dirge where it was, and they were killed as punishment. They died for nothing."

Ivy shook her head but she wasn't sure what to say to make Valian feel better. He dropped his face into his hands and they all fell silent.

It was Seb who finally spoke. "Your parents would want you to find Rosie," he said. "We're getting closer to understanding what happened to her. We just need to figure out which one of the Great Uncommon Good she has."

"Seb's right," Ivy agreed. "Are you sure you didn't catch sight of the object through the telescope?"

Valian wiped his nose and lifted his head. "No. It was small enough to fit in Rosie's pocket, that's all I know."

"If it's one of the Great Uncommon Good, there's got to be something about it in here." Ivy unfastened her satchel and withdrew Amos Stirling's journal. She began flicking through the blank pages, counting. "We know Mr. Punch has the Stone of Dreams, and the three of us destroyed the Sack of Stars and hid the Jar of Shadows, so Rosie can't have stolen any of those. Amos knew the whereabouts of the remaining two Great Uncommon Good when he wrote this in the 1960s. I just need some raider's tonic to activate the uncommon ink."

Valian pulled a small silver flask out of his leather jacket. "Like I said, I came prepared for this trip." He took a hefty sip (the uncommon concoction was normally drunk as an antidote to shock), and then he handed it over to Ivy.

The scent of lady's perfume wafted up from the bottle. Ivy drizzled a little of the liquid on page forty-two and, with a low hiss, a thick white mist seeped from the paper before words began to appear. She skimmed through till she found what she was looking for—a list of five objects and their locations.

1. The Stone of Dreams—Lundinor
2. The Sack of Stars—Unknown
3. The Sands of Change—Nubrook
4. The Jar of Shadows—Unknown
5. The Sword of Wills—Montroquer

"Numbers three and five are the ones we're interested in," she said, holding up the page so Valian and Seb could see it for themselves.

"'The Sands of Change—Nubrook,'" Seb read. "'The Sword of Wills—Montroquer.' So . . . both objects were hidden in undermarts."

Valian drummed his fingers on his knee, connecting the dots. "My parents scouted on common land, but they always visited local undermarts on their travels. They could have returned from a scouting trip to either New York or Paris."

"Is there any way to find out which one?" Ivy asked.

"Yes, but not here." He rose to his feet. "We need to go to the Bureau of Fair Trade. There's one in every undermart. It's where uncommon glove records are stored. We'll be able to see who my parents last traded with."

They left the rooftop via the Chinese rug and walked across the courtyard toward the exit from the building. The patio was flanked by rows of terracotta urns, each twice the height of Seb. As they made for the door, Ivy spotted a familiar figure step out from behind one of them.

"Quick—" She grabbed three auction catalogs from a

nearby stand and threw two of them at the boys. "Cover your faces with these."

Seb fumbled with the pages as he flapped his open. "What's the matter?"

Ivy peered over the catalog spine. Ahead of them, a bespectacled woman in a moss-green head scarf was making her way out of the building. Fixed to the lapel of her long trench coat was a glittering brooch in the shape of a forked arrow.

"Over there," Ivy whispered. "It's Curtis."

# CHAPTER FIVE

"Why am I pretending to be interested in"—Valian glanced at the page—"a set of uncommon *hair rollers?*"

"Curtis is our babysitter," Seb hissed. "We think she's working for the Dirge—that's why we left home early."

"Your *babysitter?*"

"She got the job under suspicious circumstances," Ivy clarified. "Also, she's dead."

Simultaneously, they all risked a peek from behind their catalogs. Standing in the line to leave, Curtis pushed her glasses farther up as she examined a small gold object in her hand.

"She's reading a security cufflink," Valian said. "Uncommoners use them to track stolen items. The left link shows the longitude and latitude of wherever the right link is, and vice versa. Both of you had better check your pockets—I bet she's planted one on you."

Hiding behind one of the large urns, they all put their catalogs down. Ivy rustled around inside her pockets, but they were all empty, and Scratch let her know that there was nothing in her satchel that she hadn't packed. After searching through his jeans and hoodie, Seb tried the pouch on the side of his backpack. Slowly he withdrew a square gold cufflink. "But my bag was stuffed under my bed all day before we came here," he spluttered. "How did she—?" His brows jumped as he realized. "Oh. The walking-through-walls thing."

After taking the cufflink, Valian rotated the toggle twice before placing it back in Seb's hand. "I've deactivated it now. Curtis must have used it to follow you here from London, but it doesn't make sense that she's working for the Dirge."

"That's what I thought at first," Seb admitted. "But the truth is, we've thwarted their schemes twice before. They probably want us out of the way so we can't interfere again."

"The Dirge are definitely up to something," Ivy agreed. "Think of that recent theft in Montroquer."

Valian shook his head. "If Curtis had been ordered to kill you, she could have done it while she was hiding that cufflink. She must have some other motive for tracking you here."

After checking that Curtis had gone, they walked the remaining distance to the door and left the building. In the street outside, they spotted Curtis slinking away through the crowd.

Valian began hurrying after her. "The Bureau of Fair Trade is in that direction anyway," he said. "Come on, let's see where she goes."

Ivy, Seb and Valian tailed Curtis as she advanced down the

road. Before long she ventured through the revolving doors of a huge shopping mall—or at least Ivy supposed it was a shopping mall until she saw the flying road signs.

"This is new," Seb said, raising his voice above the babble of chatter.

There were no shops inside the building. It was just a vast atrium filled with airborne road signs—everything from an octagonal red stop sign to a blue-and-white H for HOSPITAL—all ferrying passengers up and down. Depending on the size and shape of the sign, between one and three people sat with their legs dangling over the edge, like they were riding a chairlift. Ivy peered down into the void. Everything was enveloped in shadow after a few hundred meters. "How far down do they go?" she asked.

"All the way to Fourth Quarter," Valian replied. "They have these all over Nubrook. The Bureau's down in Third Quarter." He ushered them to the boarding zone, where the three of them clambered onto a large INTERSTATE 86 placard, a few signs behind Curtis's.

Ivy expected to feel a lurch when they started moving, but the ride was so smooth even Seb wasn't bothered by it. She sat between him and Valian, keeping watch on Curtis ahead of them. The atrium walls were plastered with handkerchief materializers advertising everything from stand-up comedy pogo sticks to honey dippers that "Point you exactly where you want to be."

At the exit for the Third Quarter, Curtis dismounted her diamond-shaped TRUCKS CROSSING sign and headed along a litter-strewn main road—Ivy, Seb and Valian in pursuit. The pavements were pockmarked with chewing gum, and the air smelled sour, like moldy banana skins. The area reminded Ivy of the East End of Lundinor, by far the shabbiest quarter there.

Curtis veered off into an alleyway between two dilapidated buildings. A skip near the entrance was loaded with mannequin body parts, plastic hooks and splintered shelving units. An old sign hung from a wall. "Lottie's Accessory Lounge," Ivy read.

Valian edged around the corner. "I can't see her. She must have vanished."

"I'm not sensing her either," Ivy said, extending her whispering along the alley. "Although, there is another broken soul here." A voice was murmuring nearby. Using it as a beacon, Ivy homed in on a dusty mirror leaning against the side of the skip.

The three of them gathered around it. Ivy knelt down and ran her hands over the wooden frame, rubbing off the dirt to reveal a carved emblem at the bottom: a forked arrow. "That's the same design as the brooch Curtis wears," she noted. "There must be a connection."

"Uncommon mirrors are used to hide things," Valian said cautiously. "You have to tell them a secret before they'll reveal what they're hiding. Whatever this mirror's concealing might explain why Curtis is interested in you."

Ivy tried to think of something she'd never told anyone before, but it was surprisingly difficult. She could sense the soul inside the mirror giggling breathlessly, excited at the prospect of hearing some gossip.

*Hang on . . . that's it!*

She hadn't yet spoken to Seb or Valian about her new whispering skill; she hadn't said it aloud to anyone. "I have a secret. You know how I can listen to the souls trapped inside uncommon objects? Well, now I can talk to them too."

"You *can*?" Valian regarded her suspiciously.

Ivy covered her face with her hair. "I've only spoken to Scratch—and that bell in the Grivens tournament last spring."

Suddenly their reflections wobbled. The surface of the mirror rippled in concentric circles and plunged into itself in the middle, forming the inside of a giant silver cone. Ivy yelped as her feet were dragged from under her and her vision blurred. She threw out her arms for balance.

When her sight cleared she found herself in an empty slate-tiled hallway; the alleyway had vanished. Dim spotlights cast an emblem onto a strip of carpet: a forked arrow. Seb was there opposite her, standing with his back to a door, and Valian crouched beside him. "The mirror must have been hiding a portal to this place," Seb said breathlessly.

"I can hear voices," Valian hissed. "We need to hide."

Ivy used her whispering to check: there were at least two of the dead approaching, possibly with other living uncommoners. She noticed a mirror-shaped opening in the wall behind, like a shadow cut out of the slate tiles. "Should we go back?" She could feel Scratch shivering in her satchel: he was frightened.

Seb took a long tape measure from his pocket. Ivy recognized it as the uncommon one he'd been given in Lundinor last spring. "I've got a better idea," he declared. "Stand next to me, both of you."

Ivy couldn't think what her brother had in mind but, with people drawing closer, there wasn't time to argue about it. She squashed herself under Seb's armpit as he got the tape measure ready in front of them, as if he was going to start skipping backward with it. Valian tucked himself in on his other side.

"I haven't actually tried this before," Seb confessed, "but think of it as a jump rope. On the count of three—one . . . two . . ."

"Whatever you're doing, just hurry," Ivy urged. "They're almost here!"

"Three!" Seb flicked his wrists, sending the tape measure flying up past their faces, over their heads and back down behind them toward their heels. Seb, Ivy and Valian all jumped as it scuffed the carpet under them and looped up again.

An odd sensation slithered through Ivy's body, like her skin was being pulled in different directions. "What's happening?" Her perspective warped so quickly that she felt nauseated. The hallway looked like it was getting bigger.

"It's working!" Seb cried. "Keep jumping. We're not quite small enough yet—"

*Small enough?* Ivy made a second assessment of the hallway: it actually *was* getting bigger. With every leap over the tape measure, the ceiling soared farther away.

After a few more bounces, Seb stopped. The walls loomed over them like mountain faces. "That should do it," he decided, returning the tape measure to his pocket. "No one will notice us now."

Valian swayed on the spot, looking disoriented. Ivy's mouth hung open. It had all happened so quickly. . . . She couldn't quite believe it, but judging by the carpet fibers that stretched past her ankles, the three of them had shrunk to the size of insects.

Before her senses had had time to adjust, a pair of scuffed gray sneakers the size of double-decker buses came floating around the corner toward them. Ivy craned her neck and, with a jolt, recognized their male owner: dirty blond hair, grubby skin and a wonky red-and-blue jester's hat.

"Is that *Johnny Hands*?" Valian exclaimed.

The ghoul was dressed in the same scruffy waistcoat and torn jeans that he normally wore as Hobsmatch. Ivy had no clue what he was doing there. As far as she was aware, Johnny Hands worked for Mr. Punch in Lundinor.

Next, pounding the floor with her boots, Curtis appeared at Johnny Hands's shoulder. The glittering divergent arrow brooch on her trench coat matched the design of the badge that Johnny Hands had pinned to his hat.

"Let's try one of my ideas this time," Ivy said, noticing one of Johnny Hands's laces dragging along the floor. "How are you two at climbing?"

# CHAPTER SIX

Ivy steadied her feet as a muddy cotton shoelace the width of a tree branch swung toward her. With one great leap she caught it and heaved herself up.

"I hate this idea!" Seb shouted as he made the jump behind her. The lace jerked as he and Valian grabbed hold.

Clamping her knees together to support her weight, Ivy hoisted herself higher, just like she'd once seen a tree-climber do on TV. The vibrations in the lace told her that Seb and Valian were right behind. When they all reached the top, they let go of the lace and dropped onto the surface of Johnny Hands's floating sneaker. Although the ghoul was hovering along smoothly, every bump and tremor of the ride was magnified to them. Ivy dug her fingernails into the leather, desperate to cling on.

"I don't feel right," Seb said, remaining crouched. Ivy

wondered whether the shrinking sensa-
tions had somehow triggered his motion
sickness.

"Let's secure ourselves under these,"
she suggested, tucking her legs beneath
the strung laces. "At least we won't fall
off like this."

Once they were all fastened down,
Ivy got her first real chance to con-
sider their new dimension. It was
both terrifying and exhilarating to
experience the world in such detail:
the wispy dust particles suspended
in the air, the rough threads of
Johnny Hands's stonewashed
jeans, the texture of the slate tiles—even the odors of mud and
stale carpet were richer and more intense, making her nose
twitch. Despite everything being brighter and louder, Ivy's
eyes and ears didn't feel overwhelmed: her senses must have
adjusted during her transformation.

Their ghoulish ride took them through a doorway into a
brightly lit room full of uncommoners in Hobsmatch. Some
were sitting at desks studying maps or examining images cap-
tured in uncommon snow globes; others were hurrying to and
fro distributing feathers. The noise of their movement was so
loud it sent shudders through Ivy's chest. She hoped that the
three of them were too small to be seen or heard above it all.

"What do you think they're all doing?" Seb asked.

On the wall on the far side of the room hung a patchwork
of pillowcase and napkin materializers, and projected onto

the surface of each was a live video feed. Each one seemed to be from a different place in New York—Ivy recognized one as the view over the Brooklyn Bridge and another as Grand Central Station—but most were just ordinary street corners or public spaces somewhere in the city.

"They're not viewing sites inside Nubrook," Valian observed. "They're doing surveillance on everyone in New York—on commoners."

"And they're *all* wearing those forked arrows," Ivy added. The emblem was easy to spot once you knew what to look for—some people around them had the design embroidered onto the hem of their dress, others incorporated it into the print of their scarf; Ivy even noticed one tattooed onto someone's wrist.

As Johnny Hands glided farther into the room, Ivy caught sight of a week-old copy of the *Nubrook Observer*—an uncommon newspaper—hanging over the edge of a desk. Angling her head, she just about managed to read, upside down, the headline and start of the main story:

---

### SEARCH FOR SOULMATES
#### PUTS UNCOMMON WORLD AT RISK

The number of reckless acts on common land rises dramatically as the dead attempt to become Departed. Special Branch complain of being overstretched and under-resourced.

---

She saw that several sections of the main article had been highlighted, but they were passing too quickly for Ivy to read what they said. Special Branch, she knew, were an elite contingent of underguards whose job it was to keep the uncommon world secret from commoners. She wondered if perhaps this place could be something to do with them.

"The search for soulmates?" Seb said. "That can't have the same meaning for uncommoners as it does in the common world, or else the article wouldn't make sense."

From the details in the subheading, Ivy could think of only one explanation. "If you're a race of the dead, your soulmate must be the uncommon object that contains the remaining fragment of your soul," she phrased carefully. She knew that occasionally when someone died, part of their essence transformed into a race of the dead while the other bit became trapped in an object, turning it uncommon. "That's why the dead are searching for their soulmates—to unite the two parts of their soul, so they can become Departed."

"Which, for some, is a lot better than floating around on Earth for eternity," Valian remarked. "Mr. Punch only revealed the truth about soulmates last spring. For the first time the dead now know that there is a way for them to finally be at peace."

"You could say the news was 'death-changing,'" Seb joked. Ivy glared at him, and his expression turned serious. "Although I've read that not all the dead want to Depart," he added.

Ivy thought of the somber-faced dead traders she'd seen wearing signs around their necks. The objects they were searching for must have been their soulmates. "That could be why Special Branch are under so much pressure," she realized. "The dead are so desperate to find their soulmates that they're carelessly appearing on common land, and Special Branch are having to cover it all up."

Johnny Hands and Curtis stopped at a table that had

a large gumball machine sitting on top. It was packed with multicolored bubble-gum balls, each printed with the forked arrow insignia. Standing by the desk, a tall man with strawblond hair was studying another copy of the newspaper. He had on a smart gray suit with a red pocket square and polished brogues—common dress.

"Agent Curtis"—the man tilted his head in greeting— "Agent Hands . . ."

Johnny Hands removed his jester's hat, waved it through the air and gave an old-fashioned bow; Curtis simply nodded. "A rising tide lifts all boats," they responded in unison.

The expression made Valian flinch. "A rising tide . . . *That's* who these people are—Tidemongers! My parents taught me about them. They're an international espionage guild."

"Are you saying they're uncommon *spies*?" Seb asked, grinning. "That's so cool!"

"We must be inside their Nubrook headquarters," Valian guessed. "I expect they have secret bases all over the world."

The word *Tidemonger* rattled around in Ivy's head until she remembered where she'd seen it before—on a copy of a business card that Johnny Hands had given her last spring. He didn't seem like an obvious choice for a spy; she couldn't imagine him blending in anywhere.

The blond-haired man cleared his throat. "Agent Curtis, I understand you've been unable to track the assets down?"

"They took an aqua-transport to Nubrook, Commander," she replied tersely. "It seems they are more capable than I had anticipated. Until recently, I had their whereabouts pinpointed, but they disabled my tracking device before I could make contact. To my knowledge, they're still carrying the journal."

The Commander inspected one of the bubble-gum balls very carefully before handing it to her. Ivy could sense it was uncommon. "Your orders are to continue searching. Those assets are more at risk from the Fallen Guild than most. Mr. Punch wants them—and the journal—safeguarded at all costs. We can't spare the resources to help you, so you're on your own. Updated intelligence details are inside the gum."

"Understood, Commander." Agent Curtis popped the gum into her mouth and started chewing.

"They're talking about *us*!" Ivy realized, nudging her brother's arm. "*We* are the assets. Curtis was trying to protect us, not kill us." She felt silly now for jumping to conclusions. In fact, the last time she'd seen Mr. Punch, he *had* assured her that some of his "friends" would watch over her and Seb to keep them safe. The only thing Ivy couldn't understand was why Mr. Punch had entrusted Amos's journal to her if he was worried about her having it. Surely it would have been safer with him.

"Well, how were we meant to know?" Seb protested, peering into Curtis's nostrils. "Anyway, some protection she is—she can't find us even when we're right under her nose!"

Dismissed, Curtis marched out of the hall, her trench coat flapping around her ankles. Then the Commander selected another of the bubble-gum balls and passed it to Johnny Hands before escorting him through a different door into a long passageway. They passed a rectangular shadow in the wall—the back of another mirror portal—before turning a corner. "The stakes could not be higher, Agent Hands," the Commander said gravely. "We need someone with your experience for this next mission."

Catching a hint of a smirk on Johnny Hands's lips, Ivy huffed. She doubted there were many Tidemongers with a record as extensive as his: he was more than five hundred years old.

"Last night, while performing a routine investigation in a building in Midtown, a couple of NYPD officers came across a group of selkies," the Commander briefed. "One of our friends at Special Branch happened to be passing and managed to save the policemen from being killed. While our friend was erasing their memories, he discovered several crooked sixpences at the scene—the selkies had been working for the Fallen Guild."

Ivy swallowed. She herself had had the unfortunate experience of encountering a selkie before—a vicious race of the dead with slimy bodies and mouths full of sharks' teeth. Those NYPD officers must have been terrified.

"Incidents like this are becoming more frequent," the Commander went on. "Having infiltrated several of their meetings, we've learned that the Fallen Guild are pledging to find anyone's soulmate in exchange for a year's service in their army. It's being rebuilt at a spectacular rate."

Ivy contemplated how many lives were in danger. The last time the Dirge's army had been in action, they had killed hundreds of uncommoners in Lundinor during the Great Battle of Twelfth Night in 1969.

"What kind of numbers are we talking?" Johnny Hands asked, chewing his gum.

"Details are sketchy, but we believe their forces are already large enough to launch an attack on any of the biggest undermarts," the Commander replied. "But what with this 'soulmates' crisis, Special Branch don't have the reserves to keep the uncommon world hidden *and* fight an army of the dead." He sighed. "If the Fallen Guild choose to strike now, it will be up to just us and the remaining underguard to stop them."

Johnny Hands winced. "Ah, I see the problem. So what do you want me to do?"

# CHAPTER SEVEN

Ivy gripped her shoelace tighter as the Commander accompanied Johnny Hands into a room with glass cabinets down one side and a rack of costumes along the other. She skimmed the outfits as they passed: a waitress's uniform, a business suit, a construction worker's high-vis vest and hard hat—all undercover commoner disguises. Each of the outfits had a label printed with the forked arrow insignia. "That symbol's everywhere," she observed to Seb and Valian. "It has to be the Tidemongers' crest. Every guild has a special symbol of their own."

Only the lower shelves of the glass cabinets were visible from her level. They contained a range of small objects mounted on velvet trays—everything from ballpoint pens and paper clips to scissors and rubber bands.

Seb's eyes gleamed. "*Cool* . . . uncommon spy gadgets!"

The Commander stopped at a particular cabinet filled with soldered circuit boards, USB sticks and old CDs. "Your new mission is to locate and arrest one of the Fallen Guild's most important followers," he informed Johnny Hands, collecting a disk from the top drawer. He held it aloft, at an angle. A shaft of light appeared in the hole at the center and cast a silvery outline of Europe over the surface of the ceiling. "I understand you've already crossed paths with the boy before—Alexander Brewster?"

Ivy flinched, recognizing the name. Alexander's betrayal still tugged at her heart. He had been her friend until she'd discovered he'd used his talent for mixology—the art of combining different liquids using uncommon objects—to murder two underguards and besiege thousands of uncommoners. And now he was working for the Dirge.

"We've been tracking his movements where we can," the Commander continued. "Traces of his mixology handiwork have been removed from several Fallen Guild crime scenes. Most recently, that tunneling incident in Montroquer."

*The break-in at the quartermaster's vault,* Ivy remembered. Alexander Brewster must have been the thief.

As the Commander spoke, a red dot appeared on the map and started flashing. Ivy craned her neck, watching as it moved from somewhere in Russia, over to Paris, and then finally to London, leaving a faint red trail behind. It bore a striking resemblance to the weather patterns of Storm Sarah she had seen on TV that morning. "We've intercepted several encrypted messages between Alexander and the Fallen Guild. Three phrases are repeated often—*nuevo amanacer, nyt daggry* and *fajar baru.* They all mean the same thing."

"New Dawn," Johnny Hands said, rubbing his stubbly chin.

The Commander looked surprised. "I didn't know you spoke so many languages, Agent Hands."

"Ah, well it is quite impossible to live as long as I have, Commander, and not master a few dozen at least," Johnny Hands remarked. "Do you know what this 'New Dawn' is?"

"We believe it's the code name for the Fallen Guild's latest scheme. We're not sure what it involves exactly, but based on what we've been able to decipher from their communications, we understand that the Fallen Guild have tasked Alexander with finding one of the Great Uncommon Good."

Valian went rigid. *"What?"* He threw a panicked look at Ivy and Seb. "Alexander's dangerous. We know he read some of Amos's journal. What if he's hunting for the object that Rosie has?"

"Then she's in danger," Ivy replied, "and it's more important than ever that we find her. We've got to get out of here." She began assessing the moving floor—dismounting a giant floating sneaker wasn't going to be easy. But they had another problem too. "At our current size it'll take us a day just to trek to the other side of this room," she pointed out. "We need to wait for an opportunity when no one is going to see us and use the tape measure again."

Up above, the Commander bid Johnny Hands a solemn farewell before leaving him alone to gather his equipment. Johnny Hands went through each cabinet in turn, selecting different items with his pinkie extended, like he was choosing canapés at a buffet: a pencil sharpener, two champagne corks, a pair of earmuffs . . .

Seb withdrew the tape measure from his pocket. "I've got

a plan. We slide down the laces and hide under that bin while we wait for Johnny Hands to leave"—he pointed to a large plastic container labeled RETURNS. There was a narrow gap at the bottom between the container legs and the carpet.

Suddenly, without warning, Johnny Hands made a swift about-turn, flinging Ivy's head back against the shoe leather. "He's going to go *through* the wall!" Valian shouted. "We have to jump off *now*!"

Seb yanked at the laces to loosen them and, together with Valian, scrambled to the edge of the shoe. Ivy hastened after them, trying not to imagine what death by wall-smooshing would feel like. It was only a few centimeters to the ground, but as they were the size of beetles, it looked more like five meters. She pushed her panic to the back of her mind, swung her legs over the side and slid off.

*"Ahhhhh!"* The plunge was so steep her bottom lost contact with the leather. She dropped through the air and hit the carpet with a *thud,* accidentally biting her tongue.

Valian managed to land on his shoulder and roll to his feet. "Everyone all right?" he checked, just as, high above them, Johnny Hands vanished through the wall.

"I think so," Ivy said, rubbing her jaw.

Seb lengthened the tape measure between his fingers. "We only have to wrap this around us to reverse its original effects. Now's our chance."

Within moments, all three of them had returned to normal size. From their new perspective the room looked completely different. Ivy noticed Curtis's boots stuffed inside the Returns bin they'd planned to hide under, so she guessed she must have visited the room before them.

"Hey, I recognize that," Seb said, inspecting a velvet tray resting on top of one of the cabinets. It contained pairs of cufflinks arranged in neat rows; one link was missing. Seb reached into his pocket to retrieve the cufflink Curtis had planted on them and held it against the single gold one in the tray. "Hmm, identical," he murmured. "This is the cufflink we saw Curtis reading earlier."

Before Ivy or Valian could stop him, Seb twisted it out from under its fastening. Immediately, the drone of a horn filled the air. It was deep and resonant, like an ancient war cry. Ivy clamped her hands over her ears, her ribs quaking. The lights in the room flashed as a voice bellowed over a loudspeaker: "UNKNOWN INTRUDERS DETECTED. All agents report to the Equipment Room."

Grinning sheepishly, Seb tucked both cufflinks into his pocket. "Oops, sorry . . ."

Ivy glared at him. "We need to go." They dashed out into the hallway and found the mirror portal they had passed earlier. "I can't think of another secret to tell it," she cried frantically.

"I've got one," Seb groaned, "but I'm not going to share it with you two. Cover your ears."

Ivy did as he asked. Despite her curiosity, she was determined to give him his privacy. If the situation had been reversed, she'd hate it if he listened in on her. Seb was staring at his feet as he spoke, and without meaning to, Ivy understood one word: *Judy*.

But there was no time to dwell on that. One by one they disappeared through the mirror and emerged inside a derelict block of toilets. Judging by the stale air and lime-scaled taps, the place hadn't been used for ages. Ivy spotted one of the vanity mirrors returning to normal behind them; a divergent arrow was stenciled onto the corner of the glass.

"What happened?" Seb asked, taking in the cracked floor tiles and empty cubicles. "This isn't where we were before."

"We used a different mirror," Valian reminded him. "They must each hide a different entrance to the Tidemongers' base." He went over to the only door and poked his head through the opening. "Looks like we're in some sort of depot. It's all clear."

They found an unlocked fire escape and rushed out into a quiet street in Third Quarter. There was no one around.

"Do you think the Tidemongers will know it was us?" Seb asked guiltily. "That voice said 'unknown' intruders."

Ivy's head was swimming with questions. "They're *spies*— they'll figure it out soon enough."

"And when they do, we're in trouble," Valian added. "We snuck into their base, listened to secret intelligence and stole a pair of cufflinks. We have to hope they don't catch up with us until after we've found Rosie." He stopped at a T-junction and looked up and then down the adjoining road. "I think I know where we are. The Bureau of Fair Trade isn't too far away, but we have to be quick. It closes soon."

# CHAPTER EIGHT

Valian led the way as they hurried along a deserted avenue flanked by tall, graffiti-covered buildings. Dingy alleyways with rickety fire escapes ran between them; their windows were either boarded up or broken.

Ivy shoved her gloved hands into her pockets, thinking of what they'd just learned inside the Tidemongers' base. The air was cold in this part of Nubrook, and the threat of Alexander Brewster and New Dawn only chilled her further. Worrying that they might have been pursued by Tidemongers, she extended the perimeter of her whispering senses as wide as she could. The rattling voices of broken souls trapped inside uncommon objects muttered all around, although there were far fewer than there'd been in First Quarter. There was something else at the very edge of her reach too, something *different,* only it was too far away for her to tell what it was.

"Why is the Bureau of Fair Trade all the way down here?" Seb asked. "Don't people use it that often?"

Valian shrugged. "It's more for storage than anything. Whenever two uncommoners shake hands, a record of the transaction is transmitted to the Bureau. The only time you ever really have to visit is if you're trying to settle a dispute." He scowled. "That's why I know the Lundinor Bureau so well. I once got shortchanged by . . ."

Ivy zoned out of what Valian was saying as a strange hissing voice soon became clear in her mind. It was one of the dead, moving closer. She listened intently as it chanted over and over, like a sorcerer casting a spell. It was impossible to distinguish the exact words, but whereas the broken soul inside Scratch seemed innocent and full of fun, this soul felt menacing and cruel.

She scanned the vacant shop fronts, her nerves tingling. *Scratch, you there?* she asked, reaching him with her whispering.

*Ivy's not something right,* he warned in her head.

*I know. We're being tailed, and I don't think it's a Tidemonger. Do you know what race of the dead it is?*

Her satchel shuddered against her hip. *Scratch met never before.*

Valian was still rambling on, recounting his tale of being shortchanged (". . . and the underguard wouldn't believe that I'd originally handed over seven grade . . ."), but a movement at one of the windows drew Ivy's gaze. She saw the figure of a tall man in a black suit and bowler hat silhouetted against a bright light. Ivy couldn't see much of his face, other than a wide chin and dark mustache. Was he their pursuer?

Just as she was about to warn Seb and Valian, a dozen

underguard officers rounded the corner, the stomp of their heavy boots reverberating around the street.

"They've probably just come from the Bureau," Valian said, crossing to the other side of the road.

Seb steered Ivy out of their way. "Are you all right?" he asked, studying her expression. "You look distracted."

"I . . ." She eyed the window again, but the suited figure had vanished, just as it had disappeared from her field of sense too. "It's nothing," she reassured him. "Don't worry."

Having visited a tree house department store, a windmill workplace and a circus-tent shop in Lundinor, Ivy wasn't entirely surprised when the Bureau of Fair Trade building came into view. Shaped like an American football stadium, the oval concrete structure also had a mammoth brass funnel inserted in the roof, so it almost resembled an old-fashioned gramophone.

"The glove signals are collected through that trumpet before being processed inside," Valian explained. "The system uses all kinds of uncommon objects working together."

Having passed through the automatic front doors, they found a small reception area staffed by a mustachioed gentleman sporting a rainbow wig and feather boa. Behind him were two doors: one decorated with garlands of autumn leaves, the other with large paper lanterns painted to look like Thanksgiving turkeys.

"Welcome to the Bureau of Fair Trade," he said cheerily. "What name are you looking for?"

"Kaye," Valian replied.

The receptionist signaled to his left. "Take the turkey door to hall four. Please don't forget your headwear—it's against GUT law to use any of the record rooms without it."

"I know," Valian grumbled.

Ivy and Seb walked behind Valian as they ventured along a curved corridor with numbered doors on either side. The air smelled distinctly of peppermint. *"Headwear?"* Ivy asked.

"You can't exactly *see* glove records," Valian told her. "You have to *listen* to them. Uncommoners use certain . . . devices to help them do that."

As he opened door number four, a babble of chatter erupted from the space beyond. It sounded so similar to what Ivy sometimes heard with her whispering that for a moment she thought the voices belonged to broken souls. The speakers were mostly calm-toned adults, although Ivy did catch the occasional child.

"Who's that talking?" she asked.

"Glove owners!" Valian shouted back. "This way."

The large hall they'd entered was filled with thousands of crisscrossing silvery threads. Each one was strung taut between a tiny hook on the floor and another on the ceiling, giving the impression of a vast spider's lair. Valian guided Ivy and Seb through a gap in the center of the web. Ivy watched the strands quivering around them; every time one of them vibrated, a new speaker could be heard.

"They're too thin to be guitar strings," Seb observed. "What are they?"

Ivy crinkled her nose; the smell of peppermint was so strong, it gave her a strange idea. "It isn't *dental floss,* is it?"

Valian smiled. "Spot on. Glove signals pass through the floss in here before being logged in the next chamber."

When they reached the far side, they moved under an arch into a room full of floor-to-ceiling storage chests. The noise from the dental floss hall faded slightly so that they didn't have to shout.

"Everything is stored alphabetically," Valian said, reaching into a plastic drum mounted on the wall beside the arch. "See if you can find the right drawer." While Seb searched for the label KAYE, Ivy watched Valian remove three cardboard egg boxes from the plastic container. A length of elastic was fixed to each one.

"Got it," Seb announced, pointing to a spot between KAYDOP and KAYEB.

Valian pulled the correct tray out and placed it on the floor. Inside was a stack of sheet music, stapled together in batches. "Now we put these on," he said, handing Ivy and Seb an egg box each.

Ivy flapped hers open experimentally. "*This* is the headwear?"

"Unfortunately, yes," Valian said. "You can't choose which uncommon objects do what." He made it sound like the phrase was something he'd been told a hundred times before. "If we want to hear who my parents last traded with, we have to use these." He sighed and slid the egg box over his messy hair, making himself look like a toddler wearing a homemade space helmet. Ivy stopped herself from giggling by reminding herself of the serious reason they were there, and positioned her egg box on her head, stretching the elastic around her chin.

"If this isn't a photo moment, I don't know what is," Seb said, laughing. "It would have been even better seeing those underguards wearing them."

"Just put yours on," Ivy insisted, glad that Seb's phone was out of action—common technology didn't work well in undermarts.

Once they had fitted their egg boxes, they all got to their knees beside the drawer. Valian inspected the first batch of music, put it aside and then spread the other sets over the floor. "The top one was mine, so I guess I was the last one to use this drawer. We need to check the rest until we find the ones belonging to my parents. There can't be that many other Kayes."

He studied the nearest file for a moment, shook his head and put it back in the drawer. Ivy slid a batch toward her and hesitated. She couldn't read music and she knew that, despite all his lessons and band practice, Seb couldn't either. Scanning the top page, she expected to find a meaningless jumble of swirly symbols, straight lines and long-tailed dots, so it wasn't what she *saw* that surprised her; it was what she *heard*.

"*. . . and I swear that this . . . ,*" a soft voice said in her ear.

Ivy flinched. The sound was coming from her egg box, she was sure of it. She ran her eyes farther along the notation.

"*. . . is an honest and true . . .*"

Every note seemed to account for a single syllable of speech. Ivy checked which elements around her were uncommon, trying to understand how they worked together. The sheet music, egg boxes and dental floss were the only items containing broken souls; somehow the combination of their three abilities enabled her to read the document.

She started from the beginning.

"*My name is Cherry Kaye and I swear that this is an honest and true account of my uncommon trades.*"

Ivy recognized the name: it was Valian's mum. She regarded him as he sat across from her, scrutinizing another sheet. He would have known that coming to the Bureau meant he would end up listening to his parents' voices. It couldn't be often that he heard them talking, or—thanks to the Frozen Telescope—*saw* them. Today must be making him miss them more than ever. Continuing to read, Ivy listened carefully.

*"Seven years ago, on the twenty-seventh of November, I exchanged objects worth four grade to a sky driver named Lucien Brown, for a ride to the shores of Breath Falls. On the twenty-fourth of November, I purchased two glasses of Hundred Punch in Lundinor for—"*

"Valian, I found your mum's records," Ivy blurted. "Her last trade was on the twenty-seventh of November for transport to Breath Falls. Where's that?"

He looked up from the page. "It's a famous waterfall in the First Quarter of Nubrook. I've got my dad's records here. He hired a snow-globe photographer to take a picture of him and my mum in front of the Falls on the same day. They must have finished scouting in New York and spent an afternoon sightseeing in Nubrook before coming home—the twenty-seventh of November was the date they were murdered."

"So . . . if your parents were in Nubrook before they died, then it had to have been the Sands of Change they'd found, not the Sword of Wills," Seb concluded. "Amos wrote that the Sands of Change was hidden in Nubrook. I wonder how your parents had come across it."

"I have no idea," Valian admitted, "but whatever object the Sands of Change is, *that's* what Rosie has. Did Amos Stirling write anything else about it in his journal? Without knowing what it is, we can't understand what happened to Rosie."

Fetching the journal from her satchel, Ivy cringed. "There is one thing I found a few weeks back—but you're not going to like it. Amos discovered some sentences in an ancient text that mention the Sands of Change." She found the right page and, after using more of Valian's raider's tonic, read aloud:

> *"Light to darkness, life to death*
> *Crystal droplet, bathed in breath*
> *Clasped within silver hands*
> *Deep within hide the Sands."*

"Of course," groaned Seb, dragging a hand down his face. "It *had* to be a riddle."

"We need to work out what it means," Valian said, clearing everything away. "Start brainstorming."

Ivy ran through the rhyme in her head while she gave Valian a hand tidying the sheet music. Her gaze happened to fall on the notes of one of the files, and she heard a girl talking.

"*. . . I swear that this is an honest . . .*" The speaker had a youthful, innocent voice that reminded Ivy of Scratch. Even though the file wasn't stapled, the paper felt too thick to be a single sheet. Ivy prized away the thumb and forefinger of her glove, licked her fingertip and rubbed it against the corner of the paper: two leaves separated with a satisfying crackle. Carefully, she studied the piece from the beginning.

"*My name is Rosie Kaye and I swear that this . . .*"

"Valian—" Ivy tugged on his sleeve. "This file is your sister's."

He huffed. "Yeah, but it's empty. Rosie had only just received her uncommon gloves a few days before she went missing. She never made any trades."

"Are you sure?" Ivy asked. "There are a few notes on the next page."

Valian sidled closer, frowning. "I examined her file after she went missing. There was only the one sheet."

Ivy tilted the document toward Valian so he could see too. His eyes sped hungrily over every note—

*"My name is Rosie Kaye, and I swear that this is an honest and true account of my uncommon trades."*

As the rest of the paper was blank, Ivy flipped over to the second sheet.

*"Transactions in which no goods were exchanged are as follows: seven years ago, on the fifth of December, I shook hands with Mr. Rife of Forward & Rife's Auction Company."*

The speech finished there.

"But—" Valian jabbed a fist into the floor. "Then Mr. Rife *has* seen her! He was lying to us."

Seb shot to his feet. "We should go and confront him. He has to tell us the truth now that we've got evidence."

"We can't," Valian argued with a shake of his head. "Not tonight, at least. The auction house will already be closed, and I have no idea where to find Mr. Rife if not there. We'll have to wait till morning."

There were no three-person road signs available when they got to the boarding zone at the nearest atrium. Seb took a seat on a SCHOOL CROSSING placard; Ivy and Valian shared the HIGHWAY 17 EXIT behind.

"I'll start working on that riddle in Amos's journal right away," Ivy promised. "Scratch can help me—he's good at puzzles."

Valian picked at the paint on the edge of the sign, the muscles on his face tight with nerves. "We have to hurry, though," he said. "The longer we take to figure it out, the more chance there is that Alexander will find Rosie before we do. . . .

"And I can't let that happen."

# CHAPTER NINE

*I sit splashing my feet into a clear pool of water. The zing of freshly cut oranges fills the air. Larks dart through the blue sky as my shoulders warm in the morning sun. . . .*

Ivy forced herself awake. Bird-shaped silhouettes zig-zagged across the plaster ceiling; the invigorating fragrance of citrus filled her nostrils. She pushed herself up in bed, feeling groggy.

Her room was painted mustard yellow with bold-patterned curtains hanging at the windows. All at once, the evening before rushed back to her. Valian had already organized hotel accommodation for himself, but she and Seb, having assumed their babysitter would be a commoner, hadn't planned on staying overnight in Nubrook at all. It had taken them an entire hour to locate an available room. The 1970s-themed Guesthouse Swankypants had been the first place they'd found that wasn't fully booked.

Next to her bed stood a silver lava lamp on a stylish teak table. As the wax inside it stiffened, the bird visions overhead disappeared. She read the notice beside the lamp—

DEAR GUEST,

PLEASE ENJOY THIS UNCOMMON LAVA LAMP. YOU WILL WAKE UP ENERGIZED IN THE MORNING, AND AT NIGHT YOU WILL FEEL RELAXED AND READY FOR SLEEP.

WITH COMPLIMENTS,
GUESTHOUSE SWANKYPANTS

Ivy pulled back the covers. She was wearing gingham-check pajamas embroidered with the logo of Guesthouse Swankypants—a disco-dancing woman with an afro and flared trousers. A shag-pile carpet tickled Ivy's toes as she padded into a lounge furnished with a molded plastic table and chairs in gaudy shades of orange and purple. The remains of the burgers, fries and milkshakes she and Seb had eaten last night were on a room-service trolley in the corner.

Her brother stood gazing out the window, his expression distant. "You sleep all right?"

"Yeah . . . surprisingly." It crossed her mind that the uncommon lava lamp could have suppressed any nightmares she might otherwise have had about the Dirge's army of the dead.

"I've been trying to work out what object the Sands of Change is," Seb said. "If the name is a clue, it isn't very helpful."

She joined him at the window. Beyond the veranda, the street was busy with traders doing early morning deals on everything from feather dusters to drinking straws. On the balconies of the buildings opposite, people set off for work on flying brooms and cleaning mops. The display in the window of a shop named Tierrific Ties caught Ivy's attention—an array of patterned ties around the necks of glittery, grinning mannequins. But as she watched their expressions changing from happy to sad, the ties changed color too.

"The riddle doesn't make sense either," she admitted. "I keep getting stuck on that 'bathed in breath' bit. It's so odd."

"I thought about that too." Seb gestured to Tierrific Ties. "It could mean that the Sands of Change is something you put close to your mouth, like a tie. That would explain the 'bathed in breath' line, because you'd always be breathing on it."

Gazing at the mannequins' sparkly lips, Ivy thought about which other objects might also fit Seb's theory. "What about drinking straws? Or sometimes people blow on their glasses before cleaning them too. Would that count?"

"Yeah, or pens and pencils—I always chew mine at school," Seb said.

Ivy watched a man sipping a coffee as he strolled along the pavement. "There's also teacups, chopsticks, napkins, cutlery . . ." She sagged. "I guess it doesn't exactly narrow down what type of object the Sands of Change could be." She jumped as an iridescent peacock feather suddenly appeared at the end of her nose. It floated upward and swished to and fro, writing letters in the air above her head.

*Dear Ivy . . .*

It flipped over and did a loop-the-loop. Ivy jerked her head, dodging aside.

"Who's that from?" Seb asked, shuffling back.

"I don't know," she answered. "I wasn't expecting anything."

*. . . my warning difficulty with may*

*your family*

*cannot*

"What's wrong with it?" Ivy said. "The handwriting keeps changing."

*faster than I*

*must listen gates*

The plume wiggled back and forth as if it was being tugged in opposite directions.

"I've never seen a featherlight act like this before," Seb admitted.

The feather continued jotting disjointed phrases until, with a soft *puff*, it disappeared, leaving only three words shimmering in the air:

*Yours, Mr. Punch*

Half an hour later, the message was still spinning through Ivy's head as she and Seb arrived outside the Rice Is Nice burrito van, where they'd arranged to meet Valian. Papier-mâché models of turkeys in pilgrim hats sat on the roof. Seb traded for two breakfast burritos, and he and Ivy ate them while they waited. Ivy had just swallowed her last mouthful of tortilla when she spotted Valian approaching with a girl. She had golden skin, chin-length silky black hair and a broad smile. "Judy!" Ivy's spirits lifted as she greeted their uncommon friend. "I didn't know you'd be here."

Judy gave Ivy a hug. "Valian said you needed some help, so I put together my most practical Hobsmatch ensemble and— here I am. What do you think?" She did a twirl, fanning out her denim skirt. She was wearing thick woolen tights, roller skates and a green satin bomber jacket. A sweep of matching green shadow on her eyelids made her wide hazel eyes pop.

"You look great," Seb said, hastily combing his fingers through his hair. "It's good to see you." They exchanged an awkward smile. Ivy remembered Seb murmuring Judy's name to the uncommon mirror at the Tidemongers' base. Although he'd never actually admitted to liking Judy, Ivy could guess his secret.

"Valian described to me what he saw in the Frozen Tele-scope," Judy explained, somber now, "and everything that the three of you heard at the Tidemongers' base. It doesn't sound . . . good."

"That's an understatement," Seb remarked. "We have to find Rosie as soon as possible."

Judy nodded. "Valian and I have just come from the featherlight mailhouse. We wanted to find out whether Rosie could have been traveling by pram too, like Mr. Rife. So we made inquiries with both of our trade contacts, but no one's heard of an uncommon pram being sold in the last seven years. Another dead end, I'm afraid."

By the set of his jaw, Ivy could tell Valian was disappointed.

"Still," Judy continued, smiling, "you've got one lead on Mr. Rife—you know from the sheet music that he did meet Rosie, so that sounds promising. As does that riddle in Amos's journal."

As the four of them set off in the direction of the auction house, Ivy told Valian and Judy about Mr. Punch's mysterious featherlight message. "I couldn't understand any of it," she admitted.

Valian scrunched his brow. "If there were different sets of handwriting, it almost sounds like the message was written by more than one person."

"Maybe it was," Judy commented. "Mr. Punch is a Hob, remember—his race of the dead have several broken souls trapped inside them. I only ever recognize him when he appears as quartermaster looking like a young man with a red beard, but he must have many more guises."

Ivy tried to count how many different versions of Mr. Punch she'd seen. He had appeared as an old man with a crooked back, as a softly spoken shopkeeper and as the fresh-faced quartermaster that Judy knew. His distinctive aquamarine irises were the only of his features that never changed. "I just hope he's OK," she said. "He's never acted like this before."

The streets grew busier as they walked along. It seemed that even more Thanksgiving decorations had appeared overnight—rust-colored pumpkins and gilded pinecones were now arranged on the steps leading up to most shops, and the air was starting to smell of apple pie and cinnamon. Arriving at the entrance of Forward & Rife's, they found the door to the courtyard closed. Seb grabbed the handle and gave it a yank, but it was definitely locked. He examined a note fixed to the knocker, then held it aloft for all to see.

Forward & Rife's Grand Globe-Trotting Auction of Uncommon Treasures

---

*ADVANCE VIEWING CANCELED*
*Open for auction tomorrow 12:00–4:00 p.m.*

"What could be so important that Mr. Rife and Mrs. Bees have decided to shut up shop?" Ivy asked, peering up at the roof. Security guards patrolled around the edge of the garden. "It's a pity my senses don't reach far enough to check whether that pram is still there. If we knew it had gone, then at least we'd know they'd left Nubrook."

"Mr. Rife wasn't planning on visiting his buyer, Midas, until after the auction," Valian reminded them. "Perhaps we made him nervous by asking questions about Rosie. We know he's hiding something." He bent down and squinted through the keyhole. "Great. They've got uncommon shuttlecocks inside."

Seb jerked his head up. "Those weird things you hit when you're playing badminton? What do they do?"

"They fly around acting like mobile security sensors," Judy explained. "If they detect something that appears out of place, they sound an alarm."

Ivy took a closer look. Flitting through the air as fast as dragonflies, the shuttlecocks made a whirring sound as they moved. Occasionally they hovered in one place long enough for Ivy to see how they worked—their feather skirts rotated at high speed like propellers. "So I'm guessing that means we can't sneak inside to check if the pram's still there or not? Or search for other clues either?"

"Unfortunately not," Valian said. "Even if I used my boat shoes to move through the walls, one of the shuttlecocks would likely spot me."

"What if we divert the shuttlecocks' attention?" Seb suggested. "Anyone got anything we can use to create a distraction?" He turned out his pockets, flashing his phone, a wallet and—Ivy noted—the pair of cufflinks he'd collected the day before at the Tidemongers' base. "I've got my drumsticks too, but with the amount of noise and destruction they'd cause, we'd be bound to attract the interest of the security guards on the roof—and everyone out here as well."

Valian patted the inside pocket of his leather jacket. "Same problem with everything I'm carrying."

Ivy knew her yo-yo—which generated tornados—would cause all sorts of chaos. She contemplated asking Scratch to make a loud noise, but that would only draw the shuttlecocks' attention to her satchel.

Judy hesitated. "I can't promise this will work, but I've got an idea. Can you give me some cover?" she asked, indicating the passing crowds.

Seb and Valian positioned themselves between Judy and the street, hiding her from the wandering gazes of the passersby. Judy considered the marble wall of the auction house very carefully—running her fingers over it and studying the way it looked in her shadow before flattening herself against it. She scrunched up her nose and, gradually, her skin, hair and clothes all turned a perfectly matched shade of marble gray.

Ivy blinked, unsure how Judy was achieving the effect or even whether it was permanent. The reddish-pink of the inside of Judy's mouth appeared hovering in midair. "Can you see me?" she asked.

"Not if you don't speak," Seb said. "It's brilliant."

In a streak of color, she reappeared—still with her back flat against the wall, as she had been before.

"Judy—it's better than brilliant," Valian said. "The camouflage will fool the shuttlecocks *and* the security guards, so you'll be able to slip into Mr. Rife's office easily. We can even use the cufflinks Seb took from the Tidemongers. If you plant one of them in Mr. Rife's pram, then we'll be able to track him if he does leave Nubrook."

Ivy could hear excitement rising in Valian's voice. It was a good plan. "How did you even do that?" she asked Judy.

"Well, as you know, every race of the dead has its own strengths and weaknesses," Judy explained. "Phantoms like me have the ability to manipulate light. With a little concentration I can make something appear a different color." She tucked a strand of dark hair behind her ear. "I've never actually attempted to camouflage myself before."

"You're a phantom?" Seb's face brightened. "I should have guessed sooner . . . you can touch the ground, but only on wheels; you're fun-loving and colorful . . . it makes sense now."

Ivy gave her brother a sidelong glance. All that homework

he'd been doing with Scratch now made sense: he'd wanted to know more about *Judy*.

"So . . . where do you stand on the whole 'soulmates' thing?" he asked casually—although Ivy noticed his neck stiffen, like he was bracing himself for the answer. "From what I read, the dead community is pretty divided on the issue. Not everyone wants to be Departed."

Judy arched an eyebrow. "You've been reading about the dead?" She smiled. "Personally, I'd rather be alive if all things were possible, but as they aren't, being a phantom is as good as it's gonna get. I've got no desire to find my soulmate."

"Right . . . cool." Seb's posture relaxed, although his cheeks flushed as he handed Judy the cufflinks. "Good luck sneaking past the shuttlecocks."

"I'll come find you when I've hidden a cufflink in the pram," Judy told them. "You shouldn't wait around for me; time is against us." She walked over to the door and disappeared through it, leaving behind a glittering metallic outline, as if gold dust had been sprinkled in the air.

"Judy's right," Valian said, ignoring the goofy grin on Seb's face. "If we can't question Mr. Rife right now, we need to investigate another lead. Why don't we retrace my parents' steps on the afternoon they were in Nubrook? If we can find out *where* they found the Sands of Change, we might get an idea as to *what* it is—and solve that riddle."

"The only trade they made that day was by Breath Falls," Ivy reminded them. "We'll have to start there."

Valian stuffed a hand in his pocket and retrieved his ping-pong ball. "It's not too far from here. We can bounce on the way."

# CHAPTER TEN

"Are you sure this is OK?" Seb asked, holding his ping-pong ball above a wooden street bench. "I'm not going to get arrested or anything?"

Valian aimed his ball at a nearby lamppost; Rosie's image appeared on it a moment later. "It's within GUT law to put up posters, as long as they're not being used to generate business." He pointed to the boarded-up windows of a shop on the other side of the road. "Look there—you see what I mean?"

Ivy picked her way through a river of traders on the way over. A sky driver swooped low over the street, hauling a woman up onto his flying vacuum cleaner. As the woman had been waving her hand in the air a moment before, Ivy guessed that that was how you hailed a ride in Nubrook.

Planks of chipboard covered the old shop fascia. They

were affixed with various IUC trading announcements, several lost property notices and advance warnings of road closures. There was even a poster proclaiming the opening of Strassa, the WORLD'S FIRST SKYMART! in Tibet: *The technological capital of the uncommon world! A market hidden in the clouds of the Himalayas.* She examined the picture of Strassa. It looked like a city exploding out of the side of a mountain. Brightly colored mosaic towers rose from the rock, separated by star-shaped platforms filled with fountains and market stalls.

She pushed aside a couple of trading notices and threw her ping-pong ball at the space she'd made in between, but it rebounded unexpectedly. She had to leap to catch it before it sprang out into the crowd.

"Finished," Seb announced when Ivy returned. He was standing by his bench with a smug look on his face. Not one inch of the wood remained uncovered: he'd printed so many copies of Rosie's poster that the colors bled into one another, making the prints resemble a series of Andy Warhol portraits.

"Er—thanks," Valian said, wincing. "Let's move on; the waterfall's along here."

They continued through several wide, uncluttered streets of a beautiful district of First Quarter, where all the storefronts were decorated with ornate Art Deco moldings and stained glass. Ivy noticed more of the dead traipsing around with "soulmate" signs around their necks, and she also spotted materializers playing official underguard announcements addressing the issue: "Please remain calm," a senior underguard officer announced in one video. "We are actively searching for ways to locate your soulmate."

Valian found a trio of disposable red plastic ponchos in

a rubbish bin and, handing one each to Ivy and Seb, he said, "Here, put these on. You'll need them as we get closer."

Ivy slipped the garment over her head, trying not to laugh at Seb, whose sleeves only reached his forearms. "Why do I have to wear a child's one?" he complained, dangling his arms like a scarecrow.

Ivy smirked. "You *are* a child, Seb."

They turned onto a terrace heaving with traders, all wearing the same red ponchos over their Hobsmatch. Many were clustered near a barrier on the far side, peering into a wall of dense mist. Ivy couldn't see what lay beyond, but judging by the deep rumbling noise resonating in the air, she assumed it was the Falls.

Shadowing Valian, she and Seb edged through the crowd. They passed a tall man with a shaved head wearing a bib promoting Nubrook Sights. He was addressing a group of people holding uncommon snow globes. Ivy guessed they were tourists and he their tour guide, and as she moved closer she heard him saying, ". . . Breath Falls is one of the great wonders of the uncommon world, an entirely uncommon-made waterfall in the downtown district of First Quarter in Nubrook. The silver colossus was designed in 1934 in the Art Deco style by Vermillion Spruce, the famed Danish architect. The water draws its source from Hudson Bay and is filtered by uncommon devices before reaching Nubrook. . . ."

When Ivy drew level with the railing, alongside Seb and Valian, the air felt cooler and full of the crisp scent of ice. Moisture settled on her cheeks. She blinked, gazing up through the spray. Looming above them was a gigantic silver statue of a man in a long cape; his head alone was the size of a block of apartments. He had sleek wavy hair and smooth round eyes like an ancient Greek figure. His hands were cupped under his chin so that the water gushing from his mouth fell over his fingers before tumbling into the foam below. The cascade was so ferocious, mist clouded around his lips like breath.

"I can see where the waterfall gets its name from!" Ivy shouted. She traced the statue down; the trunk of the man's body disappeared into the froth.

"I'm going to ask some of the local sky drivers if they've heard of this Lucien Brown who provided transport to my parents," Valian said. "You two see if you can find the photographer my dad traded with. The name of his company was Snowy Snaps."

Ivy and Seb dipped through the crowd, checking the lanyards of every person shaking an uncommon snow globe. Ivy watched one family posing for a photo in front of the barrier. She found it hard to believe that anything other than white mist would show up behind them in the picture. Their snow globe photographer was busy giving loud directions to the family to get the shot he wanted. "Madam, if you step to your right," he called, "that's it—we can frame you right between the statue's silver hands. . . ."

*Silver hands . . . ?*

Ivy recognized the phrase instantly. It gave her an idea. "Seb—" She tapped him on the arm. "The waterfall . . . it could be the answer to Amos's rhyme—'crystal droplet, bathed in breath, clasped within *silver hands,* deep within hide the Sands' . . ."

"What?" he shouted.

"The rhyme in Amos's journal," she repeated, more loudly.

" 'Crystal droplet' could mean water. The statue, it's got silver hands that are 'bathed in breath' . . ."

Seb tugged on his earlobe. "I still can't hear you."

"I can," Valian said, appearing over Ivy's shoulder. "I've had no luck with the sky drivers, but you're right about that rhyme—it *could* refer to Breath Falls. We know my parents flew down here. Perhaps they found the Sands of Change hidden nearby?"

The three of them hurried back to the railing and searched through the mist, looking for clues. Ivy scoured the colossus, but it was difficult to discern anything other than the rushing water and the statue's silver torso. A narrow pebble beach ran around the edge of the plunge pool. "There," Seb said. "Wait—is that something? I'm not sure." He pointed to the water's edge on the far bank. The shape of a building lurked in the mist.

"I'll ask the tour guide," Ivy suggested. Wearing his luminescent NUBROOK SIGHTS bib, he was easy to find, and Ivy returned in moments with the information. "It's a shop called the Old Seafarer's Place," she reported, "which opened in 1970. But it's closed now. The man who owned it sold nautical objects. It's the only shop down there."

Valian gazed suspiciously at the building. "My parents could have visited it, I suppose, looking for objects to trade. Let's check it out."

Ivy hailed a sky driver, who agreed to fly them down on his rug on the condition they paid extra if any water damage was caused. Dropping them on the shore, he anxiously inspected his dripping tassels before zooming away.

The Old Seafarer's Place was the size of a small bungalow.

It had barnacle-encrusted walls, porthole windows and a green mossy roof. Slimy red plastic streamers hung from the drainpipes like the bloody entrails of a monster. "What are those?" Ivy asked.

Valian peered at them as they plodded across the shingles. "They look like decorations from the Nubrook Christmas parade. I guess the shop must have still been open last winter." Seb tried the door but it was locked.

"Good, I can't see any shuttlecocks," Valian said, pressing his face to the window. "I'll unbolt it from the other side." He bent down and retied the laces of his boat shoes with more complicated knots. Ivy could see through the hole in the heel that his socks were soaking wet. "Wait here," he said, and filling his lungs with air and pushing his shoulders back, he walked *through* the wall.

Seb gawped. "He *has* to let me try those things."

There was a clatter and the door swung open. "You might want to hold your nose," Valian told them. "It stinks like a stagnant pond in here."

Ivy covered her face with her sleeve as they stepped inside. The shop had jagged, rocky walls and was filled with rope shelving units, each stocked with a variety of sea-themed objects—from anchors and lanterns to vintage life buoys. In the corner of the room stood a driftwood desk and, behind it, a large ship's wheel fixed to the floor.

"Anyone got any ideas what we're looking for?" Seb asked.

"I don't know," Valian said. "My parents didn't buy anything in here, or else it would have shown up on their trading records. They must have just browsed. Perhaps if we look around, we'll find answers."

A voice babbled into Ivy's ear, making her twitch.

"You OK?" Valian asked.

"Just another broken soul." She scanned her surroundings. "It's this ship's wheel. It's uncommon."

"Really?" Valian ran his hands over the spokes. The wood was worn smooth in places; Ivy pondered what kind of ship it had been fixed to originally. "My parents had one of these," Valian said. "They used it to protect their scout stash."

Seb frowned. "Scout stash?"

"It's a secure place where you store any objects you're waiting to sell," Valian explained. "It was one of the places the Dirge raided on the night my parents were murdered. The ship's wheel was the key to gain entry, but only if you knew the correct combination of turns. This one must be hiding something. There might be clues in here that can help us guess the correct sequence to open it."

While Seb helped Valian search, Ivy focused her senses inside the wheel, just like she did whenever she spoke to the soul inside Scratch. Unlike the rushed gabble from Mr. Rife's pram, the voice trapped inside the ship's wheel was a slow drawl. After a minute's focus Ivy was able to understand it.

*All right?* the wheel asked in a sleepy Cornish accent. *Where you to?*

Ivy wasn't sure how to respond, so she decided that honesty was the best policy. *Er . . . my friends and I need to know your combination.*

The voice chuckled. *Can't tell you that for free.*

*Would you be willing to trade?* Ivy asked. They were in an undermart, after all.

*Hmm . . .* There was a long pause before the voice said,

*'Ere, tell you what, sing me a shanty and I'll let you pass. Customers used to hum them all the time, and I miss hearing them.*

Ivy hesitated. She wasn't sure what kind of song a shanty was. "Seb, can you sing a shanty?"

He looked out from behind a set of shelves. "Say what?"

"A shanty. The soul inside the ship's wheel told me that if we sing it a shanty, it'll give us access."

Seb tilted his face lower. "There are so many things wrong with that sentence, I don't know where to begin."

"Do you know what it is or not?" she asked impatiently.

"Yeah. We learned one in music class last term. It's a traditional work song sailors sing. I could hum the tune to one, but I can't remember the words."

"So use different lyrics," Valian suggested.

Seb thought for a moment before starting to sing: "Can't take not knowing, oh, oh, oh. Give me a reason, oh, oh, oh . . ."

The tune was jolly and upbeat with lots of whistling. Ivy clamped her lips together so she wouldn't explode with laughter. She recognized the words Seb was using from a song by his favorite band, the Ripz. The combination of the two didn't exactly work. Happily she turned her senses back to the voice inside the ship's wheel.

*I've never 'eard this one before,* it remarked in a tone of surprise. *Catchy.*

Without warning, the wheel made a series of clockwise and counterclockwise turns. There was a strange groaning sound, like a heavy object being dragged over wood, and a rectangular part of the floor fell away, forming a ramp.

Seb stopped singing and walked to the edge to take a look

down inside. "There's some sort of railway under here," he told them.

The three of them ventured down carefully. Uncommon lemon squeezers were strung along the walls of a rocky tunnel, lighting it a few hundred meters into the darkness. A cart constructed from one half of a huge barrel sat on the tracks. Valian got in.

"What are you doing?" Seb asked. "We can't get into that thing—we don't know where it leads."

"Isn't that the point?" Valian argued. "What if it takes us to where my parents found the Sands of Change?"

Ivy climbed in behind, knowing Valian was right. The interior of the barrel was fitted with three narrow benches. Moisture seeped up through her trousers as she sat down.

"Fine," muttered Seb, pursing his lips as he lifted his leg over the side and took the rear position. "But don't blame me if—"

The barrel shot forward over the rails. The hood of Ivy's poncho flew back. "Hold on!" she cried. Wind blasted her face as they sped along the track, twisting left and right. She could hear the waterfall rumbling in the rocks above and presumed they were somewhere beneath it. They banked left and plunged deeper, eventually coming to a halt at the end of a short passage. Where the tracks finished, a stone door was set into the rocky wall.

Seb got shakily to his feet. "Is that . . . ?"

Ivy shuddered, recognizing the symbol carved into the door: a crooked sixpence, the guild crest of the Dirge.

# CHAPTER ELEVEN

Ivy steadied her nerves as they ventured closer to the door. "I don't understand. Was the shop owner working for the Dirge?"

"There's only one way to know for sure," Valian said. He tested the door and it creaked open.

Inside, they found a small room with brick walls. The stale air was teeming with dust, like in an attic. A chill traced Ivy's spine. "I know this place. Six walls. Six doors. We're in the Hexroom."

Seb made a swift turn for the exit. "Time to be going," he squeaked.

"Wait." Valian grabbed his arm. "This is the secret meeting place of the Dirge. We might learn something useful."

"Or we might be killed!" Seb insisted.

Ivy understood why he was worried: the last time they had

been inside the Hexroom, they'd come face to muzzle with a vicious grim-wolf, one of the races of the dead.

Valian pointed to the floor. "I don't think the Dirge use it anymore. Look at the dust—it's undisturbed. No one's been in here for ages."

Turning on the spot, Ivy surveyed the six doors in turn. Each member of the Dirge had their code name chiseled into the bricks above: Nightshade's door was carved from glittering rock; Wolfsbane (whom they'd vanquished last spring) had a stainless-steel door; the wooden door of Ragwort (now imprisoned in a ghoul hole) opened onto a featherlight mailhouse in Lundinor. The code names of Monkshood, Hemlock and Blackclaw cut into the brickwork above the remaining three doors.

Seb looked up at the stone door of Blackclaw, the leader of the Dirge, and shivered. "Still gives me the creeps that we're related to that guy."

Ivy studied the crooked sixpence carved into the surface of Blackclaw's door. The hooded face on the coin wore a mask covering its features. That mask had once belonged to their great-grandfather Octavius Wrench, before he died in the Great Battle of Twelfth Night. She speculated whether anyone else had filled the position of Blackclaw since their great-grandfather's death.

"Give me a hand with this," Valian said, shoving the Hemlock door. "I just tried Ragwort's door and it's still unlocked, so maybe we can get this one open and discover who Hemlock is."

Ivy tensed, knowing that Valian had always held Hemlock responsible for his parents' murder—hemlock was one of the poisons that had been used to kill them. "Can't you use your boat shoes?" she suggested.

He shook his head. "Not to move through uncommon doors."

Seb joined the effort, all three of them turning their shoulders against the stone to push. After a minute of sustained struggle, they straightened up again and eased their aching shoulders. Valian kicked the wall. "It's no use," he complained. "It won't budge."

"But at least we're a step closer to uncovering one of them," Ivy reminded him, and she swung back the door through which they'd first entered the Hexroom. Above it, MONKS-HOOD was carved into the bricks. "So the shopkeeper of the Old Seafarer's Place isn't just *working for* the Dirge. He *is* one of them. The dates make sense: the Dirge disappeared after the Great Battle in 1969, then this shop opened in 1970."

Valian's face darkened. "Monkshood must have had an important reason for crawling out from under his rock for the first time in forty years. Do you think it's got something to do with New Dawn?"

"Maybe. Seb and I caught a glimpse of Monkshood in Lundinor last spring," Ivy reminded him. She recalled the figure they'd seen in a long black hooded cloak. "He was trying to recruit Alexander Brewster to join the Dirge."

"Obviously he succeeded," Valian growled. "Anyway—my parents couldn't have discovered this hidden place. If they had, they would have shared the information with the under-guards, and Monkshood would have been arrested. We need to pick up their trail somewhere else."

"In that case, can we *please* go now?" Seb pleaded. "I don't want to stay in this room any longer."

Valian gave the Hemlock door a final unsuccessful shunt before returning to the barrel-cart alongside Seb. As Ivy lifted her leg over the side of the cask, a shadow in the tunnel wall caught her attention. It looked like the opening to a small cave. She ventured closer.

Seb groaned. "*Ivy, what are you doing?*"

Ignoring him, Ivy squeezed through the gap in the rock and emerged inside a small grotto lit by the silvery glow of an uncommon milk jug. The jagged walls extended into darkness many meters above.

"It's all right," she called back. "It's just an abandoned room." Filling the floor was a single table and chair, with various papers strewn across the top. Most were too water-damaged to be legible, but a few—the ones tucked within the piles—had managed to stay dry.

Valian appeared behind her, slipping easily through the slit in the wall. "Anything interesting?"

She passed him a list of strange symbols written in black ink. It looked like some sort of code. "Remember the Commander at the Tidemongers' base told Johnny Hands that Alexander Brewster and the Dirge were communicating in encrypted messages? Well, do you think this is one of them?"

"Possibly." Valian scrutinized the page.

Hidden among the other papers, Ivy found a long scroll. The words *Novus Aurora* were scrawled around the outside. " 'Aurora' is the name of the princess in Sleeping Beauty," she recalled with a shiver. "My mum used to read me that fairy tale when I was little. I remember she told me the name means 'dawn' in Latin."

"Then 'novus' must translate as 'new,' " Valian said, staring at her. "This *is* something to do with New Dawn."

With urgency, they unrolled the scroll and spread a world

map over the table. Cities on every continent had been circled and numbered. "These all have major undermarts beneath them," Valian identified. "Do you think New Dawn is a plan to attack them all with the army of the dead?"

"It can't be," Ivy said. "At least, not all at once. The Tide-mongers' Commander said that the Dirge's forces were only capable of attacking *one* of the bigger undermarts, not hundreds." She scanned the diagram, focusing on the numbers. No two were the same. "What if these numbers represent the order in which the Dirge are going to strike?" Her heart began to race as she slid her finger across the map, counting as she went. *New York is second. Moscow third. Berlin fourth . . .*

Her chest constricted as she pictured the undermarts beneath each city falling one by one to the Dirge's control. She checked on London and found it inked with the number one. "Valian—they're going to launch an assault on Lundinor *first!*"

He grabbed her hand. "We need to show this to someone, fast."

## CHAPTER TWELVE

Reversing along the track, the barrel-cart surfaced back inside the Old Seafarer's Place in minutes. Although the shop was quiet, the waterfall roared loudly outside.

"We have to contact the Tidemongers right away," Ivy said, leaping out of the barrel. Ordinarily she would have suggested they speak to Mr. Punch, but after his worrying message earlier, she wasn't so confident he'd be able to help. "Do either of you have any feathers?"

Seb shook his head.

"I used the last of mine to send inquiries to my trading contacts this morning," Valian replied sullenly. "We can get hold of some if we get back to the main part of Nubrook. We just need to hail a sky driver to take us up there."

"I'll go," Seb offered, striding toward the door. "I'm the tallest; they're more likely to see me waving."

As Seb disappeared into the mist outside, Ivy rolled up the Dirge's map and stuffed it into her satchel, contemplating whether they could arrange to have it ghost-couriered to the Tidemongers' base. "We should send a feather to Johnny Hands first," she decided. "Lundinor's his home." Without wanting to, she pictured the Dirge's army of the dead tearing through the cobbled streets of Lundinor, destroying shops and houses, and killing those traders who stood in their way. "Why do the Dirge have such a vendetta against that undermart in particular?"

"The one time the Dirge tried to take control of Lundinor all those years ago, they were humiliated," Valian stated, perching on a driftwood bench in one corner of the shop. "So perhaps it's not so much a vendetta as a need to succeed where they previously failed?"

Ivy recalled her uncommon history. In the lead-up to the Great Battle of Twelfth Night, the Dirge had committed hundreds of crimes around the world, conducting a global campaign of fearmongering. "You could be right. These last six months the Dirge have been responsible for all kinds of offenses—burglary, arson, blackmail—it's similar to what they did before."

"I bet that's why they're searching for one of the Great Uncommon Good," Valian hissed. "The Dirge wouldn't want to risk losing again and being made to look weak. Whichever object they're chasing—the Sword of Wills or the Sands of Change—it might have the ability to bolster their power and ensure they win."

Just then, several brass lanterns rattled as Seb returned through the front door. "Well, that was a waste of time," he moaned, wiping spray from his forehead. "No one can see me through the mist. We need to draw attention to ourselves in another way—"

Suddenly the entire shop quaked, sending smaller items rolling off shelves. "What's happening?" Ivy cried, steadying herself against a chair.

With a loud crackle, two creatures—roughly gorilla-shaped—peeled themselves off the craggy walls and dropped to the floor with a thud. Their bodies were made of jagged rocks; they had large, featureless boulders for heads. Despite having no eyes, one creature turned for Valian, the other for Seb. As they stamped their feet, sand spilled from their joints, making a horrid crunching sound.

"Gravellers," Valian breathed. "I've crossed paths with one before. Run!"

Ivy dashed for the door, but a third graveller dropped from the ceiling, blocking her path. Seb drew out his drumsticks.

"Those won't work!" Valian warned. "Gravellers are only damaged by fire."

Ivy backed away as the third graveller lumbered toward her, pounding its fists together. "I don't have anything that creates flames!" she yelled, trying to dispel a horrible vision of being ground to smithereens with a mortar and pestle.

Valian ducked behind some shelves as one of the gravellers made a swing for him. "Seb, give us an exit! I'll try to distract them." He took something from his pocket, but Ivy was too far away to see what it was.

Seb thrashed his drumsticks angrily in the direction of the window. Ivy dropped to the floor as glass shattered around her. But Seb's aim must have been slightly off, because several floorboards splintered too, leaving a hole in the ground. Amid all the chaos Ivy noticed that the tunnel leading to the Hexroom had disappeared—there was only earth and concrete foundations below now.

"Everyone—get to the window!" Valian shouted. He was holding what looked like a rubber stamp in his hand, wooden with a brass handle. "I'm about to give the gravellers a whole lot more targets."

Sand showered Ivy's face as a graveller stomped at her head. With a yelp, she rolled aside and scrambled to her feet. "What the—?" she spluttered. The shop was unexpectedly crammed with clones of themselves: the figures looked like exact replicas of Ivy, Seb and Valian, only all facing in different directions. Ivy raised her arm; her mimics copied the movement.

The graveller pursuing Ivy dithered, turning its boulderhead left and right. It seemed confused, and Ivy saw her opportunity to escape. She hopped over a broken shelf, sidestepping the graveller's reach, and leaped through the empty window frame. Spray from the waterfall coated her face as she sprinted across the shingles toward the water. She checked over her shoulder. Seb and Valian were following, kicking up stones as they ran. A graveller thundered out of the Old Seafarer's Place in pursuit, roaring and beating its chest.

*We need a way to escape,* she communicated to Scratch urgently.

He vibrated. *Soap dish beings here still.*

*Yes—good idea!* She jabbed a hand into her satchel and grabbed the soap dish, tickling Scratch in thanks. Skidding to

a halt at the lake's edge, she placed the dish in the froth, where-upon it instantly expanded to the size of a paddleboat. "Er—get in!" she urged Seb and Valian.

"That gravel guy is still coming," Seb warned as they all

jumped aboard. With a foot against the shore, Valian kicked off. A hood of bubbles sealed them in as their silver boat glided across the water. Ivy just caught sight of a graveller hopping up and down angrily on the shore before the soap dish finally submerged.

"Everyone OK?" Valian asked, brushing sand from his leather jacket.

Ivy peeled back her gloves. The heels of her hands stung where she'd grazed them, but they weren't badly bleeding.

"Still alive . . . ," Seb grumbled, ". . . just."

The same robotic voice as before echoed around the vessel: *"Welcome aboard this aqua-transport vessel number 2895. What is your desired destination?"*

"Forward & Rife's auction house," Valian replied, adding, "We can get feathers near there *and* check whether Judy's seen Mr. Rife and planted that cufflink."

They rocked backward as the dish suddenly accelerated through the water. Outside, Ivy could see foam and the occasional flash of silver as they sailed by Breath Falls. The vessel shuddered as it entered a large pipe, and everything went black outside. After a moment there was a loud squealing noise, like a car breaking, and from out of nowhere bubbles surged up Ivy's nose, making her snort and shut her eyelids. "What's happening?" she gulped.

"Hold on!" Valian cried.

Something cold and heavy shoved against Ivy's side and, when she opened her eyes again, she found herself slumped under a wide stone arch. Immediately ahead of her, a fountain spurted, set inside a small circular garden next to a busy road. The roar of a huge city filled the cold air. Next to her Valian was rubbing his ribs as he sat up; Seb appeared opposite from under a pile of leaves.

"This isn't Forward & Rife's," Seb mumbled, stating the obvious.

"No," Ivy said, staring at the skyline. "I think we're in New York."

# CHAPTER THIRTEEN

The late-afternoon sky was gray and getting darker. Ivy noticed clouds swirling around as if they were sizing each other up before a fight. She trod carefully between the trimmed yew hedges surrounding the fountain. Something silver glinted between the leaves. Ivy reached down and picked up the dolphin-handled soap dish and examined it.

"Anything?" Valian asked.

"Yes—there's a crack in one side. It must have gotten damaged when we were escaping the gravellers."

"That explains why we've ended up here," he told her. "Broken soap dishes will throw you out at random points on your journey, wherever the nearest water outlet is."

Seb removed his plastic poncho and brushed off the wet leaves that had stuck to his jeans. "So what do we do now? If we want to contact Johnny Hands, we have to get back to Nubrook."

"I know of one entrance beneath a disused subway platform," Valian said, collecting all three of their ponchos and stuffing them in a nearby recycling bin. "We just need to navigate our way to the nearest subway station. We'll be able to access the disused platform once we're underground."

Seb reached for his phone. "I'll find us a route," he offered. "At least we already know where we're starting from—" He pointed behind them. Flanking the stone arch were steps leading up to the veranda of an impressive building with a sloping red roof. Engraved across the balustrade in capital letters were the words:

### THE AMERICAN MUSEUM
### OF NATURAL HISTORY
### FOUNDED 1869

For the briefest of moments, Ivy wondered what it would feel like simply to be in New York on holiday. She'd love to explore the museum and see the city's other sights, just as a normal tourist.

"The nearest subway station is on the corner of Eighty-First Street and Central Park West," Seb said, tapping at the screen. "It's a five-minute walk from here. Follow me."

The noise of a crowd greeted them as they headed onto Seventy-Seventh Street. People crammed the pavements, laughing and pointing: the road was filled with a line of giant inflatables, secured under nets in preparation for the Thanksgiving parade the next day. As the road was closed in the other direction, they kept the museum building on their right and ventured along Columbus Avenue. "I'm glad we dressed warm," Ivy commented, watching her breath condense in the frosty air. "It's freezing up here."

"Minus two Celsius, according to my weather app," Seb told her. "Apparently, Storm Sarah is due to hit the city today. New Yorkers have been advised to stay inside."

"You mean the same Storm Sarah that was in London yesterday?" Ivy wasn't a meteorologist, but it seemed impossible that a storm could travel as quickly as that across the Atlantic Ocean and still be as powerful.

"Yeah," Seb said. "They're calling it a phenomenon."

Ivy remembered noticing the similarities between Storm Sarah's path across Europe and Alexander Brewster's crime trail. She hadn't given it any thought since first spotting it back at the Tidemongers' base, but now she considered whether the two might be connected. Could Alexander Brewster somehow be controlling the storm? But before she had time to share her theory with Seb and Valian, she caught the murmur of a sinister voice in her ear. It was chanting, over and over.

. . . *The sun will rise, the night is done, what is lost will be won.*
*The sun will rise, the night is done, what is lost will be won.* . . .

Her skin prickled as she realized it belonged to the dead creature who had been following them the day before in Nubrook. She shook her head clear and shuffled closer to Seb and Valian. "We need to get out of here," she said simply. "*Now.*"

Straightaway, Valian looked alert. "What's wrong?"

Ivy scanned the road. A tall man in a black suit and bowler hat was walking steadily through the parade floats, an ebony cane swinging in his left hand. He was too far away for Ivy to see him clearly, but his face was pale with sharp cheekbones and a dark mustache. Nobody seemed to be paying him any attention; perhaps the spectators thought he was part of the show. "A strange race of the dead was tailing us yesterday," she said. "Scratch warned me away from it. It's here again now. We've got to move."

It started to rain as they turned the corner and hurried down Eighty-First Street toward the subway station. People opened umbrellas, making it more difficult to dodge between them. Ivy sensed the dead creature behind, the voice of its broken soul growing louder. "It's coming in this direction!" she cried.

"We've got to lead it away from all these commoners," Valian decided. "Central Park's emptying, so let's turn off into there."

Crossing the road, they dashed toward one of the entrances of the park. New Yorkers, seeking shelter, darted past them in the opposite direction. Inside the park, a few joggers bobbed by, some with dogs leashed to their belts scampering beside them. Men and women in business suits paced along, the steam rising from their coffee cups.

Seb, his cheeks flushed from hurrying, said accusingly, "Why didn't you tell us about this dead creature before?"

"Because it vanished as soon as some underguard appeared," Ivy replied. She looked over her shoulder and saw their dark-suited pursuer emerge onto the puddled path, fifty paces behind them. She couldn't understand how he was so close when he was only walking. He stopped and tapped his cane twice on the ground. As she watched, his nose extended into a long snout, his skin grew coal-black fur and he sprouted pointed ears and a tail. His suit disappeared completely as he dropped to all fours.

"OK, now he looks like a *grim-wolf*," Valian said. "What's going on?"

"I don't know," Ivy admitted, "but he'll be able to chase us even faster now. Run!" She swung her satchel around to her back as they broke into a sprint. Her arms pumped by her sides, her feet pounded the wet concrete. Valian and Seb raced ahead.

When Ivy looked next, the grim-wolf was no more and, in its place, stood what looked like yet another race of the dead. This one had a bulky body dripping with black slime and a head featuring two hollows for eyes. Ivy shuddered as it fixed its gaze on her and grinned, flashing a mouth of shark-like teeth.

*A selkie.* Ivy had escaped one before . . . just.

With a loud *slurp,* the selkie dived into a puddle and disappeared. Ivy had a horrible feeling she knew what was coming next. "You two—wait!" she yelled, skidding to a halt. Seb and Valian came to a standstill just in time as the sludge-covered body of the selkie rose from the water on the path ahead. Rather than being the color of seaweed, its hairy scales were charcoal black. An acrid whiff of chemicals hit Ivy in the face, making her gag.

"Don't move," the selkie warned, in a voice so clear and deep it made Ivy's ribs shake. Selkies normally sounded as if they were speaking underwater; whatever race of the dead this one was, it was nothing like any she'd encountered before. Lifting a slimy finger, the creature pointed to a trail of sludge encircling them on the pavement. Valian and Seb stumbled back as the substance fizzed and a wall of mist rose out of it, obscuring Central Park. The tarmac beneath frothed like harsh chemicals reacting.

"Acid rain selkies are by far the most useful breed to transform into," the selkie remarked in the same sonorous tone. "Remain within the ring of acid, and we may all talk without any of you getting burned."

They all took a nervous step toward the center. Ivy projected her senses inside Scratch. *Do you know what race of the dead this is? I know it looks like a selkie now, but it was a grim-wolf before.*

*Nothings ideas,* Scratch replied shakily. *Farrow knowings might; Scratch can readings Guide.*

It took Ivy a moment to realize what Scratch meant. *Farrow's Guide* to Nubrook was still in her satchel; it contained an index of the dead. Ivy wasn't sure how Scratch could read it inside her bag. Then again, Scratch not having a brain or eyes, she wasn't sure how he read it at all.

Seb angled his body defensively, slipping the ends of his drumsticks out from his sleeves. "What do you want with us?" he growled.

"Only to become more acquainted," the creature said charmingly. "We are family, after all."

*Family?* Ivy racked her brains and came up with two names: Silas Wrench and Norton Wrench—Granma Sylvie's two missing brothers. They'd both disappeared after the Great Battle of Twelfth Night. She hesitated. "Are you . . . one of our great-uncles?"

The creature laughed, spilling drool from its lips. "Guess again."

She felt her satchel vibrate against her leg.

*Has findings Scratch.* He read from *Farrow's Guide:*

*"Augrits are the only creatures able to transform into any race of the dead at will, allowing them to take advantage of their respective strengths. Although immensely powerful, they have a major weakness—they draw their power from natural light and are therefore only able to operate aboveground. Many scholars argue about their existence, claiming*

*that it would be easier to find a fresh-smelling selkie than it would a real Augrit. . . ."*

"It is disappointing that you are having trouble working it out," the selkie muttered. "I had hoped you'd inherited my intelligence."

Ivy ignored him, trying to analyze the information from *Farrow's Guide.* If this creature was powered by natural light, they might be able to escape it if they could get underground. Squinting through the veil of acid smoke, she scanned the park. They hadn't ventured in too far; she could still make out the road. The subway station they'd been heading toward couldn't be that much farther.

"Why don't you try the generation above?" the selkie suggested. "That should narrow it down."

Ivy went cold. There was only one person he could be: "*Octavius* Wrench?" she gasped. "But—you were killed in 1969!"

"Indeed I was," Octavius Wrench agreed, with a hint of amusement. "And here I am. You could say that I've enjoyed the ultimate last laugh: the underguards I fought in the Great Battle thought they'd vanquished me, when in actual fact they had only made me stronger. It was a perfectly executed plan with a satisfying conclusion."

Seb rocked on the spot. Ivy could see him piecing together the information: this *monster* was their great-grandfather. "But—you died in a shower of uncommon bolts during the battle," he said, recalling what he and Ivy had learned last winter. "It was an accident."

"I can see *you* lack the family imagination," Octavius Wrench muttered. "Shame. Listen to me: my death was conceived in advance. With all the forbidden knowledge the Dirge have . . . collected over the years, effecting my transformation into my chosen race of the dead was easy: I simply had to die by revealing my darkest secret . . ."

". . . that you're Blackclaw," Ivy finished, "the leader of the Dirge." She clenched her jaw, wishing she'd considered before now the possibility that their great-grandfather had never become Departed. She looked over at Valian; his hands were curled into fists, his expression seething.

"Do you know why members of the Dirge are named after poisons?" Octavius Wrench asked them, slithering forward. "In the natural world, certain plants are poisonous to stop creatures from eating them. Animals with the intelligence to identify plants that are dangerous survive; animals that are weak or stupid will be killed. The Dirge exist to protect the uncommon world from weakness and stupidity. People like your friend Mr. Punch, or the Tidemongers I saw you visiting yesterday, are weak—they lack vision." He bared his jagged teeth. "Muckers are the same. Their numbers need to be controlled."

Ivy stiffened. "Muckers" was a nasty term for commoners.

*"Murderer!"* Valian charged forward, reaching for something in his inside pocket, but Octavius Wrench was too fast. His gloopy selkie body dissolved into a sheet of black powder, which swooped closer. Valian dropped to his knees, gasping for air.

Seb ran forward to help him.

"Wait—he's a wraithmoth!" Ivy warned, recognizing the flakes of skin and hair within Octavius Wrench's new dusty form. Wraithmoths were toxic up close.

Valian's skin was turning blue-purple; his eyes rolled back inside their sockets. Seb, protecting his mouth with his arm, shuffled toward his friend, trying to reach him. "He's choking!" he cried.

The dust shivered as Octavius Wrench spoke. "If only you could see the truth as I do: uncommoners shouldn't scurry around underground like rats, as if we've got something to be ashamed of. There is no need to hide from muckers—*we* are *their* superiors."

Valian gasped for air. Ivy squealed: "Stop it!"

"It is a pity that neither of you have the insight to join me," Octavius Wrench continued, "I do so like to keep the Dirge in the family." He sighed. "Still, New Dawn is coming, whether you like it or not."

"We know you're planning to attack all those undermarts, but you won't win!" Ivy shouted. "Everyone will stop you."

"Attacking undermarts?" Octavius Wrench sneered. "Oh, our ambitions are far greater than that. New Dawn will change the future of the entire planet, not just the uncommon world. Now, your friend's brain will starve of oxygen in moments unless you answer me this: where is Amos Stirling's journal?"

Ivy's fingers twitched toward her satchel, but she remained calm. "We don't know! Let Valian go."

"You're lying," Octavius Wrench snarled. "I was reading your mind as a selkie: you've seen the journal recently. Sources assure me that Mr. Punch doesn't have it anymore, and without the instructions inside it, I cannot wield the sword."

*The sword?*

Ivy's mouth went dry. Octavius Wrench could mean only

one thing. "*That's* what you've been looking for—the Sword of Wills?"

"Of course," Octavius Wrench answered. "Only with that blade's unique powers can I forge a new path for this planet. The sword will be used to complete a series of specific tasks. Ah, but I understand your confusion." His sheet-like body crinkled, pointing in Seb's direction. "You are far more concerned with another of the great five, aren't you? The Sands of Change . . ."

Seb's face flashed with fear. "We don't know what you're talking about!"

"Come now, I've seen inside both your heads," Octavius Wrench teased. "A small girl with pale hair possesses the Sands . . . someone you care about. But who is she?"

As Valian spluttered for breath, Octavius Wrench hovered closer to Ivy and Seb. Ivy's lungs heaved as the air thinned. She stumbled back.

"If you don't tell me," he boomed, "I will kill you, family or not."

Ivy realized that the river of acid encircling them had vanished, now that Octavius Wrench wasn't a selkie anymore. Remembering that Seb had once been able to keep a wraith-moth at bay using his drumsticks, she hurriedly began to formulate a plan.

Lightning flashed overhead. Octavius Wrench tilted, as if he was peering into the sky. "Ah, Monkshood arrives and New Dawn draws closer," he muttered.

Ivy took a deep breath and shouted, "Seb—chuck me your drumsticks. Then get Valian. We need to get out of the park!" Seb hesitated for a second before hurling his drumsticks through the air. Ivy caught one in each hand and began clashing them in Octavius Wrench's direction. At once, his powdery body ripped open with holes, but he quickly started to change form—back into the suited man with the bowler hat.

Seb had just enough time to throw Valian's limp body over his shoulder before he and Ivy both turned and ran.

# CHAPTER FOURTEEN

Ivy heard the crackling wing beats of a pyroach. Octavius Wrench was chasing them, now as a nasty flesh-eating race of the dead—but she didn't dare look over her shoulder. Sprinting through the freezing rain, she led Seb in the direction of the subway station they'd been aiming for earlier. Her pulse throbbed against the shoulders of her jacket.

As they approached the road, a stout figure in a long trench coat came hurtling out of the crowd toward them.

*Curtis?*

Their babysitter-spy had a look of grim determination on her face—her mouth drawn into a straight line, her brow lowered beneath the edge of her moss-green head scarf. "Keep going!" she shouted, turning to run alongside them. "These should slow that creature down"—she dropped what appeared to be silver safety pins in their wake—"I've fought pyroaches before with them. They unfold into insect traps."

Ivy didn't risk looking around to see how they worked in case it affected her speed. As they reached the street, they began elbowing their way through the mass of people on the pavement.

"This way," Curtis told them. "I've already called for a ride."

A yellow cab pulled up alongside them. The driver's window lowered and Johnny Hands's disheveled head poked out. "Get in!" he cried. He was wearing a flat cap and grubby white shirt with the sleeves rolled up to the elbows.

Seb slid Valian off his shoulder while Curtis opened the rear door, and together they propped Valian's limp body between them on the back seat. Ivy got in the front, slamming the door shut. "We need to go underground," she wheezed, peering behind them to see if Octavius Wrench was chasing after them. "Somewhere without natural light."

"There's a basement garage a few blocks away," Johnny Hands said, fiddling with the cab's sat-nav. He swiveled the steering wheel; the car made a sudden turn and sped forward.

Ivy checked on Valian. He looked pale and weak, but he was conscious. Seb fumbled for the flask of raider's tonic in Valian's jacket pocket and helped him take a sip. "Just breathe slowly. You're going to be OK."

Curtis inspected Ivy and Seb for wounds. "Are either of you injured?"

Seb shook his head while panting heavily. Ivy's heart was still going a hundred miles an hour. *Octavius Wrench is back. He's here, in New York.* She pushed off her hood and scraped the wet hair away from her face, trying to clear her head. From what Octavius Wrench had said, Ivy wasn't sure whether he already had the Sword of Wills, or soon would have. Either way, it didn't bode well. And now he knew who had the Sands of Change. . . .

They headed along Seventy-Ninth Street before driving down a ramp into a basement car park. A car horn sounded behind, quickly followed by another. "All right, all right!" Johnny Hands depressed the accelerator. "Honestly, I'd forgotten how tedious driving is. Give me a horse, I say. Those fine beasts got me around for hundreds of years before the motorcar was invented."

Ivy noted the lighting in the garage, all of it artificial.

"Won't Octavius Wrench be able to attack us in here?" Seb fretted as they cruised around, trying to find an empty bay.

"*Octavius Wrench!*" Johnny Hands squeezed the steering wheel. "What on Earth do you mean?"

"He's back, and he's an Augrit now," Ivy explained, shakily. "They're powered by natural light."

Curtis scowled. "Yes. I've never crossed one before, but you're right—as long as we're underground, we should be safe."

Ivy pondered how Octavius Wrench had been able to chase them underground, through Nubrook, the day before. Perhaps it had something to do with the bright light she'd seen behind him. If that was what was helping him, she had to hope he hadn't followed them here, or their defenses would be useless.

Valian rubbed the back of his head and tried to sit up. Ivy examined his face; the color was slowly returning to his cheeks. "How do you feel?" she inquired.

"Like someone tried to strangle me," he slurred. "We were lucky to get away."

Johnny Hands snorted as he slid the cab into a parking space. "Luck had nothing to do with it. Agent Curtis had an alert put out on your aqua-transport vessel. As soon as you hit the waterways she was able to trace you. Do you know what Octavius Wrench wanted?"

"Information," Ivy said. "As a selkie, he looked inside our heads, trying to uncover what we knew about Amos Stirling's journal."

"And . . . ?"

She fixed her gaze on Valian, her heart breaking. "I'm so sorry—he must have seen Rosie's image. He knows what she's carrying."

"What?" Valian's voice faltered.

"I don't think he's realized who she is yet," Ivy added, hopefully—though she knew it was only a matter of time before he found out.

Valian's face flooded with panic. "I've got to get out of here," he declared, and stretched across Seb's lap, reaching for the door.

"You're not going anywhere," Curtis said firmly, pushing Valian back in his seat. "It's not safe for the three of you to be going off alone anymore."

"It's not safe for anyone," Ivy said. She pulled the Dirge's map out of her satchel and thrust it at Johnny Hands. "We found this at an entrance to the Hexroom near Breath Falls. The Dirge are going to attack hundreds of undermarts, one after another."

Johnny Hands's face darkened as he examined the

document. "Nevertheless, you are in more danger than you know, Ivy Sparrow." Opening the glove compartment, he withdrew a small red wooden box with a brass crank on one side. "Agent Curtis installed this uncommon jack-in-the-box in your house before she left for Nubrook on your trail. The voices inside were recorded last night."

Ivy didn't know what uncommon jack-in-the-boxes did, but, based on what Johnny Hands had said, she thought she could guess. She hesitated before turning the handle. A creaky, high-pitched tune played from somewhere within. On the final note the lid popped open to reveal a bouncing clown puppet on a spring. Its fat red lips moved as it spoke with two different voices. The first was low and grisly, making the box shudder. "You have done well to bring the Dirge *this,* but without being able to control it, we cannot initiate New Dawn. Prove your loyalty by sharing what you read inside that journal." The voice was familiar to Ivy, but she couldn't place it.

"How many times do I have to tell you?" whined the second, younger-sounding voice. Ivy recognized it as Alexander Brewster's instantly. "I don't care about your New Dawn. What does it matter if muckers know the truth or not? I want vengeance." Then came the sound of things clattering to the floor. "Why aren't they *here*? This is where they live."

"This grudge of yours is a waste of your energy," the first speaker snapped. "Your enemies will soon be scorched in the light of the New Dawn. Once we give this to Blackclaw, New Dawn can be—"

"You don't understand!" Alexander interrupted, almost shouting now. "This won't be over till I've avenged my father. I'll tell you what I read in that stupid journal as soon as you do what you promised and help me exact revenge. *Ivy Sparrow* and her friends must pay."

With a rattle, the puppet finished speaking. Ivy swallowed as she watched it bobbing up and down, Alexander's last words ringing in her head.

"Perhaps I should have warned you about that bit at the end," Johnny Hands said. "It's a trifle personal. We know the identities of both speakers, and I'm guessing you do too. Mr. Punch told me you might be familiar with the voices of some of the members of the Dirge."

Ivy's skin still tingled with shock from Alexander's threat. But she ran through the handful of occasions she'd ever heard members of the Dirge talking and realized who the first voice belonged to. "Monkshood," she growled, remembering his gruff tone. "Both he and Alexander Brewster are at our house?"

"*Were* at your house," Johnny Hands said with a sigh. "Alexander Brewster took a flight to New York from London, arriving here this morning. He's been traveling on common transport to avoid detection; we had to hack commoners' airport security to find him." He snapped the lid of the jack-in-the-box shut and rammed it back inside the glove compartment. "Now you see why Mr. Punch is so concerned about keeping you safe."

"But we didn't kill Alexander's dad," Seb protested. "Why does he want revenge on us?"

"We were there when it happened," Ivy said sadly, remembering the dreadful events that had taken place in Lundinor the previous spring. A blast from Alexander's weapon—meant for Ivy—had hit his own father instead. "I guess it's easier to hold us responsible than admit it was an accident that was his own fault."

Johnny Hands slipped a feather out from under his cap. "I'll let Agent Curtis explain what's going to happen from here. I need to send a communication." With the Dirge's map tucked under his arm, he stepped outside. Ivy watched him walk behind a nearby car to write a message. She wondered who he was contacting and hoped it was someone who could warn every undermart on that map of the Dirge's intentions.

Valian sat with his arms folded. "You cannot hold us here against our will. We haven't broken any GUT laws."

"I assure you, theft from the Tidemongers' base *is* a crime," Curtis insisted.

Ivy squirmed in her seat. The Tidemongers must have discovered their trip through the mirror.

"Although, in this instance, it's more for your own security," Curtis continued. "You heard Alexander Brewster: he's looking for the three of you, and it's quite possible that Monkshood is traveling with him. My orders are to bring you all back to Nubrook, where you'll spend the night at an underguard station. Tomorrow morning, when we deem it safe, I'll escort you to your hotels to collect your belongings."

Valian scowled at her, but he stayed quiet. Ivy suspected he was hatching an escape plan for when they arrived back in Nubrook. Now that Octavius Wrench had seen Rosie's image in Ivy's and Seb's minds, time was running out for them to find her before the Dirge did.

"While we're aboveground," Curtis continued, addressing Ivy and Seb, "the three of us need to video-call your parents, to reassure them that everything's OK. It's eight-thirty p.m. in

London right now. I've told them we were going to the cinema this evening, so they'll think we're in the back of a taxi on our way home." She squinted at the rain-smeared windows, blurring the car park outside. "If we all play along, they won't suspect a thing."

Ivy contemplated being uncooperative, but she decided it would be better to participate in Curtis's ploy. She and Seb couldn't leave Valian, so smoothing things over at home would allow them to remain in Nubrook by his side without fear of their parents' worrying.

Curtis took a mobile phone out of her coat pocket; it was so new it still had the protective film covering the case. She held down the power button and studied the screen carefully as the light came on. Judging by the lines of concentration on Curtis's face, Ivy guessed she didn't use common technology all that frequently.

"Hmm . . ." Curtis muttered. "The device is having difficulty getting reception." She waved it around, growing more and more frustrated.

"It's probably because we're underground," Seb told her. "You might get a signal somewhere else in the garage."

"Yes, you could be right," Curtis agreed. She opened the door. "Stay here," she growled. "I'll be watching the car. If any of you move, I'll know."

As soon as she'd left the vehicle, Ivy lowered her voice. "Valian, I'm so sorry." Her stomach twisted with regret, wishing she could turn back time and undo their encounter with Octavius Wrench. "The Dirge were never looking for the Sands of Change at all, but they will be now. I should have realized sooner what Octavius was up to."

"You're not to blame," Valian said firmly. "Mr. Rife is our last chance now. We have to focus on finding him and hope he'll tell us something that can lead us to Rosie."

Ivy wondered if Judy had managed to plant that cufflink in Mr. Rife's pram. If she had, they'd be able to trace Mr. Rife's location and catch up with him. She made a mental note to send Judy a message about it as soon as they were back in Nubrook.

"Did anyone else think it was weird," Seb asked, "what Octavius Wrench said when that lightning struck? It was like he knew straightaway that Monkshood had arrived in New York, as if the storm was a signal."

Ivy shared her theory with them about Storm Sarah being uncommon. "It started in Paris, four days ago," she explained, "right when Alexander broke into that vault in Montroquer. Now the storm is here, and so are Alexander and Monkshood. Perhaps whatever they stole from that vault generated the storm? Although . . . I can't see why they'd want to do that."

"The only uncommon object I know that can affect the weather is a bag," Valian said. "And that's only when thousands of them are used to travel to the same place all at once."

Gazing at the raindrops on the front windshield, Ivy remembered something she'd been taught at school. "Rain and wind are only ever caused by a change in temperature in the atmosphere. Is there something uncommon that can manipulate that?"

"What about a knife like the one I used to alter the state of water?" Seb suggested. "Mr. Rife said that uncommon blades all do the same thing—they control forces."

*Blades . . .*

Ivy's mouth went dry as understanding crept through her. "The Sword of Wills! *That's* what Alexander stole! We know the sword was hidden in Montroquer . . . and Octavius Wrench told us he's going to use it to begin New Dawn . . . so Alexander and Monkshood must be bringing it to him."

"Whatever they're planning to do with it," Seb muttered, "it's gotta be a lot worse than a bit of thunder and lightning. Mr. Rife said that the higher the grade of the blade, the greater the number of forces it can control, so I guess there's no limit to the things the Sword of Wills can manipulate—the laws of physics, emotions . . . people's minds?"

Ivy considered what the Dirge might be plotting. Octavius Wrench had said that he was going to use the sword's "unique powers" for a series of tasks. She replayed the jack-in-the-box conversation in her head and had a sinking feeling it was something to do with what Alexander had said about "muckers" knowing the truth. "Remember what Monkshood said: the Dirge can't wield the sword without Amos's instructions." She clasped her satchel firmly. "That means we have to keep the journal protected at all costs. Maybe we should go along with Curtis after all?"

There was a loud *click* and the car door flew open. "Quick, get into position," Curtis said, shuffling in. "It's ringing."

# CHAPTER FIFTEEN

The next morning, after complying with the Tidemongers' protection scheme, Ivy sat tapping her feet against the polished ebony floor of the underguard station. The windowless waiting room was a lot bigger than the one in Lundinor but featured comparably creepy décor: pumpkins with carved screaming faces adorned the flint gray walls, and uncommon lime squeezers spilled eerie green light over the ceiling. Officers in navy blue uniforms peered out from behind the main desk, which was constructed from three lacquered coffins stacked on top of each other. If it wasn't late November, Ivy would have thought they were getting ready to celebrate Halloween.

"I cannot believe they put us in the cells overnight," Seb growled, folding his arms. "I had to sleep on a bench made out of an old gravestone with a blanket that only came up to my knees."

Valian huffed. "At least you had fresh air. I was sharing with a sootsprite named Claude who had a serious wind issue." He scrunched up his nose and shuddered, as if revisiting the experience.

For Ivy, the hard bed and small blanket had been the least of her problems. Without the lava lamp at Guesthouse Swankypants to soothe her to sleep, she'd been haunted by nightmares about the Dirge's army of the dead. At one point, she'd dreamed of Octavius Wrench rising from the bowels of the earth as a giant—his bowler hat as big as a football stadium—  stomping around the planet, gobbling up undermarts. It made her shiver just thinking about it.

Over by the main entrance, Ivy spotted Judy skating through the automatic doors. A pair of underguard officers stopped her before she could come any closer. With the handles of their toilet brushes resting over their shoulders, they looked like soldiers holding bayonet rifles. They grumbled a few words, and Judy shook hands with them. Finally she was allowed to pass.

"I can't stay long," Judy whispered as she reached them and took a seat opposite. "Visiting time is half an hour, apparently."

"This is ridiculous," Seb muttered. "You'd think *we* were the criminals."

"Did you manage to plant one of the cufflinks in Mr. Rife's pram?" Ivy asked.

Judy patted the pocket of her patchwork waistcoat. She was wearing a new Hobsmatch combo with her roller skates—a tutu, tiger-stripe leotard and ankle warmers. Her hair was braided away from her face, so her cheekbones looked even more prominent. "I've got the other one safe here. I'll keep checking the coordinates to see if anything changes."

Ivy caught Seb staring at her and gave him a subtle elbow.

"Mr. Rife didn't set foot in the building all day yesterday," Judy continued. "But while I was sneaking around, I found something interesting in one of his cardboard boxes. Hidden beneath a collection of *Farrow's Guides* was a whole pile of old newspaper articles about the murder of Valian's parents."

"Old?" Ivy's brow crinkled. "You mean—he'd had them for a while?"

"So he must have known exactly who I was when I walked into his office," Valian said angrily.

Judy checked the skull-clock on the wall. "The auction house opens in two hours, at midday. I'll go straight there from here. You three need to figure out a way of breaking out so you can come and join me."

Over her shoulder, Ivy noticed an underguard officer escorting a prisoner through a black door labeled DISCO-COMMUNICATOR. "What's through there?" she asked Valian, knowing he'd seen the inside of many underguard stations. "I've never heard of a discommunicator before."

He turned to look. "You're reading it wrong," he corrected

her. "There's an extra 'co' in the middle: it says '*disco*commu-nicator.' Every underguard station has one. It's a device that allows you to send live images to and from anywhere on the planet."

"Like an uncommon video call?"

"It's a bit better than Curtis's phone," Valian replied with a smirk. "Discocommunicators can transmit light, sound, aroma and taste; and they work thousands of miles underground. They're used exclusively by underguards to give them more powers during an emergency."

*Like the flashing blue light on an ambulance,* Ivy thought. Underguards were also permitted to use uncommon body bags inside undermarts when, for everyone else, bag travel was forbidden; she guessed this device had a similar purpose.

"This discocommunicator . . . ," Ivy continued, ". . . if it's that powerful, do you think we could use it to contact Mr. Punch? I'm worried that his featherlight yesterday contained an important message and we haven't worked out what it is."

Judy's expression darkened. "That might be a good idea. I wrote to him this morning, asking if he knew any more about Mr. Rife. I've had no reply yet."

"They won't just let us use it," Valian said, considering the black door. "We'll need a distraction before sneaking in."

The four of them huddled closer, making a plan. Ivy observed the flow of people in and out of the discocommu-nicator room. As soon as it was empty, Seb and Judy stood up and went over to the coffin desk. A pair of stern-faced male underguards sat behind it.

"Ooh . . . er . . . I'm not feeling well," Seb slurred, hold-ing his tummy. He convulsed just enough to make the performance realistic. Ivy wasn't surprised how convincing he could be; he'd had enough practice at it, after all. One of the guards—a young man with dark hair and glasses—looked up and startled. Seb's face was pea-soup green. Ivy could tell by the set of Judy's jaw that she was concentrating hard to achieve the effect. "I think it might have been a dodgy burrito," she explained, rubbing Seb's back. "Can you call your medical officer, please?"

The officer exchanged a suspicious glance with his colleague.

"*Please?*" Judy begged. "I don't want your lovely clean reception area to be spoiled."

The young man wrinkled his nose. "Wait here," he said, and he rose from his seat and disappeared through a door at the back.

Ivy and Valian hopped a few chairs closer to the discocommunicator door.

Seb leaned over the coffin desk. "Urgh . . . ," he gurgled, approaching puke mode, "I can feel it coming."

"There, there," Judy soothed. "Perhaps we can find a bag?"

The remaining officer leaped from his chair and yanked open the rear door. "Frank!" he yelled. "Hurry!"

While his back was turned, Ivy and Valian shot to the door of the discocommunicator room and, using Valian's boat shoes, unlocked it from the inside. The room was circular with a slanted floor that dipped in the center. Rows of benches ran around the perimeter; in the middle a glittering disco ball was suspended from a wire in the ceiling. *That explains the name,* Ivy thought. She was surprised Guesthouse Swankypants hadn't acquired one.

A steel truss rigged with various stage lights and spots stood on one side. Valian fiddled with the controls on a few of them, and the room filled with tiny squares of light. "I once tried to use one of these to speak to Rosie, but it can't dial people; only places," he clarified. He pressed a button to start the ball rotating and the lights began sweeping across the walls. "I've set it up to give us a direct view into Mr. Punch's Curiosity Shop. If he's not there, we'll have to try a few other spots in Lundinor."

A hot-tub-sized circular hologram sputtered into life above the mirror ball. It showed a room with curved gray stone walls and narrow slits for windows. Outside it, Ivy caught glimpses of castle turrets and battlements made from the same smooth, square stone blocks. The floor was dotted with various trunks, crates and cases, all stamped with Mr. Punch's logo: a black top hat. Valian was right about the discocommunicator being able to transmit smells, because the scent of rain lined Ivy's nose.

"This is it?" she said, surprised. The last time she'd seen Mr. Punch's shop it had looked like a giant purple tent. Before that, it had been a brick-built shop with leaded windows.

"The Stone of Dreams is in the corner, over there," Valian whispered, pointing to a gray plinth carved with winged horses and five-pointed stars. A battered copy of *King Arthur and His Knights of the Round Table* by Roger Lancelyn Green lay open on top.

Ivy was familiar enough with the fairy tale to know that it was set in medieval England. "That explains the castle," she muttered, knowing that the Stone of Dreams had the extraordinary power to manifest certain aspects of whichever book rested on its surface. Mr. Punch used it to change the appearance of Lundinor every trading season; Ivy was curious to see what the rest of the undermart looked like.

As she and Valian waited, a tall man dressed in a black tuxedo strode into the room. The short fuzz of brown hair on his scalp was the same length as that on his chin. "Mr. Punch," Ivy said quietly. "He might not be wearing his usual Hobsmatch, but it's definitely him." She could tell because, as she watched, his appearance kept shifting—a phenomenon she was able to perceive using her whispering. First he was slim with freckles and a dimpled chin; then he was short and hunched with a wrinkled face and white hair. She'd only seen him change this quickly when he'd been under extreme pressure. She wasn't sure what Valian could see.

When the red-bearded quartermaster took shape, he turned to face them. "Ivy? Valian?" He squinted toward what Ivy presumed must be a hologram of herself and Valian in the castle tower.

Before they could respond, however, Mr. Punch altered into a beefy-looking man with a stubbly beard, who grunted, "Why are we talking to them?"

"This is a waste of time," said the next guise—a smartly dressed gentleman with a cravat. He had a well-spoken voice. "I don't see how we can make progress."

Ivy double-checked, but there was no one else in the room. Mr. Punch was talking to himself . . . if you could call it that. "Are you OK, sir?" she asked. In all her experiences with him, he'd still only ever felt to her like one person.

"Let me find my soulmate and become Departed, and this won't be an issue!" demanded another guise.

"That could destroy us," the next pointed out. "I, for one, vote we don't risk it. Some of us want to stay around."

"*Some of us* shouldn't have kept the knowledge of soulmates from others," one of them stated bitterly.

Ivy understood from the snippets of conversation why they were arguing. Some of the souls within Mr. Punch wanted to be reunited with their soulmates so they could become Departed, while others didn't. It sounded like they weren't even sure what would happen if one of them did depart. Perhaps the conflict between them explained the strange featherlight Mr. Punch had sent Ivy, the one that had looked like it had been written by multiple people.

"Mr. Punch, sir? Can you hear or see us?" Valian asked.

The quartermaster appeared again. His top hat sat off-kilter, his red beard was ruffled and there were dark circles under his swirly green-blue eyes. "I don't have long," he warned. "At the moment, it takes a lot of persuasion for my other friends to allow me to talk to you."

Ivy imagined what it might be like to share her body with several broken souls. You would all have to compromise with one another in order for one of you to assume control. It would need to be a relationship based on trust and understanding.

Valian asked hurriedly, "Do you know anything about Mr. Rife? Why did you give me the invitation to the auction house?"

"For the same reason I gave Amos Stirling's journal to Ivy. Because fate decided you should have it." He looked over his shoulder, as if expecting someone to sneak up behind him. "A powerful uncommon clock foretold to me that you and Mr. Rife would meet. The invitation was to point you in the right direction."

Valian gritted his teeth. "Mr. Rife lied to us. We know he shook hands with Rosie on the day she went missing, but he said he'd never seen her before."

"He is not your enemy," Mr. Punch said firmly. "The vision I had was of you two embracing as friends."

"That doesn't make sense," Valian said. "I don't even know him."

"I received another premonition yesterday morning," Mr. Punch continued, urgently. "I sent you a featherlight to explain—" His words were cut short as his face widened into that of the beefy man with the stubbly chin. Before *he* could say anything, the quartermaster returned for a split second. "It was a warning—"

Ivy grew more and more frustrated as the quartermaster continued to vanish and then reappear briefly, struggling against his colleagues. On each occasion he managed to utter a single word or short phrase.

"*. . . Great Gates . . . Blackheath . . . using the sword . . . commoners in danger,*" Valian repeated. "The sword must be the Sword of Wills; and Lundinor lies under Blackheath in London. Any idea what the rest of it could mean?"

"It's got to be something to do with New Dawn," Ivy decided. "Perhaps that's what Mr. Punch saw a prophecy about; he said it was a warning."

Valian shivered. "'Commoners in danger' . . . That would fit with all that rubbish Octavius Wrench said in Central Park—about commoners being inferior and their numbers needing to be controlled."

The door behind them thudded open. Ivy spun around to see a red-faced underguard officer standing in the opening. "Out," he barked. "NOW!" He flicked a switch on the wall and the disco ball began to slow down.

"No, wait!" Ivy studied the flickering hologram, trying to capture every detail. Just before the transmission died, Mr. Punch appeared as the red-bearded quartermaster one last time. Ivy tensed as he uttered two final words:

"*. . . attack London.*"

# CHAPTER SIXTEEN

Six heavily armed underguard officers escorted Ivy, Seb and Valian along the road toward Guesthouse Swankypants. Ivy caught the nervous expressions of traders peering at them through shop windows. With everyone watching, it wasn't going to be easy to slip away.

"I'm very disappointed," Curtis said, stomping behind them. "I had assumed, given the seriousness of your situation, that you'd conduct yourselves properly."

As Curtis continued to scold them, Ivy reached for Scratch with her whispering. *Mr. Punch saw a prediction about New Dawn in the face of an uncommon clock,* she told him. *The Dirge are going to attack London.*

Her satchel trembled. *But what Dirge stoppings can we do?* Scratch replied.

*I don't know.* Ivy's mind was racing. She remembered

Octavius Wrench boasting that the Dirge had far greater ambitions than attacking undermarts. Now that she thought about it, the Dirge's map hadn't actually shown any undermarts on it at all . . . perhaps it was the common cities above them that were the real targets.

*Scratch beings scared,* he said in a little voice.

*Me too,* Ivy admitted.

The lobby of Guesthouse Swankypants fell silent as they all marched in. A cleaner looked up from polishing the marble floor only to leap up from his knees and scamper away. A similarly quick exit was made by a porter tidying a vase of orchids. One of the underguard officers went over to reception; the others waited for instructions.

"Their suite is on the second floor," Curtis told them. "I'll need you covering the windows, doors and fire exits. Nobody goes in or out until we've left." The officers promptly dispersed. One went outside, while another stationed herself by the front door; the remaining three ran to the stairwell.

Curtis guided Ivy, Seb and Valian to the central elevator. "You'll have fifteen minutes to get packed. Take everything you need; we're not coming back."

"Why the rush?" Seb asked, checking his watch. He stared pointedly at Ivy and Valian. "It's only just *midday.*"

Ivy tensed. The auction house had opened; they needed to get there fast.

"No more questions," Curtis said dismissively. "Just do as I say." When they got out of the elevator, she marched them along the corridor and paused outside their room. "I'll be stationed here, covering the hallway. Your time starts *now.*"

Ivy swiped her glove against the door handle; it buzzed

loudly before opening, and the three of them stepped inside. As Valian shut the door behind them, Ivy saw immediately that something was amiss: fragments of colored glass lay scattered across the thick carpet, cabinet drawers hung open and curtains had been ripped down. She spotted her pajamas hiding under the upturned coffee table. Someone had been in and ransacked the place.

A rustling noise sounded in one of the bedrooms. Seb reached for his drumsticks.

"Wait," Ivy whispered, pulling him back. "Shouldn't we get Curtis?"

"Not till we're sure we need her," Valian hissed. "This might be the only chance we get to escape."

They crept toward the bedrooms; the door to Ivy's was ajar. Valian put a finger to his lips and signaled for Ivy and Seb to get back.

"Who's there?" he shouted. There was no reply, but the rustling stopped. Valian nodded at Ivy and Seb, and then burst in, and they hurried after him.

Ivy stopped dead in her tracks when she saw Alexander Brewster standing at the foot of her bed. In one hand he held a test tube filled with transparent liquid. In the other was a small round tin painted with a geometric pattern; a steel handle protruded from the top of it.

*"Alexander—"* She lost her breath.

His Hobsmatch—a simple shirt and trousers—were baggier than before, and his skin and fiery-red hair were dirtied with oil and blood. He blinked once, then, with a menacing grin, smashed the test tube on the floor. As Ivy, Seb and Valian shuffled back to avoid the spillage and shards of glass,

Alexander rotated the handle on the colorful tin. It emitted a high-pitched, tinkling tune that made the hair on Ivy's neck stand on end. Worse, at the sound of the music, the puddle at her feet crystallized with a loud crackle, and tiny spores of chalky powder began lifting from its surface.

The air turned cloudy. A dry chemical coated the roof of Ivy's mouth, reeking of plaster. She heard Seb coughing, but when she tried to reach for him, her arms wouldn't budge. Her limbs felt numb, as if the flow of blood had been cut off. As

the room cleared, she saw that Seb and Valian were having the same problem: their bodies had ground to a stony halt, like robots drained of battery power. Ivy wanted to shout to them, but her mouth was frozen shut.

Alexander snorted with laughter. "Brilliant!" he cried gleefully. He was clutching the tin music box in his hand. "You look ridiculous!"

Terror squeezed at Ivy's chest, but she breathed through her nose, trying not to panic. Her internal organs seemed to be functioning fine: it was just the rest of her body that felt like wet clay.

"I've named this formula 'Statue Salt,'" Alexander announced boastfully. "After much experimentation, I discovered that the tune from an uncommon music box activates the liquid, which solidifies into a powder that invades people's lungs. The genius thing is that the paralysis is instantly reversed if you listen to an uncommon music box played backward—and as I've already heard this one in reverse, I'm immune!" He tucked the music box inside a battered leather doctor's bag, which lay open on the bed. Inside, Ivy could see test tubes containing various substances, some with what looked like more of the same transparent fluid. One was labeled DAYLIGHT BURST, and below it was scribbled *Blackclaw*. Ivy guessed Octavius Wrench had made use of that particular potion in order to briefly appear in Nubrook two days ago.

When he turned around again, Alexander was still smiling smugly. Ivy growled at him—her vocal cords were still working, it was just that she couldn't get any words out—and the joy dissolved from Alexander's face. "You're back earlier than I anticipated," he snapped. "You can wait there while I continue searching." From the state of the bedroom, Ivy reckoned Alexander had been there awhile. The pillows had been slit open, and the wardrobe drawers tipped out. A soft mulch of feathers covered the floor.

"But wait . . ." Alexander smiled greedily as he noticed the satchel hanging across Ivy's shoulders. "What have we here?" Stepping closer, he easily slid the bag over Ivy's head and opened it up. "Useless, useless," he muttered, throwing Scratch and Ivy's yo-yo away and into the next room. Finally he came upon Amos's journal. "Aha!" he exclaimed. "Just where you kept it last time! I only got a peek before."

There was nothing Ivy could do except watch. With Amos's journal in his grasp, Alexander drew so close to Ivy that she could feel his breath against her face. He smelled foul, as if he hadn't washed for weeks. Ivy weighed their options. She couldn't shout for help from Curtis, and Scratch was too far away to whisper to for aid. Perhaps she could try communicating with an object that was closer?

Alexander's eyes flashed hungrily. "The information inside this will help me build my own guild, far more powerful than the *Dirge*." He said the name like it belonged to an idiotic rival. "In exchange for a few formulas of mine, they've been telling me their secrets. Their only strength is their leader. He manipulates all the other members, getting them to do his bidding so that he can take all the glory for New Dawn. But *I* will be a greater leader than even Blackclaw. . . ."

Listening to him gloat, Ivy filled with anger. Alexander hadn't seemed as unhinged as this the last time they'd met. She reckoned that spending time with the Dirge had been a destabilizing experience for him. She scanned the room with her whispering, searching for an object that could help them escape.

"Good leaders set an example to their supporters," Alexander continued. "You and your family must be punished for destroying mine, and for making a fool of me in front of the whole of Lundinor!"

There was a rustle by the door, and a figure in long dark robes glided into the room. Alexander hastily hid Amos's journal behind his back. "You're late," he snapped, glaring at the sunburst clock on the wall.

The stranger turned to face Ivy. His head was covered by a hood and a scaly mask with slits for nostrils. All Ivy could see were his black lips and emaciated neck, as if his body was made only of skin and bone. She had no idea what race of the dead he was. "What's this?" the stranger demanded. "I thought we were leaving Nubrook to meet Blackclaw."

Ivy recognized his hoarse voice immediately: *Monkshood*. Curious, she searched him with her senses. He was carrying several uncommon items. Imprisoned inside one was a broken soul with an old, croaky voice. She thought it might be speaking Japanese, since it sounded like the characters in the anime movies Seb watched. Her heart stirred strangely as she listened to its weary muttering. Ivy had been in the presence of three of the Great Uncommon Good before—the Sack of Stars, the Jar of Shadows and the Stone of Dreams—and she knew what they sounded like. They all had strange, penetrating voices that filled her with emotion. This voice sounded like it had been around for a very long time. It had to be the Sword of Wills . . .

. . . which meant Blackclaw didn't have it yet.

"You should have stuck to our original plan," Alexander retorted.

"The only plan that matters is the one that brings about New Dawn," Monkshood said dismissively. Ivy noticed the fingers of his black gloves were creepily thin as pencils. "Have you found the journal? I have just received a message from Blackclaw: he has almost acquired the Sands of Change."

*Rosie!* Ivy tried struggling again, but it was no use.

Alexander's arm twitched behind his back. "You must use the sword on their friend first. That was our agreement."

The dark eyeholes of Monkshood's mask fell upon Alexander's elbow. Ivy had a feeling he had guessed what Alexander was holding. "Why are you wasting your time with these three uncommoners when New Dawn will change the lives of every uncommoner in the world?"

"You know why!" Alexander barked. He removed another test tube from the leather doctor's bag, this one labeled TELE-PORT, and held it threateningly close to his own lips. "I suggest you cooperate before I disappear out of here. I'm the only one who's read the journal. I can tell you Amos's instructions for handling the sword in a way that maximizes its power."

Ivy had a strong suspicion that Alexander was bluffing. She'd been reading and translating the journal for months now and she hadn't discovered any sword-operating guidelines. Alexander had only possessed the journal for a few minutes.

"You might be able to use the sword for small tasks," Alexander sneered, "but if you try wielding it to start New Dawn, you'll cause another storm. You need me."

Monkshood made a hissing, snarling noise. His robes flickered.

From what Alexander had said, Ivy realized she'd been right about a connection between Storm Sarah and the Sword of Wills. It *had* been responsible for the storm—but it had been an accident. Without Amos's advice, Monkshood had lost control of the sword, and Storm Sarah had been the consequence.

"So be it," Monkshood replied. From within the folds of his dark cloak, he withdrew a long black sword with a single-edged, curved blade. The circular guard and grip were patterned with silver stars. It looked a lot like a Japanese katana that Ivy had seen on the cover of one of her dad's books, *Weapons from History.*

Monkshood held the blade horizontally in his nimble fingers, just as Seb had done when he'd been using the uncommon paper knife. After a moment's concentration he released the sword. It hovered away from his gloved hands, the point toward Valian, and started spinning. . . .

# CHAPTER SEVENTEEN

Adrenaline shot through Ivy's numb body. Her mind sharpened. She focused her whispering senses inside the Sword of Wills, desperately trying to communicate with the resident soul. After it failed to understand English, she tried sending it relaxing images, hoping to encourage it to slow down—a wave gently lapping the sand, a bird landing on water . . .

. . . but the blade persisted.

Eventually, Monkshood controlled the sword to a stop. There was a leather cord attached to the scabbard, which he slipped over his head so that the blade hung at his back. Except it wasn't exactly "hanging"—Ivy could see the handle hovering above Monkshood's shoulders, powered by some invisible force.

*Valian, no—!* Ivy shouted inside as Valian stepped into her line of sight. His movements were stiff and robotic as he stood to attention before Monkshood. Valian's dark eyes had glazed over and his expression was blank, as if he'd been hypnotized. Ivy understood what had happened: the Sword of Wills had broken the effect of Alexander's Statue Salt and taken control of Valian's mind.

"You will do exactly as I say," Monkshood told Valian. "Climb to the top of Breath Falls and jump off."

Ivy's heart flinched—*No!* She tried to wrestle her limbs free again, but it was no use.

Valian nodded once and, with Monkshood—and the Sword of Wills—carefully accompanying him, he marched out of the room without looking back.

A satisfied grin spread across Alexander's face. Desperately, Ivy skimmed the room with her whispering senses. The soul within the lava lamp spoke with an American slow Southern drawl. *Help me,* she begged. *I have to save my friend.*

Then, without waiting for a reply, she moved her senses on and reached for the tin music box in the old doctor's bag. *Please turn backward,* she pleaded. *My brother and I are trapped. We need to save our friend. You've got to help us.*

The lava lamp responded first, darkening the room with images of an erupting volcano. Fiery ash rained from the sky; the stink of sulfur filled Ivy's nostrils. Alexander looked confusedly from the walls to the door like he didn't know whether to run or applaud. Visions of pterodactyls roared through the black sky before dive-bombing him. He ducked and covered his head, knocking his doctor's bag onto the carpet. . . .

And that was when Ivy saw the music box roll out and the handle rotate backward.

The shrill tune sounded eerie played in reverse. As the melody penetrated Ivy's ears, she felt her limbs loosen and her muscles rush with blood.

"No!" Alexander blurted, hastily recovering the music box from the floor. He fumbled for the handle and yanked it, but by then it was too late.

Ivy kicked with all her might and stumbled forward. Seb punched his arms free, as though he was breaking out of a block of ice. He grabbed the object nearest to him: Alexander's leather doctor's bag.

"That's for Valian, you loser!" he yelled, swinging it into Alexander's side.

Alexander thudded hard against the bed. Ivy heard the smash of glass, and a cloud of green vapor started rising out of the top of the bag.

"Seb, we've got to save Valian!" Ivy gasped as Alexander wobbled to his feet, looking stunned. Collecting her satchel, she dragged her brother into the lounge and grabbed Scratch, who had rolled under a coffee table.

"Ivy curtains yo-yo beside," he told her helpfully.

Dashing to the window, she collected her weapon from the floor. She stuffed the yo-yo in her right pocket and Scratch in her left. Glancing at the buildings opposite gave her an idea. "Help me open this. We need to get out onto the veranda."

Seb slid up the pane of glass so they could both squeeze out—

Behind them there was a sudden loud clatter as Curtis burst through the door. She made a split-second assessment of the scene: the suite in ruins; Ivy and Seb about to escape through the window; Alexander Brewster on his feet hurtling through from the next room . . .

. . . and she rugby-tackled him to the ground. "Go!" she cried to Ivy and Seb.

With one hand on the railing, Ivy waved a thumb in the air, and a worn and dusty carpet appeared a moment later, hovering at the same level as the balcony.

"Where you off to?" asked the woman with dark curly hair riding on top.

"The summit of Breath Falls," Ivy said, climbing over the railing. She heard Curtis and Alexander shouting as she and Seb sat down on the rug. "We need to be quick."

"You'll have to pay extra for water damage," the lady noted firmly.

"We know!" Ivy insisted. "Please, hurry!"

As they zoomed over Nubrook, Ivy and Seb tried to pick out Valian in the crowded streets below. Everywhere Ivy looked, Thanksgiving festivities were in full swing: troops of dancers paraded through the streets; music and confetti filled the air; and huge uncommon ribbons floated between buildings, writing messages of celebration.

"Ivy, Alexander is after us!" Seb warned. "Something must have happened to Curtis."

She checked over her shoulder. Alexander was pursuing them on the back of a cylinder vacuum cleaner, the nozzle flapping in the wind.

Ivy hoped Curtis was OK. "He's still got Amos's journal," she observed, catching sight of it tucked under his arm. She was annoyed at herself for not grabbing it earlier. "We've got to slow him down. We can't fight him *and* Monkshood."

She whipped out her yo-yo and, aiming it carefully, flicked her wrist. Twisting torrents of air formed on either side of the spinning toy and merged into a single whirlwind, which surged toward Alexander. Sucking clumps of confetti from the air, the cyclone quickly took on the appearance of a giant spool of rainbow cotton candy.

Just as it was about to collide with Alexander, he managed to dodge aside . . . right into the path of an uncommon ribbon looped into a "Happy Thanksgiving!" message. Alexander tried to bat the ribbon away, but it got tangled around his arms, causing him to lose control of the vacuum cleaner. He went spinning across the road and landed on the awning of an Italian gelato stand. Two men wearing gelato-splattered aprons appeared below, shaking their fists and shouting furiously.

Relief washed over Ivy as she turned back around. "Now we just need to rescue Valian," she said. "Next stop, the Falls."

As the silver colossus came into sight, their sky driver soared toward Nubrook's concrete ceiling and then swooped down to land on the statue's head. Water gurgled over the surface from where the mist condensed into shallow streams. Up close, the structure was made of gray metallic rock that undulated with ripples, giving it the appearance of hair. The sky driver lowered them onto the surface.

Here, the roar of the falls was so loud that Ivy couldn't hear herself think. "Can you see Valian?" she hollered, searching for any solid form in the mist. Her coat and skin were soaked in seconds.

Seb pointed toward the statue's hairline, where two dark shapes hovered in the spray. "Over there!"

The ground was slippery underfoot so Ivy trod carefully, grasping the peaks of the statue's hair to steady herself. As they got closer, the outline of Monkshood's dark robe became clear. His hood had been pushed off in the wind: a few straggly dark hairs clung to the rear of his skull; the skin on his scalp looked like bathroom mold. Ivy could see the Sword of Wills floating at his back. "How do we release Valian from the influence of the sword?"

"I think we just have to force it away from Monkshood," Seb said. "I only lost complete control of the paper knife when I wasn't concentrating on it anymore. Perhaps we need to cause a distraction?"

Ivy grasped her yo-yo. "We need to be careful not to make Valian topple over the edge by accident. He'll be trying to leap off the whole time."

"Do you think you could use your whirlwinds," Seb said, "to push him away from the edge, while I tackle Monkshood?"

Ivy had never used her yo-yo to do that before, but they were low on options. "I'll do my best," she replied.

They quickened their pace over the rest of the distance, concentrating hard to stay balanced—it was like running on selkie slime. Valian finally became visible when they were almost within reach of him. He stepped closer to the edge, his expression vacant.

"Now!" Seb shouted, striking out with his drumsticks. Monkshood tumbled back, sliding across the floor.

Aiming more carefully than she ever had before, Ivy generated a trio of tornadoes with her yo-yo. One by one, they lined up at the statue's hairline and forced the mist back. The water under Ivy's feet began to ripple in reverse and, slowly,

Valian glided to safety. "It's working!" she cried, although she could see Valian already leaning forward, trying to use his weight to resist.

Monkshood pulled a steel can opener from his cloak and pointed it at the ground, where a glittering pile of metal filings appeared. From out of the filings, six steel-bodied crabs the size of small dogs came to life and scuttled toward Seb. They had razor-sharp pincers and beady black eyes that wiggled around on silver stalks on their heads.

"Ugh! Get away!" Seb yelled, trying to smash them with beats from his drumsticks.

The glinting crabs gripped onto the wet rock as well as real crustaceans, dodging Seb's blasts, snapping their pincers and drawing ever closer. Down through the mist, Ivy glimpsed a crowd looking up at them. Their presence hadn't gone unnoticed; several people were already approaching on flying carpets.

Too late, she heard the *whirr* of machinery—

Alexander Brewster dropped from the sky and clattered to the ground. His vacuum cleaner smashed into several pieces and washed over the side. "You will not ruin this!" he shouted as he limped to his feet. His outfit and the journal tucked under his arm were smeared with several different colors of ice cream. "You and everyone you love will pay!"

Ivy checked on Valian, who was wobbling a few feet from the edge, and sent another carefully positioned tornado to keep him in place. Seb was still trying to fend off Monkshood and the steel crabs.

"I'm sorry that you lost your pa!" Ivy shouted to Alexander. "But it wasn't us who killed him."

Alexander wiped his face dry, scowling. "You didn't save him!" he spat.

Just then, one of the steel crabs caught Alexander's heel with a snip of its pincer. Alexander howled and hopped onto one leg. His foot slipped—

—and, in a streak of shadow, he washed over the side of the waterfall. Ivy hurried to the edge. The nozzle of Alexander's broken vacuum cleaner had become wrapped around one of the statue's eyelashes; Alexander was hanging from it one-handed, his limbs flailing in the wind.

"Drop the journal!" Ivy shouted, catching sight of it in his fingers. "You need two hands to climb up."

Alexander's face flashed with fear, but, rather than taking Ivy's advice, he scowled and attempted to haul himself up with one arm. Ivy tried to think of a way to save him. Perhaps if she aimed a tornado under his feet, it would keep him from falling. . . .

"Ivy, look out!" Seb shouted.

She turned. Monkshood was gliding straight toward her. He swiped the Sword of Wills from his back and pointed it at Alexander, who was still dangling in the mist. The katana rotated in midair, faster and faster.

Valian fell to his knees. His gaze sharpened.

"Valian!" Seb hollered, walled in by metal crabs. "Get away from the edge!"

When Ivy looked back at Alexander, his body had gone taut and his face was expressionless. She understood what had happened: the Sword of Wills had relinquished its control over Valian and focused on Alexander instead.

"Throw me Amos Stirling's journal," Monkshood demanded.

With all the strength he could muster, Alexander hurled the journal toward the top of the colossus. His body was left swinging precariously. The vacuum nozzle creaked.

"Foolish boy." Monkshood laughed as he caught the journal and tucked it securely inside his robes. Then, with the Sword of Wills in his grasp, he turned and vanished into thin air—his crab army dematerializing with him.

Alexander's face twitched; light returned to his eyes. "What—?" In the confusion of remembering where he was, his hand slipped—

Before Ivy could shout, however, a carpet emerged from the spray. Riding atop was Curtis, gripping the shirt collar of a wriggling Alexander.

Ivy slid over to Valian and threw her arms around him, burying her face in his shoulder. "It's all right. You're safe."

But, despite having been just moments from death, there was only one thing on Valian's mind. "Rosie . . . ," he murmured. *"We have to find Rosie."*

# CHAPTER EIGHTEEN

The underguard station was buzzing with activity when Ivy, Seb and Valian returned. A constant stream of Tidemonger agents—Ivy could tell because of the divergent arrow symbols on their clothing—flitted to and fro across reception, disappearing through different doors. Short puffs sounded every few moments as featherlight messages arrived for the underguard officers on duty behind the coffin desk. Scribbling feverishly, they sent responses while other guards hurried in and out of the discocommunicator room. The walls of the building vibrated with the rumble of the growing crowd outside, eager to learn what was happening.

Water dripped from the hem of Ivy's duffle coat as she shifted in her chair, drawing the unwavering stares of three underguard officers standing opposite. Their hands rested threateningly on their toilet brushes, their expressions unflinching. Valian and Seb had been made to sit a chair apart in the same row so they could all be watched closely. Judy—who arrived after hearing what had happened from a street vendor near Breath Falls—had been allowed to sit beside Ivy.

"Seeing as we're not allowed to leave here again," Seb muttered, shivering, "can one of you officers get us some hot drinks? Or maybe even a dry blanket?"

The underguards didn't react. Ivy wondered if the post-ordeal care package had been canceled in the aftermath of her and Valian's break-in to the discocommunicator room. Or maybe these three just weren't the warm fuzzy types.

"What do you think they're doing?" she asked, squinting at the darkened glass door through which Johnny Hands, Curtis and several senior underguards had stepped almost an hour ago. "They've been in there for ages."

"They're probably contacting more Tidemongers and other underguard cohorts to tell them about Monkshood," Valian said, folding his arms. "They've got to plan their response to stop people from panicking."

Ivy wished she could un-see the stunned and terrified faces of the traders in Nubrook's streets as they'd flown down from the waterfall on Curtis's carpet. Everyone knew that another member of the Dirge was out in the open. Security would be heightened throughout the uncommon world. Thanksgiving celebrations would be canceled.

"What about the Dirge?" Seb said quietly. "Monkshood will soon give Octavius Wrench the Sword of Wills *and* Amos's journal. After that, New Dawn could start at any moment."

Ivy thought of all those cities around the world that would be overrun by races of the dead . . . and London first. Her nerves felt as damp as her clothes. She sniffed and looked at Judy. "We have to find Rosie and the Sands of Change," she said firmly. "Did you see Mr. Rife at the auction house?"

"Not personally, no," Judy said, sounding irritated. "Uncommon bridal veils have been placed around the building since yesterday—they prevent any travel through the walls. Without an invitation I couldn't get in, but, according to a couple of guests I asked outside, Mr. Rife *is* there. He just doesn't want any unwelcome guests."

"Even if we do somehow escape from this place, we'll be too late to catch him." Valian sounded almost defeated. "The auction is due to finish any moment now. We know Mr. Rife is going to visit Midas, his buyer, afterward. As soon as he gets in that pram, we have to be ready to go after him. He's the only person who might know what happened to Rosie."

Just then, the darkened glass door opened and Curtis and Johnny Hands emerged. Ivy scrutinized them to see if she could work out what had happened. Curtis's head scarf was blotchy from water stains, the sleeves of her trench coat rolled up past her elbows to reveal another layer of clothing beneath. A sheen of sweat coated her skin. It looked like she'd been busy. Johnny Hands looked no less exhausted. Even his wobbling red-and-blue jester's hat didn't detract from the grim look on his face.

Curtis marched over to the reception desk and spoke urgently with the underguards sitting behind it. The officers watching Ivy and the others stood up and went over to join them.

"We don't have much time," Johnny Hands said, sitting down on a seat opposite them. He leaned forward, gathering them around. "Alexander Brewster's been charged. The officers here believe there's plenty of evidence to have him convicted, so I doubt he'll be trying to kill you again anytime soon."

Ivy felt conflicted at the news. She knew that Alexander needed to pay for his crimes. And yet . . . the overwhelming feeling she had when she thought about him wasn't anger; it was pity. She wanted to believe there was still hope in the future for him.

"Turns out Alexander wasn't very loyal to the Dirge," Johnny Hands added. "He actually gave us the identity and location of Nightshade in exchange for a nicer cell. We've deployed a team of agents to go and arrest her."

*So Nightshade was a woman,* Ivy thought, but then her surprise and relief were tainted by another thought: having another member of the Dirge unmasked was a positive step, but it didn't solve the bigger problem. "What about Monkshood and the Sword of Wills?" she asked.

"That *is* slightly more complicated," Johnny Hands admitted. "But it's not for you to worry about. My orders are to send you and your brother home."

"Home?" Seb's voice faltered. "You mean, London?"

"London, the Old Smoke, Thames City—whatever you want to call it. Agent Curtis has organized everything with your parents, who are expecting you back today. I thought you'd be concerned about them, so I've pulled a few strings and arranged for a couple of Special Branch officers to be stationed outside your house in case Octavius Wrench turns up." He gave Valian and Judy a wonky smile. "You're both free to join them, if you'd like."

Valian shook his head. "Er—thanks, but I've got some-where to be."

"Me too," Judy said, her shoulders drooping as she looked across at Ivy and Seb.

"We can't go home yet," Ivy told Johnny Hands. "There's something we need to do."

He winced. "I thought you might say that. The thing is . . . your parents aren't considered high-priority assets, but you are. The only way to protect them is for you all to be in the same building. So if you remain here, those Special Branch officers will be deployed on other duties, and your parents will be all on their own."

Ivy flashed her brother a panicked look. The Dirge could attack London at any moment and their parents would be defenseless. . . . Then again, they couldn't abandon Valian now. Four heads were better than two: they'd have a better chance of finding Rosie if they stuck together.

"Curtis has arranged for you to travel to London via uncommon drawer," Johnny Hands explained. "Whatever your decision, I wish you luck. In the meantime, I have work to do. Goodbye, Ivy Sparrow."

After the furor of the morning's celebrations, the streets of Nubrook were quiet now. The shops had shut early, but a few bars and restaurants were open, a sprinkling of custom-ers watching sports on huge materializers inside. Steam fra-granced with roast turkey escaped from the occasional kitchen window, and chatter spilled from terraces. Ivy considered how many of Nubrook's residents might have changed their traditional Thanksgiving Day plans after the events on top of Breath Falls.

After returning from Guesthouse Swankypants with a small bundle of singed clothes, Curtis escorted Ivy and Seb to the drawer-station. Walking alongside them, Judy and Valian were unusually quiet.

"Keep up, you four!" Curtis called from up ahead.

Every time Ivy caught the look of disappointment on Valian's face, the bagel she'd nibbled at the underguard station that morning threatened to reappear. With time running out, in the end she and Seb had agreed to Curtis's plan. Her legs tightened as they walked by a troop of severe-looking underguards marching in the opposite direction. There were more around than normal. Groups of two or three stood on street corners, patrolling with their toilet brushes on show. Ivy guesstimated how big the underguard force was in Lundinor and whether there would be enough of them to defend London from the Dirge's army.

They passed the bench that Seb had turned into an Andy Warhol installation with Rosie's Missing posters. As Ivy studied the different-colored versions of Rosie's picture, a new detail suddenly jumped out at her. "Seb, hold still," she said.

She took out her ping-pong ball and threw it at his back: Rosie's poster appeared on his hoodie. He yanked it up at the shoulders to see what she'd done. "Ivy!" he spluttered.

"It's important," she told him. "I need to take a closer look at the photo and I can't slow everyone down."

As they walked, Ivy examined Rosie's necklace with fresh

consideration. It had a metallic rope chain and a large pendant featuring a black crystal in a silver mount. "Valian," she asked, "that necklace Rosie is wearing—do you have another photo of it?"

Valian took a fifty-pence coin from his pocket and flipped it over between his fingers. A different image of Rosie appeared with each turn. Ivy knew that uncommon coins were used a bit like photo albums. "No, I don't think so," Valian said. "She's not wearing it in any of these." He looked again at Seb's back. "Why do you ask?"

Ivy hesitated, thinking of the discussion she'd had with Seb about the strange "bathed in breath" phrase from Amos's riddle. "The rhyme in Amos's journal—'crystal droplet, bathed in breath, clasped within silver hands' . . . well, Rosie's necklace would fit the bill perfectly. Her crystal pendant has a silver frame; and wearing it around her neck, she'd breathe on it all the time."

"You think her *necklace* is the Sands of Change?" Judy had skated closer and was resting a hand on Seb's shoulder to examine the photo too.

"Look, I could just take my hoodie off," Seb pointed out as they continued to peer at his back. "That way we could all see."

Valian rubbed his forehead. "I wish I could remember more clearly what I saw through the Frozen Telescope. There *might* have been a necklace on that table. . . ."

"If there was, it could easily have slipped off when you and Rosie jumped out at your parents—and it would be the right size to fit in Rosie's pocket," Ivy said, easing the facts into place. "Is it something she would have been likely to take?"

"She liked glitter and sparkly stuff, so yeah." He looked again at Rosie's photo, his brow hardening.

"Hold everything," Judy said, lifting an uncommon cufflink closer to her face. "The coordinates on this have changed—Mr. Rife has moved. Here, take this—"

Without stopping, she unfolded a world map from her pocket and gave it to Valian, then relayed the numbers. "He's in Tibet," Valian said, tracing his finger across the page. "Strassa."

Ivy peered closer. The gradient lines on the map were compactly spaced, indicating steep mountains. She remembered seeing the advertisement for Strassa on the boarded-up shop two days ago—the WORLD'S FIRST SKYMART! "That's aboveground," she observed. "It'll have natural light, so Octavius Wrench could exist there without help from Alexander's potion."

"There's no time to lose," Valian said, folding the map away and stuffing it back in his pocket. "Judy, we have to leave *now*. Ivy, Seb . . . get home safe." Then he turned in the opposite direction. Judy smiled weakly at Ivy and Seb before she and Valian hurried away.

Ivy's legs twitched, wanting to join them. She felt awful.

Curtis, Seb and Ivy turned into a marble courtyard where stationmasters in red uniform were standing in a grid formation. Resting beside each of them was a set of drawers labeled with a different number. Uncommoners stood waiting between the chests, fidgeting and chatting. Ivy assumed it was the equivalent of a major transport depot.

Curtis approached a mirrored dressing table with six drawers. The stationmaster dipped his head. "Miss?"

"These two are to travel to drawer 262 in London," she told him. "I will be accompanying them." She gave him a piece of paper stamped with the divergent arrow crest.

The stationmaster read it quickly. "As you wish." He handed them a ticket each and signaled to chest number 36. "Please join that line."

Curtis herded Ivy and Seb over, checking the faces in the crowds. Ivy examined her ticket. It had been stamped with two words: ONE JOURNEY.

"I wonder if there's a drawer in one of these chests that goes to Strassa," Seb whispered in her ear.

"What difference does it make?" Ivy asked, watching Curtis double-check she had her common mobile phone stowed in her pocket. "Mum and Dad are at home, waiting for us. You heard what Johnny Hands said: they'll only be protected if we're with them."

"We can't just sit at home waiting for New Dawn to happen," Seb argued. "I've been thinking: maybe the *best* way to safeguard our parents is to help save Rosie first. The Dirge are still hunting for her and the Sands of Change; if we can find her before they do, we can stop them from using another of the Great Uncommon Good. That might give the Tidemongers and the underguards a better chance of defeating them."

"I don't . . ." Ivy hesitated, feeling torn. The last thing she wanted to do was destroy the one chance their parents had of being safe when New Dawn began . . . but Rosie's life was at stake too. And Seb was right: if the Dirge got hold of the Sands of Change, they would be unstoppable.

*London or Strassa?* Both options seemed like the right

thing to do, but she could only pick one. In the end she listened to the sinking feeling in her gut that had started when Valian and Judy left. "You're right," she told her brother. "We should be with Valian. We've got to see this through to the end."

Seb lowered his head to Ivy's pocket. "Scratch, buddy, you listening? Can you read *Farrow's Guide* and see which one of these things goes to Strassa?"

Ivy's bag vibrated. "One hundred and sixty-six," Scratch said in a muffled voice.

"I can see it." Ivy pointed to a rickety wooden chest with a fabric top, a few chests along in the same row. "We'll have to switch drawers at the last minute, once Curtis is inside the drawer to London."

The stationmaster checked his pocket watch before finally opening the top drawer in the chest. Ivy scrutinized the uncommoners lining up in front, who took turns boarding. "Adults to load first, please," the stationmaster instructed. "They take up more space."

The pavement rumbled as their bodies turned into tiny golden lights that flew into the drawer, like dust being sucked into a vacuum cleaner.

Ivy nervously adjusted her coat as they approached the head of the line.

"First time?" the stationmaster asked Ivy and Seb. "You won't feel a thing. Just place your hand inside the drawer. After you, madam."

Curtis assessed Ivy and Seb carefully. "I'll be waiting for you in there. Just be quick." She scanned the nearby faces one last time before moving her hand into the drawer.

Ivy noticed Curtis's head scarf ruffle as a strange wind passed over her, and then, with a golden flash, she disappeared. Ivy went leaden with guilt, hoping they were about to do the right thing. "Come on," she said, grabbing Seb's hand. "Let's go save Rosie."

# CHAPTER NINETEEN

The drawer to Strassa was dark and smelled overwhelmingly of talcum powder, making Ivy's nose twitch. She tried to peel her foot away from someone's thigh, but there was no other space to put it. She understood now what Valian had meant by "those *impossibly cramped* drawers."

"Scooos me," Seb mumbled in a muffled voice. Ivy glimpsed him a few bodies away, his sweaty forehead pressed against the shoulder of a woman wearing a flamenco dress. She wondered how Curtis was faring in the drawer to London, and whether she'd yet realized that Ivy and Seb wouldn't be joining her.

There was a loud rumble, and then clear light appeared in the cracks between passengers. Other people started shuffling; Ivy felt a stream of hot air circle around her. Light flashed all around, and before she knew it, she was crouched on an area of pavement, surrounded by people in Hobsmatch.

"I can't believe uncommoners actually pay to travel like that," Seb grumbled next to her, wiping his face clean with the sleeve of his hoodie.

Ivy could see the pores of his skin as clear as if they were under a spotlight. She looked up and her ankles wobbled. "Seb, are you seeing this?"

He craned his neck. "No. Way."

They were on a star-shaped platform jutting out from the side of a craggy mountain. Its snowy brothers rose into the blue sky for miles in either direction. *The Himalayas!* Ivy's heart stirred with emotion; it was the most spectacular sight she had ever seen.

"Look over there—camels!" Seb cried.

Ivy groaned and turned to where a small enclosure of packhorses, donkeys and camels were being offered to traders needing help to carry goods. All around, uncommoners were wrestling with overflowing boxes or towing heavy carts. She cast her gaze through the crowd, looking for anyone in a black suit and bowler hat—all this natural light would be perfect for Octavius Wrench.

"This must be the equivalent of the arrivals chamber," Seb decided. "So . . . where's the skymart?"

On the opposite side of the platform, a doorframe the size of a three-story building stood astride one of the star's points. In place of a door there was a brightly colored beaded curtain decorated with chrysanthemum flowers and hanging chimes.

"Through there, I guess. Whatever's behind it must be invisible." Ivy angled her head and caught flickers of a thin dome of light surrounding them. From the poster she'd seen of Strassa, she knew the skymart was constructed from a number of different platforms slotted together. Maybe the reason they couldn't see the adjoining one was because each had its own invisible covering. That would also explain how commoners couldn't see the skymart.

Seb stripped off his hoodie and tied it around his waist. "Hopefully Valian and Judy haven't already gone inside; we'd better start looking." Ivy removed her duffle coat; the sun was surprisingly warm.

Meandering through the crowd, Ivy caught alternative wafts of manure and sweet incense. She scanned for Judy using her whispering, but there were so many races of the dead around, it wasn't easy. Seb picked up a freshly printed copy of *Strassa: Farrow's Guide for the Traveling Tradesman* and borrowed Scratch from Ivy's pocket in order to read it.

" '. . . *advanced uncommon technology controls the temperature and air quality inside Strassa and offers year-round protection from wind, rain and snow,*' " Scratch read. " '*The control hub of the skymart is situated inside the mountain, where technicians also manufacture uncommon equipment for other undermarts in the world. Officials estimate that the skymart will be finished in two years, once expansion inside the mountain is comp*—' "

"Found her!" Ivy interrupted, picking out the soothing voice of Judy's broken soul among the crowd. "This way." She stuffed Scratch and *Farrow's Guide* in her pocket and dragged Seb in the direction of the giant beaded curtain, where a mass of people were waiting to pass through.

Valian's face lit up when he saw them running over. "You're here!" Without thinking, he hugged them firmly. "What about your mum and dad?"

"They'll be OK," Ivy said. That heavy feeling in her gut

hadn't gone away, but, seeing how much their being there meant to Valian, she knew they'd made the right choice.

"Glad you came," Judy said, smiling at Seb. "Strassa is twelve hours ahead of Nubrook. Right now it's seven in the morning on the first day of trade. There are ID checks to get in—it'll be busy."

Ivy saw men in green-and-silver uniforms standing in a line across the entrance. Large silver bells etched with a fingerprint symbol stood on tables beside each officer.

"Must be a reaction to Monkshood's appearance on top of Breath Falls," Valian commented. "There are more skyguards on duty here than I've ever seen before."

While they got in line, Ivy nervously fingered the copy of *Farrow's Guide*, hoping that their last-minute drawer-hopping hadn't raised any alarms in Nubrook. The paper felt crisp and unwrinkled. Curious, she took a look at the author's biography on the back cover. "Frederick Ignacio Farrow," it said, "is the pseudonym of a writer who started traveling at a young age, after the death of his intrepid explorer parents left him an orphan." The Strassa guidebook was the most recent Mr. Farrow had written.

"Gloves on?" Seb asked. Everyone in line around them was pulling on a different pair.

Ivy cringed at her dress gloves, now mud-stained and grubby. "Yeah."

At the front of the line, she was asked to ring one of the large silver bells. *"Ivy Sparrow. Junior trader. Primary undermart: Lundinor in the United Kingdom,"* the bell said in a clear, high voice.

The skyguard stepped aside to let Ivy pass. As she waited

for the others to join her, she listened to the bells announcing their details. Instead of "junior trader," Valian got "scout" and Judy "waitress." The bell also told everyone that Judy was "Dead. Classification: Phantom."

The four of them walked through the beaded curtain together. The chimes tinkled as chrysanthemum petals fell into everyone's hair. On the other side, Ivy saw a city of modest wooden buildings arranged around a stunning jade temple on a hill. The structure had translucent green walls and a roof decorated with silver crescent moons. In the streets below, Tibetan writing decorated the brightly colored shop fronts, and rich fabrics embroidered with gold thread hung from the balconies. Ivy noticed that, like Lundinor and Nubrook, Strassa had its own special streetlamps—shaped like tall flowers with white petals. Every door had a colorful rope knocker.

"Does that include a map?" Judy asked, pointing to *Farrow's Guide*.

The Lundinor guide didn't, but Ivy flipped through the Strassa guide anyway. Inside she found what she assumed was a street plan. The names were all written in code, but the grids were numbered. Judy checked the coordinates on the cufflink against the map. "Looks like Mr. Rife's pram is not too far away. Follow me."

She led them to a stable courtyard filled with yurt cafés selling everything from yak meat wraps to thenthuk—a Tibetan noodle soup. The stables were used to store various vacuum cleaners, doormats and rolled rugs. Seb spotted Mr. Rife's pram in one corner, and after checking the coast was clear, they crept over.

The pram was covered by the same see-through silvery

sheet that Ivy had seen draped over it before. "The covering is uncommon," she told the others. "What does it do?"

Valian took a step back. "It must be a security blanket. They read fingerprints. If anyone other than the official owner touches it"—he pulled a gross face—"imagine being covered head to foot in a sticky spiderweb, unable to move from the spot."

Ivy looked closer, careful not to make contact. The gold magnifying glass, which Mr. Rife had said he was delivering to the mysterious Midas, was wrapped in a neat bundle inside, along with Mrs. Bees's flowery apron and Mr. Rife's feathered hat. "If that magnifying glass is still here, they can't be meeting the buyer yet. Where do you think they've gone?"

"I don't know," Valian said. "We'll have to stake out the site until they return."

They took a table outside Yak-Attacks Yurt House. Seb brought over some fried meat dumplings and two jugs of water. Ivy tucked in: she hadn't eaten since her bagel that morning . . . or rather yesterday morning. She kept forgetting it was Friday in Strassa now.

"If it's called the Sands of *Change*—it must be able to transform things," Seb guessed, guzzling from his glass. "Perhaps you wear it around your neck and it changes your appearance."

"That might explain why no one's ever seen Rosie," Valian said. "She could look completely different."

As they cleared up their empty plates, they heard cheering from the street. Ivy and Judy went to investigate. A parade of costumed dancers was moving along the road, performing a series of solemn movements. They each wore a crown of small skulls and a menacing mask painted red, yellow and black.

Musicians clashed cymbals and banged drums at the rear of the procession. Ivy overheard a few English-speaking tourists discussing how the traditional Tibetan costumes were meant to represent demons and angry spirits.

"Must be a celebration for the opening day of trade," Judy guessed. "Wait—look." Watching the dancers from the other side of the road were Mrs. Bees and Mr. Rife . . . with the gold magnifying glass in his gloved hand.

As if on cue, Valian and Seb came running out of the courtyard. "It's gone!" Seb said. "The pram. The blanket. Everything. We must have missed them."

"Not quite." Ivy pointed. Rather than tapping his feet to the beat, Mr. Rife was carefully scrutinizing the parade. One of the masked dancers broke formation and slipped to the side of the road. The dancer nodded at Mr. Rife and Mrs. Bees before guiding them away, wheeling the pram beside them.

"That must be the buyer, Midas," Valian said. "Let's go."

They crossed the road and trailed Mr. Rife, Mrs. Bees and the masked dancer at a distance, ducking behind stalls and snaking through the crowd. Skirting the jade temple, the masked dancer turned toward the mountain and ventured into an area of the skymart still under construction. It was eerily quiet in this part. Trucks and diggers stood idle, piles of earth lay abandoned beside the sandy makeshift roads. Ivy noticed cotton reels, kitchen whisks and high-heeled shoes dotted about the site—all uncommon building tools. She guessed that all the workers had taken the day off, as it was the first day of trade.

Suddenly Mrs. Bees screamed. Valian pulled them all behind a stack of paving slabs and they looked out. Mr. Rife, his hands held up in defense, was edging away from the masked dancer. "Midas?" he spluttered. "Is that really you? What is the meaning of this?"

The dancer held a long white electric cord as if it were a whip. On the tip was a three-pin plug . . . except the pins looked more like stainless-steel claws. They gave a hissing laugh and lashed the cord through the air, striking Mr. Rife in the leg and tearing at his flesh.

"*Gah!*" Mr. Rife cried, and fell to his knees, trying to protect his head with his arms. The dancer threw something toward Mrs. Bees, and her wrists sprang together as if they were connected by elastic. An uncommon paper clip. Ivy had been restrained in a similar manner before. She fumbled for her yo-yo as the dancer began to drag Mrs. Bees away.

"Come on, we have to do something!" Dashing from her hiding place, Ivy spotted Mrs. Bees and the masked dancer vanishing around the corner of a newly laid brick wall.

"No!" Mr. Rife yelled, staggering to his feet. "Whoever you are, take the necklace and let the girl go!" Judy and Valian hurtled past him in pursuit; Ivy and Seb stopped to help Mr. Rife.

"Slow down or you'll make your leg worse," Seb said, pushing his shoulder under Mr. Rife's armpit to keep him upright. "You're too weak to chase after them." Ivy tried to brace Mr. Rife's other side. His trousers were torn and soaked with blood from his wound, which was bleeding badly.

"I've got to help her," Mr. Rife persisted, dragging his injured leg forward, but it wouldn't support his weight and he crumpled in Ivy's and Seb's arms.

After a few minutes, footsteps sounded as Judy and Valian came running back. "They've flown into a dark tunnel on the back of a carpet," Judy said. "It leads into the mountain. We tracked them to a T-junction, but it was impossible to tell which way they've gone from there—they were too far ahead."

Valian marched up to Mr. Rife. "Where is my sister?" he demanded.

Mr. Rife muttered a curse, rubbing his bad leg.

"Tell me!" Valian kicked the floor in frustration, possibly to avoid kicking Mr. Rife himself. "You lied to us— you *have* seen her. You shook hands with her on the day she disappeared."

Ivy noticed something glittering in the sand and bent down to pick it up. "A crooked sixpence . . . ?" She beheld Mr. Rife. "*You* are a member of the Dirge?"

"Wh-what?" he stuttered. "No . . . no—the dancer in the mask dropped that."

Ivy wasn't sure whether to believe him, until she remembered that Mr. Punch had told them he'd seen Valian and Mr. Rife embracing as friends in the face of an uncommon clock. Surely Valian wouldn't do that if Mr. Rife was lying now?

"The dancer must be a member of the Dirge," Ivy realized. "But—I thought they were your mysterious buyer, Midas?"

"As did I, at first," Mr. Rife said, "but the real Midas wouldn't have done this; I've traded with Midas before. Whoever the dancer is, they're an imposter."

"I don't get it," Seb said. "What would the Dirge want with Mrs. Bees?"

"You don't understand"—Mr. Rife rubbed his face with his hands—"I've failed her."

Ivy considered what Seb had suggested when they were eating dumplings—that the Sands of Change must have the power of transformation. "You said just now, 'Take the necklace and let the girl go,'" she reminded Mr. Rife. An idea lodged in her head. It seemed unlikely, and yet . . .

"Is Mrs. Bees . . . *Rosie?*"

# CHAPTER TWENTY

"Steady," Seb warned, trying to keep Mr. Rife upright. "Let me help you sit down." He carefully lowered Mr. Rife to the ground and propped him up against a wooden post that formed part of a building frame. The pram creaked beside them.

Ivy rolled up Mr. Rife's torn trouser leg and considered what their mum—a nurse—would do. "I think we need to put pressure on his wound to stop the bleeding."

"Here, we can use this—" Judy tore off a section of her waistcoat and ripped it in two. Ivy tied one strip around Mr. Rife's thigh to stem the flow of blood; the other she wrapped firmly around the wound. Judy pressed down on the lesion with both hands.

Valian hadn't moved a muscle. "Is that *true*? Is Rosie really Mrs. Bees?"

Mr. Rife rubbed his hip and took a long sigh. "Six years ago, I found a girl hiding in the Dead End of Lundinor. She was all alone and crying, kept muttering something about her murdered parents and brother. I shook her hand to reassure her. She told me her name was Rosie."

"*What?*" Valian swayed. Ivy took his arm and helped him sit down.

"I heard underguards calling her name and assumed she was in trouble," Mr. Rife continued. "Being an orphan myself, I took pity on her and offered to help her escape. You must believe me, Valian: I didn't know you were alive. I thought Rosie's entire family was Departed."

Ivy could feel Valian trembling, but whether with shock or anger she wasn't sure. A lump formed in the back of her throat.

"Rosie was wearing a necklace that I'd only seen once, seven centuries ago, in China: the Sands of Change—one of the Great Uncommon Good. I knew how it worked, so I decided to use it to disguise Rosie so that she wouldn't be recognized leaving the Dead End."

*Seven centuries ago . . .* Ivy contemplated how long Mr. Rife had been dead. It didn't surprise her that he'd heard about the Great Uncommon Good if he'd been around for *that* long.

"Disguise?" Valian retorted. "You turned her into a different person! I met Mrs. Bees—she didn't know who I was."

Mr. Rife studied the ground, his voice weary. "Please, just let me explain. There's no time. A principle of some ancient philosophies is the belief that the natural world consists of pairs of interconnected contrary forces—summer and winter, fire and water, yin and yang—which all rely on each other to exist. These opposites are present inside every one of us too. The Sands of Change works by taking one of these forces and flipping it around."

. . . *Light to darkness, life to death,* Ivy thought, remembering the words from the rhyme in Amos's journal. "The most obvious difference between Mrs. Bees and Rosie is their age," she said carefully. "Did the locket convert Rosie's youth into old age?"

"Yes," Mr. Rife answered. "Only, that wasn't all. Unbeknownst to me, the clasp on the necklace had been sabotaged, so I was unable to remove the Sands of Change from around Rosie's neck after we had escaped. The pendant continued to alter more aspects of who Rosie was until only Mrs. Bees remained. Mrs. Bees isn't aware that she has a brother. She doesn't even know who Rosie is."

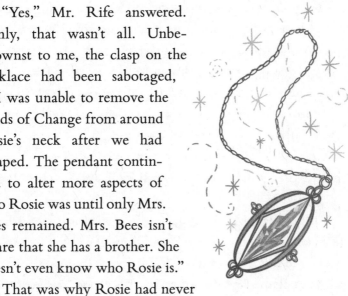

That was why Rosie had never come looking for Valian, Ivy realized. She scanned his face. His expression was taut. "There's got to be a way to undo the transformation and get Rosie back," he said decisively.

Mr. Rife sighed. "The process could be reversed if the Sands of Change clasp was repaired. I spent my fortune trying to find someone with the knowledge to fix it, but eventually it became too risky. That's why I didn't contact you when I learned you were alive—I was worried it would put Mrs. Bees in danger if anyone discovered what she was wearing around her neck."

Valian scowled, his hands curling into fists.

"Amos Stirling knew more about the Great Uncommon Good than anyone," Ivy said. "I bet he had a theory in his journal about how to fix the necklace. Mr. Punch must have read it before he gave it to me—*he* might be able to help us. We need to work out where Mrs. Bees and that dancer went."

"It sounds like they took one of the engineering passages into the core of the mountain," Mr. Rife said. "They all lead to the control center of the skymart."

Ivy wondered how he knew so much about Strassa. She lowered her voice in Valian's ear. "If we get close enough, I can use my whispering to track Mrs. Bees by listening for the broken soul inside the Sands of Change."

"Good idea," Valian agreed, getting to his feet. His mouth twitched as he looked back at Mr. Rife. "Will you be all right on your own?"

"I'll be fine." Mr. Rife gave him a weak smile, pushed a shaky hand inside his cape and withdrew the gold magnifying glass. "Hold this over your heart and it will amplify your abilities," he explained, passing it to Ivy. He tapped his ear. "I'm a Sasspirit: we have exceptional hearing."

Ivy, Seb, Valian and Judy entered the mountain via a craggy dark hole between the timber skeletons of two half-finished buildings. The pebbly tunnel floor sloped down, into darkness. They read a sign nailed to the rock:

The crackle of Judy's roller skates reverberated around the mottled brown walls. The cool air carried the odor of damp clay. Ivy untied her coat from her waist and pulled it back on, her heart thudding in her rib cage. Despite her nerves, she was glad to move away from natural light and the increased danger of Octavius Wrench.

Judy rolled to a halt at a fork in the passageway. "This is where we lost Mrs. Bees and the dancer. Ivy, can you tell which way they went?"

Ivy broadened her field of sense. She caught the pleasant whisper of Judy's broken soul and the voices of the uncommon objects they were all carrying, but the tunnels were vacant. "No, sorry," she said. "Nothing yet."

She lifted the uncommon magnifying glass over her chest, just as Mr. Rife had told her to do. The backs of her arms prickled as her senses spread farther. She winced as the gibbering voices of every fragment of soul, all the way to the jade temple, filled her head. "I think I can pinpoint the control center of Strassa, ahead of us," she told the others in a strained voice. "It's along the left-hand passageway. The other feels empty." She concentrated a moment longer, trying to identify any individual voices. "I can't isolate the Sands of Change yet. I'll keep trying as we go, though." There was no time to waste.

They jogged along the left-hand passageway, the blue-tinted glow from Valian's uncommon trowel lighting the way. Soon the stony walls turned into gleaming steel panels, lit by uncommon lemon squeezers. A door labeled ENGINEER'S ENTRANCE appeared up ahead.

"We need to come up with a plan to get inside unnoticed," Judy decided. "The facility might not be fully staffed, but there will be people working around the clock to keep Strassa running. If we're seen, we'll blow our chance of finding Rosie."

Valian put his trowel away and patted his jacket pocket. "I can use my boat shoes to escape if I'm spotted, and Judy can use her camouflage," he told Ivy and Seb, "but I don't have any liquid shadow for you two."

"I've got an idea for us," Seb said, reaching into his hoodie pocket. "Only, it'll require one of you two giving us a piggyback."

"What do you mean?" Valian asked.

But Ivy knew exactly what her brother was thinking.

*Not again . . .*

# CHAPTER TWENTY-ONE

Ivy stamped on the cotton lining of Valian's outer top pocket, checking it was strong enough to hold her weight. The zipped opening was at neck height, so her head protruded above the top. As Valian turned a corner, she fell into Seb's shoulder.

"Will you please hang on!" he snapped, gripping the zip pull. They were both about ten centimeters high—bigger than the last time they'd shrunk themselves using the measuring tape, but still the size of hamsters. "The last thing we need is for you to fall out and get hurt."

"Sorry, but it's difficult when I'm holding the magnifying glass over my heart," she countered.

"Can you sense anything yet?"

She listened for broken souls in the surrounding area. "There are uncommon objects everywhere in this place, but none of them are the Sands of Change." She communicated with Scratch, who relayed the information to Valian and Judy since she and Seb were too small to be heard naturally.

Valian continued along the corridor, holding Scratch close to his ear. Glass doors on either side led to empty offices. Judy offered them a wobbly smile of good luck before turning invisible. Ivy caught Valian's reflection. He was wearing her satchel across his body, his ratty dark hair tucked behind his ears and his boat shoes fastened with fancy bows. Ivy and Seb looked like strange dolls sticking out of his top pocket.

Just then, light flickered at the end of the passageway. Before either Ivy or Seb could react, Valian darted through the nearest wall to avoid being seen. Ivy felt a cold, ticklish sensation all over her body, like silk gliding across her skin, and realized she was moving *through* the wall. She guessed the abilities of Valian's boat shoes extended to her and Seb also. Valian emerged into a large laboratory, where the strange shapes of machinery loomed all around and white coats hung on a hook beside the door. A shadow drew across the glass. Ivy and Seb bashed heads as Valian nose-dived behind a desk to hide.

The door creaked open and a tall woman in a green-and-silver skyguard uniform stepped in, brandishing her toilet brush. She scanned the gloom carefully. Ivy could feel Valian's heart racing, as fast as her own. Eventually the skyguard scowled and muttered something in Chinese before leaving. Ivy wished she could have understood. Valian took a deep breath, tossing Ivy and Seb forward.

"This is worse than hitching a ride on Johnny Hands's sneaker," Seb complained, rubbing his forehead. "Where are we?"

As if on cue, Valian rose to his feet and looked around. Hanging from a track on the ceiling were a dozen silver bells engraved with a fingerprint symbol—like the one used to ID Ivy at the entrance to Strassa. A robotic arm had its fingers frozen around the waist of one bell. Ivy followed the track across the ceiling and down the wall, where it passed over a large cylindrical vat. Valian climbed a stepladder beside it and peered over the rim.

The drum contained a transparent liquid.

Ivy wrinkled her nose as a chemical tang filled the air. "Is it just me, or does that smell like Alexander Brewster's Statue Salt to you?"

Seb scrutinized the identity bells. "It looks like they're coating the bells in the formula." He sniffed one of his drummer's gloves. "Yeah—they must be. I rang the bell when we were IDed with this hand, and it smells the same."

Ivy hurriedly passed the information on to Scratch, who explained it to Valian. "Hmm, Alexander mentioned that he'd given the Dirge several of his recipes," Valian said. "They must be behind this somehow; perhaps one of them works here. But why?"

Just then Judy shimmered into sight beside them. She looked flushed. She brushed a wisp of hair away from her nose.

"The bells have been coated—sabotaged, you could say— with one of Alexander Brewster's concoctions," Valian told her. "It turns people to living stone."

"I know," she replied in an ominous tone. "I found another lab just like this one on the other side of the hall. From the labels, the staff must think that the mixture is ever-shine polish. And that's not all they've done." She held up a wad of papers.

The top sheet was printed with a list of numbered addresses. "I came across this in one of the office rooms. Last week, Strassa shipped these identity bells to every undermart in the world. That means anyone who has entered an undermart in the last seven days will have contaminated their gloves."

The heavy clutches of dread fell around Ivy's shoulders. "This has got to be part of New Dawn," she told Seb. "It would only take the sound of an uncommon music box to turn the chemical on everyone's gloves into powder, and then they'd freeze, like we did. The Dirge would be able to immobilize the majority of uncommoners in the world . . ."

". . . meaning they could attack the common cities above without anyone trying to stop them," Seb said. "Ivy, we can't let that happen!"

The hairs on the back of Ivy's neck stood to attention as an unsettling voice crept into her ears. It hummed somberly like a meditating monk, filling her with a deep feeling of emptiness. She knew immediately what it was.

"Findings Ivy the Sands of Change!" Scratch announced. "Is fast movings; hurry follow Scratch, please."

In Scratch's voice, Ivy directed Valian and Judy away from the laboratory, through a staff canteen, across a large atrium and out of the Strassa control center altogether. They had worked their way back to the mottled-brown rocky tunnels they'd started in when Ivy brought them to a stop. The broken soul inside the Sands of Change had settled in one position.

Ivy tried to pinpoint its location.

*Strange . . .*

It sounded like the object was *inside* the rocky wall just to the left of them. Ivy wondered if there was a secret chamber on the other side. She explained it via Scratch.

"I can try walking through it," Valian said. "But just to warn you: I've never used the boat shoes to pass through something that thick before, so I don't know what may happen."

He took a deep breath before stepping forward. The cool, slippery feeling over Ivy's skin lasted longer than before, but they eventually emerged into a dimly lit lounge. She tingled with relief, examining the Tudor-style beams running across the ceiling and the tapestries adorning the mahogany-paneled walls. The room was decorated in the style of an old English stately home. Logs had been laid in the cold fireplace, and the air smelled medicinal, like bitter herbs. Valian lifted Ivy and Seb down onto the ground so they could use the measuring tape to return to normal size.

"This is the right place," Judy hissed, inspecting a brightly colored mask and costume dumped on a sofa in the center of the room. "This is the outfit that dancer was wearing."

"I wonder where the real Midas is," Seb said. "The Dirge must have gotten rid of them in order to assume their identity."

Ivy fixed on the location of the Sands of Change as Valian handed her back her satchel. She could tell the necklace was close by. "This way," she told the others.

They padded across the room toward a door in the far wall. Beyond it was a workbench scattered with uncommon equipment: crystal prisms, conical flasks, a Bunsen burner and an alchemist's crucible. It didn't exactly fit with the rest of Midas's décor.

"This looks out of place; it has to belong to one of the Dirge," Valian said in a hushed voice. A lab coat identical to the coats Ivy had seen hanging in the Strassa control center was draped over the back of a chair. "It's all starting to make sense now," he muttered bitterly. "After Octavius Wrench read our minds, he must have instructed another of the Dirge to hunt for Rosie and the Sands of Change. Somehow *they* discovered the truth about Mrs. Bees before we did and posed as Midas in order to lure Mrs. Bees and Mr. Rife away." He nodded to the lab coat. "Maybe the Dirge member knew who Midas was because they work in the control center. That would explain how they were able to interfere with the bells."

Ivy examined the items on the table. "Looks like they've already been trying to fix the clasp on the necklace," she said. "Come on, the Sands of Change is behind that door."

Seb and Valian positioned themselves, one on each side of the door. Behind the melancholy, droning voice of the Sands of Change, Ivy caught a faint whisper and identified the tapestry hanging beside the door as uncommon. "Careful," she muttered as Seb brushed the fabric with his shoulder by mistake.

"Hang on," he said, frowning. "There's something behind this." He heaved aside the wall hanging to reveal a gray stone door engraved with a crooked sixpence. Ivy tensed. It wasn't the tapestry she'd sensed after all.

"It must lead to the Hexroom," Seb decided. "But whose door is it?"

From her coat pocket, Ivy fetched the crooked sixpence that she'd picked up at the building site and flipped it over between her fingers. With every turn, a new face appeared. She recognized Monkshood's scaly mask and the two pointed tusks of Blackclaw's. After a few more turns she found the mask that matched the one carved on the stone door. "Judging by the design, I'd say it was . . . Hemlock."

Valian's nostrils flared. "I should have known it would

be Hemlock behind this! Probably wants to finish what they started when they killed my parents."

Just then, light flickered under the other doorway, and they heard a clatter of metallic objects. Ivy reached for her yo-yo. She wasn't sure what to prepare for if they really were about to fight a member of the Dirge. They'd only survived their encounter with Monkshood at the summit of Breath Falls because he'd chosen to leave.

Valian nodded at everyone, and then flung the door open.

Ivy stared as she beheld the space beyond. She had never seen so many gold objects in all her life. Gleaming ornate swords and pistols decorated the walls; sparkling jewelry, coins and clocks were displayed in cabinets; military flags embroidered in gold thread hung from the ceiling; and a headless suit of gilded armor stood in one corner.

Mrs. Bees sat in a chair in the center of the room, her wrists fastened to the armrests with thin metallic wire. Light glowed around her, blinking on and off like an emergency beacon. With every flash of light, some aspect of Mrs. Bees was reverting to Rosie. Her dark hair tumbled down and went blond. Her skin darkened, and the wrinkles disappeared from her forehead and around her mouth. Her scowl smoothed into a wide-eyed look of fright, and her clothes sagged like a collapsed tent around her bony shoulders. She became so scrawny that she was soon able to try wriggling free from her paper clip shackles.

As she did so, a raven-haired person wearing a lab coat stepped forward, grabbed Rosie and retightened her bonds. For a split second, the aggressor's surgical gloves were peeled back in the struggle. Ivy caught sight of their shriveled, blistered hands—a deformity she had seen before, and it meant one thing:

They were a member of the Dirge.

Just then, Valian barged through the doorway and charged in. "Get away from my sister!"

# CHAPTER TWENTY-TWO

Valian knocked Hemlock over and they both slammed into a case of jewelry. The glass front shattered, sending precious gems rolling across the floor.

Hemlock twitched. Ivy saw her face—a hawkish nose, pale blotchy skin and hooded brows. Her dark hair was scraped back into a taut bun. She bounced to her feet and pulled out the electric cord she'd used to attack Mr. Rife. Valian leaped back as she lashed it toward him. The metal claws in the plug tore splintering holes in the wooden boards.

Her voice, however, was soft and sweet. "Stay where you are," she warned, moving to Rosie, who was still strapped to the chair. She held the plug threateningly close to Rosie's trembling chest. The claws splayed with the sound of a knife being sharpened.

Rosie's cheeks were wet with tears, her eyes drawn so wide

it looked to Ivy as though she was seeing the world for the first time. "Valian?" she squeaked.

"Rosie, it's me," he said, his eyes shining. "Don't worry."

Ivy hoped Valian had a plan. Judy used her camouflage to disappear; Seb was frozen, a drumstick in either hand, waiting to see what would happen.

"Come any closer and I'll kill her," Hemlock assured them calmly.

Ivy couldn't sense any broken soul within her, so Hemlock must be alive.

"I have no use for the girl, now that I have this," she explained. Dangling from Hemlock's free hand was the Sands of Change. The pendant was just as Ivy had seen it in Rosie's photo—a black crystal set in a silver mount. The rope chain was unfastened, the clasp undone.

"Leave her alone," Valian growled, his face contorting with anger.

Hemlock leered. "Or you'll do what? You are no match for me, especially in this room." She signaled with her surgical gloves to the hoard of golden objects on display.

Ivy broadened her senses. Almost every item present was uncommon—from the jeweled crowns and trophies, to the gold bars and Olympic medals. She had a bad feeling that they would all have unfriendly powers.

"Your parents defied me," Hemlock continued. "You don't want to make the same mistake."

"You murdered them . . ." Valian's voice fractured. Ivy noticed him squeezing something behind his back.

"Yes," Hemlock declared, lifting her pointed chin. "Even after a dose of tongueweed, they couldn't tell me where the Sands of Change was. It wasn't till they were dead that I finally believed their assertion that they'd lost it through carelessness."

Valian was shaking. "They were my mum and dad!"

Ivy curled her hands into fists, liquid welling in her eyes. Valian's pain was written across his entire body.

"They were in my way," Hemlock replied simply. "I would have poisoned you and your sister also, but your parents wrestled the hemlock away from me and drank the last of it. So you see, there was nothing left to leave as a trap for you."

Tears streamed down Valian's cheeks. Ivy wanted nothing more than to throw her arms around him, but she didn't dare move. At least Valian knew now that his parents' death hadn't been for nothing: they had died to save him and Rosie.

"Now, let's see if this device is correctly mended, shall we?" Hemlock fastened the clasp of the necklace and then swiveled the pendant once clockwise. A beam of shifting sand about the width of a broomstick shot out of it, glowing with golden light. Within the swirling dust, Ivy recognized the shapes of Chinese characters. Hemlock angled the pendant so that the beam moved across the floor toward Seb. Where it touched the boards, it left behind a bizarre trail of changes. In some places the wood appeared rotten or burned; in others it became metal or glass.

Without warning, Judy materialized over Hemlock's shoulder and snatched the Sands of Change from her grasp. Hemlock jerked with surprise and lashed her electric cord, but Judy dodged the flailing plug before vanishing again.

It took the others a moment to react.

Then Seb smashed his drumsticks and Hemlock was thrown into the headless suit of armor in the corner of the room. Valian ran to Rosie, wrapped his arms around her, and then hurriedly began removing both their shoes. Ivy had seconds to formulate a plan. She couldn't risk using her yo-yo: a room full of flying golden weapons would be as dangerous for themselves as it would be for Hemlock.

Cackling with amusement, Hemlock pushed herself

upright. There was a fresh cut across her cheek. "OK, little lambs. If you really want to fight . . ."

At her feet, the disassembled pieces of the ancient suit of armor convulsed and reshaped themselves into the body of a huge golden beast. Four strong legs, a barbed tail and two clawed wings formed in quick succession. The individual leaves of gilded metal became scales, covering the belly of a headless medieval dragon.

Ivy edged back as the dragon stretched its wings. Cold sweat trickled down the back of her neck. She saw Rosie move her hands free of her restraints as if they were made of nothing more than wet tissue paper. Valian's boat shoes were fastened to her feet. *Ingenious!* He'd used them to enable Rosie to pass through the unbreakable wire in the same way they allowed him to pass through walls.

With a flick of her wrist, Hemlock turned on them, striking the ground with her electric cable whip. Valian jumped aside and lobbed a bath plug into the air. Ivy had seen him wield one before; when activated, they behaved like tiny black holes, sucking in all matter for a short amount of time.

Where the plug landed, a crack of darkness opened and began dragging everything toward it. Ivy dodged aside as a rapier sprang free of its fastenings and sliced through the air on its way toward the maelstrom. She went to grab the edge of a table to stop herself sliding forward—*"Humph . . ."* —and received a blow to the ribs from the dragon's tail, which sent her spinning.

Her satchel fell open and Scratch bowled onto the floorboard. "Watch out, Ivys!" he cried.

Before she could roll aside, a fan of daggers came loose

from the wall above and careered toward her, points first. She shielded her head with her arms as they stabbed the floor all around, sounding like a battering ram. Shaking with fear she waited for one to strike, but, miraculously, she didn't feel a thing.

When she looked again, she saw Judy's bright face hanging over her, wincing. Two daggers had stuck in her ribs and shoulder, but she wasn't bleeding. There was no time to say thank you, as, just then, Valian cried out in pain. Ivy got to her feet as Judy hurried over to help, the Sands of Change swinging in her grasp.

The bath plug black hole had vanished. The room filled with the repeated crash of metal as Seb battled the headless dragon in one corner and Valian defended Rosie from Hemlock in the other. But, as Judy ran, the tip of the dragon's wing caught her in the arm with enough force that the Sands of Change was knocked from her hand. Ivy watched the necklace fly across the room almost in slow motion. The pendant spun clockwise and the flowing stream of sand burst from inside.

First it passed over the headless dragon, which clattered to the floor in a pile of lifeless armor.

Next Judy leaped to catch the necklace, but the shaft of glowing dust touched her, and the pendant rotated yet again. She rolled away, apparently unscathed.

Finally the sandy beam fell onto Scratch, and the pendant rotated twice more. Ivy threw herself toward him, but, when she got there, the bell had gone and a scrawny little boy with gray eyes and freckles had taken its place. A large white scar ran from his left temple up into his light brown hair. "Ivy?" he asked in Scratch's high-pitched voice. "What be happenings?"

Ivy wobbled. *"Scratch?"*

Overhead, there came a loud *whoosh* like the blades of a fan, and they saw the necklace had become tangled in the ribbon of a medal hanging from the ceiling. The dangerous beam of sand spun around the room, creating havoc. It missed Ivy by a few centimeters as it glided over Scratch once more. With a little shriek he vanished, and a bicycle bell reappeared in his place.

Ripping the necklace down, Valian turned the pendant counterclockwise, shutting off the beam of sand. But in doing so he'd left Rosie unguarded. . . .

"Give the necklace to me or I'll kill your sister!" Hemlock was holding Rosie tightly around her shoulders, the jagged claws of the three-pronged plug lifted to her throat.

Ivy gripped Seb's hand. She could feel him shaking, but both of them stayed silent.

"Don't do it, Valian!" Rosie squealed. Her voice was determined, but her face shone with fear.

Valian's body was like stone, his expression unreadable. Ivy had no idea what he was going to do. He'd be protecting thousands of lives if he kept the necklace—including those of her own parents—but he'd also lose the sister he'd spent almost half his life looking for. An impossible choice. Ivy felt her heart might tear in two, whatever he chose to do.

"I . . . I'm sorry," he muttered, glancing at Ivy, Seb and Judy. He carefully unfastened the clasp of the Sands of Change before throwing it to Hemlock, where it landed by the foot of her lab coat. With Rosie still locked in one arm, she bent down and scooped up the necklace in her free hand.

"Now let Rosie go," Valian demanded.

Hemlock snickered and held the plug claws closer to Rosie. "Foolish children, just like your parents!"

"PUT THE CHILD DOWN!" bellowed a voice from over Ivy's shoulder.

She turned to see Mr. Rife standing in the doorway. With his head down, he bull-charged Hemlock, grimacing through the pain in his leg.

There was a creak and a slam. When Ivy looked up again, Rosie was collapsed in a heap on the floor, sobbing.

But Hemlock and the Sands of Change were gone.

# CHAPTER TWENTY-THREE

Valian threw his arms around Rosie, both of them sobbing so hard they were shaking. Deciding to give them some privacy, Ivy and the others rushed over to check on Mr. Rife.

"Are you all right?" Ivy asked as Seb and Judy helped him sit up against a wall. The dark patch of blood on his trousers had grown bigger.

"I'll be fine," he replied. His gaze flicked to Rosie. "She's OK?"

"Yes, thanks to you," Seb told him. "I don't think Hemlock would have released Rosie if you hadn't charged in. How did you know where to find us?"

"I discovered a cufflink in my pram," Mr. Rife croaked. "I assumed one of you was carrying the other, so I was able to locate you." He took a few deep breaths, still staring at Rosie. "I . . . hadn't really considered what it would mean to have

Rosie back and Mrs. Bees gone. I'd grown quite fond of the old woman really. If it wasn't for her, the reputation of my business would still be in tatters."

Ivy remembered what Valian had uncovered during his research on Forward & Rife's auction house. It must have been thanks to Mrs. Bees that they'd stopped making false claims about the items they were selling.

At the sound of sniffling, Ivy turned to see Valian and Rosie approaching, holding hands. Rosie looked just like her picture, except older—as scrawny as her brother but shorter, with sloping cheekbones and deep-set dark eyes. Using the belt from Valian's jeans, she'd fashioned Mrs. Bees's oversized shirt into a dress. Her shiny iceblond hair appeared gold as it reflected all the objects in the room.

"Thanks for saving me," she said, wiping her nose on the back of her arm. "Valian told me you're all his friends."

Ivy smiled. "It's great to meet you at last, Rosie. I'm Ivy. This is my brother, Seb, and this is our friend Judy."

"Hi," Judy said. Seb waved gingerly.

"And this is Mr. Rife," Ivy said cautiously.

"Hello again, Rosie," Mr. Rife rasped. He raised a shaky glove to Rosie's face, but she backed away. The lines around his eyes deepened.

"It's all right," Valian reassured her. "This is the man who looked after you while you were lost." Ivy, guessing Rosie didn't remember much of the last six years, smiled encouragingly.

Rosie shuffled closer, curious. "I know your face," she said softly. She held his fingers to her cheek. "You're hurt. You need to be treated at a hospital."

"She's right," Valian said, assessing Mr. Rife's wound. "We've got to get you up and get you back to the main part of Strassa right away." He bent down and lifted Mr. Rife under his shoulders, hugging him around his middle to help him to his feet. Ivy pondered if that was the very snapshot Mr. Punch had seen in the face of the uncommon clock.

They emerged from the side of the mountain a short while later, Seb supporting Mr. Rife under one arm as he limped along. Ivy squinted at the blue sky through Strassa's shimmering dome. The defiant afternoon sun warmed her face and neck, although her insides felt cold. The Dirge were now in possession of the Sword of Wills *and* the Sands of Change. She wasn't sure if anyone was powerful enough to stop them now that they had two of the Great Uncommon Good.

She looked from face to face around her as the five of them traipsed back through the building site. No one had spoken since leaving Midas's gold-filled room. In the quiet, her mind had filled with worries about the fate of her parents and of everyone else in London.

Valian and Rosie trudged a little way off from everyone else, Valian with his head lowered. Ivy wanted to tell him that she didn't blame him for giving the Sands of Change to Hemlock—she would have done the same thing had it been Seb's life under threat—but she thought it better to give him and Rosie some space.

*Weird beings in squidgy body was,* Scratch said in Ivy's head.

Opening her satchel, she brought him out into the sunshine. "Do you feel OK?" she asked.

"Like strange dream happened," he said, "not back yet to normals."

Ivy couldn't get the image of Scratch as a little boy out of her mind. He'd been dressed in metallic-gray jeans and a T-shirt with an orange-and-white logo—the same colors he sported as a bell. She thought of all the instances when his quick thinking had saved her life or when his words had filled her with courage. And yet she'd never realized before just how young he was.

"It might take a while," she reassured him, "but you'll feel better eventually."

She deliberated how the pendant in the Sands of Change worked. It had rotated twice while focused on Scratch, transforming him from a bell into a human, but that hadn't been all. . . .

"I . . ." She hesitated. While Scratch had transformed, she hadn't been able to sense him. "Your broken soul wasn't inside you back there, Scratch. Was it made whole? Were you alive?"

He went quiet for a moment. "Thinkings so me yes; Scratch never knowings it was possible."

Ivy gazed over at Judy, who was skating ahead. She realized with a jolt that she couldn't sense Judy's soul anymore either.

*Light to darkness, life to death . . .*

The words in Amos's journal certainly rang true. Judy was alive, Ivy was sure of it. She didn't understand why Judy hadn't told anyone yet, but Ivy knew that it wasn't *her* information to share. She held Scratch to her chest, giving him a hug. She'd never once considered if he minded being a bell or if he'd prefer to be a human boy. As she tucked him back into her bag she decided that, when this was all over, they'd talk about it and she'd help him with whatever he wanted.

"Ivy," Mr. Rife wheezed, struggling to fetch something from the pocket of his crushed velvet jacket. "Please, give this to Rosie. I want her to have it."

Ivy helped him pull out a familiar silver object. "The Frozen Telescope—"

"There's so much for Rosie to understand," Mr. Rife said sadly. "By looking through the device, she'll be able to see everything that's happened to Mrs. Bees these past seven years."

As Ivy carried the telescope over to Rosie, she considered how crucial it had been in their search for her. If Valian hadn't peered through it three days ago, they never would have learned the truth about the Sands of Change, and none of this would have happened.

Rosie gazed up at Valian, listening carefully as he explained how the telescope worked. Ivy liked watching the two of them together. It was obvious how much Rosie idolized her big brother, and in her company Valian seemed more relaxed. There was a playful, easy swagger to his walk that Ivy had never seen before.

But when they reached the edge of the construction zone, an alarm sounded, wailing like an old World War II air-raid siren. The timber building frames rattled, and the dome overhead turned an alarming shade of red, transforming the sandy roads into Martian earth. An announcement crackled over a loudspeaker, first in Chinese and then translated into English: "STRASSA IS IN LOCKDOWN DUE TO AN INTERNATIONAL EMERGENCY. All guests are to remain inside the protective domes for safety."

The red light of the dome flashed, making Ivy's temples ache.

"Something's happened," Valian said, pulling on Rosie's hand as he sped up. "Come on!"

As they reached the main part of Strassa, they saw skyguards lining the streets, directing people inside buildings and helping stallholders lock up. Yurt flaps were being rolled down; music was replaced with nervous chatter. Judy made a hasty trade at an uncommon button stall before it shut. She brought back two buttons and popped them both in Mr. Rife's jacket pocket. "One to help heal the wound, the other to soothe the pain," she explained briefly. "They'll have to do for now because we don't have time to visit the hospital." (Ivy had been treated by uncommon buttons before and knew there was a different button for every ailment. You only had to tuck them in your pocket for them to take effect.) Mr. Rife nodded to Judy in thanks.

Valian scanned the road and fixed his gaze on a group of skyguards. "Something's happening to all the skyguards," he said in an unsteady voice. "Look, their bodies are going rigid."

Ivy examined their faces. Their eyes had glazed over.

"They look like you did when you were under the influence of the Sword of Wills," Seb observed.

Ivy grabbed the magnifying glass from her pocket and held it over her heart, using her whispering to listen hard. "Neither the Sands of Change nor the Sword of Wills is here," she said. "The Dirge must be controlling the skyguards from somewhere else in the world. . . . How is that possible?"

"The powers of the Great Uncommon Good are limited only by the user's knowledge of them," Mr. Rife croaked. "If Blackclaw has read and understood the directions in Amos Stirling's journal, he will be able to control the minds of anyone, even across oceans."

There was a loud crackle and another announcement sounded over the loudspeaker. This time, the voice was strained, making Ivy wonder whether the announcer was under the control of the Sword of Wills too: "THIS IS A SECURITY UPDATE. A dangerous criminal has been discovered masquerading as a quartermaster in Lundinor, in the United Kingdom. Underguards have been dispatched to arrest one Mr. Punch. ALL UNCOMMONERS WILL BE PLACED IN TEMPORARY PARALYSIS IMMEDIATELY. This measure is being taken for your own safety and will last until the criminal, Mr. Punch, has been detained. PLEASE REMAIN CALM. You will be released from your paralysis once our work is complete."

"*What?*" Ivy exclaimed. "Mr. Punch? No—they've got it all wrong!"

The air rippled as several giant materializers dropped from the sky and hovered into positions where all the remaining uncommoners in the street could see them. The same video image appeared on every one: a figure in a black suit and bowler hat standing in a moonlit field. His face was masked by the shadows of the surrounding trees, but Ivy knew who it was immediately. She gritted her teeth as he started speaking.

"As of this moment, every undermart in the world is under the Dirge's control," Octavius Wrench announced triumphantly. "We are the pioneers of a new future for uncommonkind, a future that will see commoners submit to our superior wisdom and technology . . . or *die*."

Before anyone could make any comment, the tinkling melody of a music box began seeping out of the loudspeaker . . . and wisps of noxious dust burst from everyone's gloves.

# CHAPTER TWENTY-FOUR

"Everyone, take your gloves off, NOW!" Seb shouted, ripping open the Velcro tabs around his knuckles. "The Statue Salt will start seeping from the material. We'll only be affected by it if we breathe it in."

Ivy pulled on the cotton fingers of her dress gloves, scrunched them into a ball and lobbed them several meters away. Valian and Judy did the same with their gloves; Rosie helped Mr. Rife remove his. A puff of white powder arose from where they hit the ground.

All around in the street, pale dust motes swirled into traders' faces. Coughing and spluttering, they wiped at their mouths and clawed at their throats. Some people stiffened within seconds; others got as far as running a few paces before their legs locked. Ivy saw a mother go to grab her young son before freezing in midair with her face caught in a wide-mouthed expression of terror. As the air clouded with Statue Salt, the only people left moving were the skyguards, who looked on impassively.

"We need to get as far away from here as possible," Ivy said, covering her nose and mouth with her bare hands. "We can return to the construction zone—there's no one there, which means there are no gloves covered in Statue Salt. The air there will be cleaner."

They turned and sprinted back the way they'd come. Valian and Seb each shouldered one half of Mr. Rife's weight, helping him hobble as fast as he could. A veil of Statue Salt had developed over the rooftops of Strassa, obscuring the sky through the red dome. Ivy listened to the eerie tune of the music box and knew that, in every undermart around the world, at that very moment, adults and children were being paralyzed. She remembered the sickening panic she'd felt at Guesthouse Swankypants as her limbs had gone numb. People would be terrified.

"Look out! There's a patch of Statue Salt ahead," Valian cried. "I can't see a way around it." A haze of the deadly powder lingered across their path, seeping into the shells of unfinished buildings. Two traders stood immobile by a cement mixer at the roadside. The path behind them sloped upward; beyond them, the air looked clear. "We'll have to hold our breaths and run through it," Valian decided.

Ivy filled her lungs with clean air before charging ahead. . . .

"*Argh!*" On the other side, Judy fell to the ground, wincing. "One of my knees has gone solid—I can't move it!" She tried dragging herself forward, but her bad knee was like an anchor, weighing her leg down.

Seb left Mr. Rife with Valian so he could help Judy up. "It's a good thing you're on wheels," he said, gripping her around the waist. He went behind her and pushed, rolling her over the gritty road.

Together, they all ran, hobbled and skated into a clear area of the construction zone. Standing atop a small hill was a partially painted Chinese pagoda. It had a square base and seven gradually tapering tiered eaves. These supported a cobalt blue roof that came to a thorny point at each corner. Ivy speculated that the structure was destined for use as a featherlight mailhouse, as there were small holes in the walls for feathers to fly in and out of, just like the wobbly brick tower in Lundinor.

"Let's stop here," Valian wheezed, hauling Mr. Rife into a seated position at the base of the pagoda. "The one good thing about this Statue Salt is that you can't miss it: we'll be able to see any approaching clouds from this height."

"It's only a matter of time before one of us inhales enough of Alexander's formula to paralyze our entire body," Seb pointed out, leaning Judy against a wall. "We need to find a way to protect ourselves and free all these other people."

*That's not our only problem.* Ivy thought of Mr. Punch; somebody had to help him, and their parents, and all the other citizens of London.

"When Alexander Brewster used the Statue Salt on us, he said that its effect could be reversed if the victims listened to an uncommon music box played backward," Valian recalled. "There's probably a few for sale in Strassa, but there's no way to trade for them now. And it'll be the same in every other undermart."

Ivy had a sudden inspiration. "There was an uncommon music box on display at your auction house," she reminded Mr. Rife. "It used to belong to Queen Victoria."

He nodded. "I know the one. Mrs. Bees and I—" He shook his head. "Sorry, I mean *Rosie* and I didn't pack away the sale items before leaving. That music box will be right where we left it in the garden."

"I've been in an undermart in lockdown before," Valian shared. "All methods of uncommon transport stop operating; every border and possible exit is monitored by underguards. Even the movements of the dead are restricted. I don't know how we'd get to Nubrook to fetch it."

Ivy racked her brains, trying to come up with something. By the empty looks on everyone else's faces, they were just as stumped as she was.

"I'm afraid leaving this place under lockdown will be about as easy as finding a fresh-smelling selkie," Mr. Rife remarked, rubbing his bad thigh. "Perhaps we could get a message to someone in Nubrook who can retrieve the box for us?"

*A fresh-smelling selkie* . . . Ivy had heard that turn of phrase before. She reached for Scratch with her whispering: *Didn't Mr. Farrow write that in the guide to Nubrook?*

*Certainlys did,* the bell replied in her head. *Need Scratch readings again?*

*No, it's OK.* Ivy recalled what Mr. Rife had told them: that he'd helped Rosie because he was an orphan too . . . just like Mr. Farrow. Now that she considered it, there were quite a lot of similarities between the auctioneer and the travel writer who went under the pseudonym "Frederick Ignacio

Farrow" . . . They both traveled a lot. They both knew a great deal about Strassa. They both were dead. . . .

*Perhaps,* Ivy thought, *Mrs. Bees isn't the only one who's been fostering a secret identity.* . . .

"Mr. Rife, do you know Frederick Ignacio Farrow at all?" Ivy questioned.

Mr. Rife tilted his head, a coy smile on his face. "Ah, what gave it away—the anagram?"

"Anagram?"

*Jumbly letters,* Scratch said. *Forward & Rife beings Fred I. Farrow.*

Ivy understood Scratch's meaning: minus the ampersand, the letters of "Forward" and "Rife" could be rearranged to spell—

"*You* are Fred I. Farrow!" Ivy cried.

"There aren't many people who know," Mr. Rife admitted. "The guides are given away free, so the auction business is my real livelihood. It makes sense as we travel . . ." He paused, and a wide grin broke across his face. "What am I *saying*? There *is* a way for us to get to Nubrook!"

Valian stepped closer. "There is?"

"My uncommon pram should be right where I left it, not two minutes from here," Mr. Rife said. "It will allow us to journey to Nubrook, but it only carries two. Everyone else will have to take their chances in Strassa."

From the conviction in Mr. Rife's voice, Ivy gathered that he had successfully used his pram in a similar situation before. She was about to volunteer for the mission when he cleared his throat. "I'll go. I'm the only one with access to the auction house. I'll have to be careful that no underguards spot me moving around. You should all head into the mountain.

Hopefully you'll have a better chance of avoiding the Statue Salt from in there."

"You're too injured to operate the pram on your own," Rosie said, laying a gentle hand on his shoulder. "I remember what to do. You and I've made hundreds of journeys together. I'll come with you." She turned to Valian. "Don't worry. I know what I'm doing, I'll be fine."

Ivy caught a flicker of worry on Valian's face, but he nodded.

"OK, that settles it," Mr. Rife said, lifting his chest and taking a shaky breath. "We'll be as quick as we can."

Rosie hugged Valian tightly. "Stay safe." And with a solemn nod, Mr. Rife and Rosie left.

Fear gripped at Ivy's chest as she, Seb, Valian and Judy hurried toward the tunnel that burrowed into the mountain. "It's going to be OK," she told everyone. "For all we know, Johnny Hands, Curtis and the rest of the Tidemongers are working on getting everything back to normal as we speak." Truthfully, however, she had never felt so uncertain about anything. She glanced at Valian, who was scowling so hard she decided that he might be trying to stop himself from crying. It must have been so difficult for him to let Rosie go after he'd just found her again.

"Everything the Dirge have done so far has been to neutralize their enemies," Seb remarked, pushing Judy into the mouth of the tunnel. "Anyone who might try to fight them— the underguards, and now Mr. Punch—is powerless. There's no one left to prevent New Dawn."

"If all the broken souls inside Mr. Punch weren't arguing, he would be able to stop them," Ivy said. "I wish we could help him."

"Me too," Judy agreed. "But there's no other way to get to Lundinor from here."

As they advanced down the tunnel, Ivy sensed they were approaching a large collection of uncommon objects on their left. They turned a corner and she recognized a crumbling hole in the rock. It was where they had all broken out of Midas's gold-filled chamber using Seb's drumsticks after they had rescued Rosie. Under the surface of the speckled tan stone was a layer of brick wall. A gentle whirring noise sounded within as the swords, jewelry and trophies left over from their battle with Hemlock stirred.

Ivy had a thought—"Maybe there is a way to travel out of here," she blurted. "If we can get into the Hexroom, we could use Ragwort's door, which opens onto the featherlight mailhouse in Lundinor."

"Ivy, you're right!" Valian's face brightened. "If we're quick, we might be able to prevent Mr. Punch's arrest."

They stopped where they were. Seb withdrew his drumsticks and moved toward the opening. Judy tried to follow, but her bad leg wouldn't budge. "I'll have to stay here," she said. "You're on your own."

"Why don't you try vanishing and then coming back?" Seb suggested. "Your knee might return to normal that way."

"I . . ." Judy hesitated. "I can't." Very slowly, she looked over at Ivy. "Do you know?"

Ivy nodded. "Yes, I can sense it."

"I didn't want to say anything," Judy explained. "It seemed too good to be true."

"What did?" Seb asked. "What's going on?"

Judy fixed him with a stare, her eyes glistening. "While we were fighting Hemlock, I got caught by the Sands of Change. . . ." She took a deep breath. "I'm alive, Seb. Living, heart beating, the works."

"*What—*" Seb assessed Judy from her messy braids right down to her vintage roller skates. "Seriously?"

Her lip wobbled; a smile spread through her entire face. "Seriously. I'm not a phantom anymore. I'm just a girl."

His jaw dropped. "That's . . . brilliant!" As he threw his arms around her, Judy blushed. Ivy noticed her patting her cheeks, sensing the blood under the surface of her skin. She guessed blushing must feel different when you're dead.

Valian gave Judy a friendly pat on the shoulder. "Really glad to hear you've left planet zombie, but we need to hurry," he said, not unkindly.

Ivy stuffed her yo-yo in her pocket before handing her satchel to Judy.

"Judy really needs a friend right now," she told Scratch as she stroked him goodbye. "You have to stay here and help her."

"Doings best will Scratch," he promised. "Ivy's stay safe?"

"I'll do my best too."

They traipsed through the messy remains of Midas's room, stepping over the shattered glass and dented pieces of golden armor. Valian shoved open Hemlock's door to the Hexroom with surprising ease, considering it had been impossible to move from the other side, and they went in. They crossed the Hexroom and stood facing Ragwort's wooden door.

Seb laughed nervously. "What's so funny?" Ivy hissed. Her

nerves were pulsing through her skin; she could do with a joke to relax her.

He shrugged. "I was just thinking—if the Dirge haven't killed us by the time this is all over . . . I'm actually gonna have to ask Judy out on a date. I don't know what's more terrifying."

# CHAPTER TWENTY-FIVE

"Lundinor will be a hostile place if Mr. Punch has already been arrested," Valian warned, curling his fingers around the handle of Ragwort's splintered wooden door. "We've got to be prepared for anything."

Ivy squeezed her yo-yo. With a long creak, Ragwort's door swung open, revealing the shadowy interior of Lundinor's featherlight mailhouse beyond. The curved walls were made of the same gray ashlar as those in Mr. Punch's Curiosity Shop. Floor-to-ceiling shelves held jars of every imaginable kind of feather. Ivy read the labels of some of them as she ventured in: SPECIAL DELIVERY FLAMINGO and ULTRA-FAST FALCON caught her notice.

The air was cool and damp, as if it had just been raining. Valian emptied a pot of feathers labeled CHRISTMAS GREETINGS ROBIN and wedged it between Ragwort's door and the doorframe—just in case they needed to make a speedy exit.

"Ready?" Seb asked, pausing by the door that opened into Lundinor.

Ivy could hear the wind whistling outside, rattling the hinges. She steadied her nerves as the door flew wide.

"No way." Seb's voice was soft.

Unable to believe what she was seeing, Ivy followed him out in a trance. What had once been a paved square bordered by cafés was now a grassy mound sloping down to the banks of a lake.

Lundinor had been *flooded*. Green islands poked through the murky water as far as the eye could see. Some were crowned by stone castles and connected by wooden bridges; others stood isolated in the thick mist, covered in forest. Ivy spotted the crumbling arches of a ruined abbey on one hill and a huge stone circle on another. She remembered then that a battered copy of *King Arthur and His Knights of the Round Table* had been lying open on top of the Stone of Dreams: Lundinor had transformed into a version belonging to a mythical England of old.

Other than a few boats bobbing in the reeds and a line of swallow-tailed pennants waving from distant battlements, the place was still and quiet. Over her shoulder Ivy glimpsed the featherlight mailhouse, which now formed the wobbly turret of a medieval fortress. A wooden sign erected on the drawbridge listed the names of shops and restaurants you could find inside the courtyard. The portcullis was down; there was no one around.

"I've never been in Lundinor when it's closed," Valian

admitted. "I'd guess the only people here would be under-guards and a handful of officials, but stay alert all the same."

Seb examined a map on the side of the featherlight mail tower. It was constructed from odds and ends of string, rub-bish, plastic bags and random objects used to represent dif-ferent landmarks. "If I'm reading this correctly, Mr. Punch's Curiosity Shop should be"—he moved his thumb between the strange map on the wall and the green island in the distance—"in that castle over there. The one with the red bunting."

Ivy squinted through the mist. Sure enough, she spotted Mr. Punch's symbol—a black top hat—on the flags. "How are we going to get over there? It's not as if we can hire a mop from a sky driver."

"Look, down there." Valian pointed to a small wooden rowboat, anchored in the weeds at the lake's edge. They clam-bered down as quietly as they could and climbed in. Seb took the oars. As they moved through the water, Ivy gazed at the empty market city.

"This place is seriously creepy," Seb muttered, scanning the shadows as he rowed. Only the splash of the oars broke the silence. Valian opened his leather jacket and they saw inside the pale light of his glowing trowel, which meant, Ivy knew, that it was sensing the presence of the dead.

"We're not alone," Valian whispered. "There must be races of the dead lurking nearby. We need to keep our voices down. If we're discovered, we'll have no chance of saving Mr. Punch."

Ivy pushed her whispering senses as far as she could, using the magnifying glass to increase her reach. An overwhelming number of voices darted into her ears, making her jump. It felt as if she was standing in a huge crowd, with everyone talking through a loudspeaker. A shooting pain coursed down to her eardrum, and she had to lower the magnifying glass away from her heart. "The dead are congregated inside the castles," she said, wincing. "I've never sensed so many together in one place before. They've got to be part of the Dirge's army."

"Great." The oars vibrated in Seb's hands. "Anyone else thinking we should have stayed with Judy in Strassa?"

They moored the boat under the drawbridge of the castle where Mr. Punch's Curiosity Shop was located. Ivy attempted to sense him, but, with so many of the dead around, it was difficult to isolate one set of souls, and too painful to listen for any length of time.

"From what we saw in the discocommunicator, that could be Mr. Punch's shop," Valian said, signaling to a tower at one corner of the castle. Ivy studied the squat, circular stone structure. It was the right size and shape, and the positions of the arrow slits in the walls would offer a similar view to the one Ivy had seen in the discocommunicator hologram. Underguards in swishing black cloaks and three-cornered hats patrolled up and down the ramparts, their expressions blank.

"They're still under the control of the Sword of Wills," Seb murmured. "We can't just knock and expect them to lower the drawbridge. How are we going to get in?"

"Did you bring your tape measure?" Ivy asked in a hushed voice. "I've got an idea."

They waded as quietly as they could through the shallows of the moat, using the tall reeds and grasses for cover. Ivy checked with her whispering until they reached a part of the castle wall with no dead around; Seb climbed up on the bank, his tape measure in his hands. He frowned at Ivy, a grim expression on his face. "Are you sure about this?"

"The tape measure has the power to resize things, to make them not just smaller but bigger too," she said. "We skipped backward to grow smaller, so, theoretically, if we skip forward . . ."

"OK, OK, I get the idea." Seb flicked his wrists and sent the tape flying up behind him, over his head, toward his toes. On the first jump, his head bulged like it was a balloon being inflated. His cheeks turned chubby and his feet swelled.

On the second, his legs grew taller, as if he was wearing stilts.

"It's working," Ivy whispered to Valian. "He won't be able to stay that size for long or he'll be seen. We have to be quick."

She and Valian crawled out of the water. Once Seb was around twenty feet tall, they climbed onto his sweaty hand, and he lifted them up to one of the battlements. Lowering their heads below the embrasures, they scurried along to Mr. Punch's tower. The door to the shop was already wide open. Ivy couldn't sense any dead within the immediate vicinity, so they sneaked inside. Mr. Punch was nowhere to be seen, but there were no signs that there had been a struggle. The room and all its contents appeared the same as when Ivy had seen them in the hologram of the discocommunicator.

"Perhaps he fled before they could arrest him," Valian said hopefully. "The Stone of Dreams has gone too."

They heard some shuffling outside and hurried to one of the arrow slits. A small group of underguards was assembled down in the courtyard, just in front of the gatehouse. Two of them were guarding the Stone of Dreams, while another

three detained Mr. Punch. Ivy could see him flicking between several appearances, faster and more out of control than ever. She tried to catch what his different guises were saying to each other, but they were changing too fast.

"Is that who I think it is?" Valian said, squinting.

"The souls within Mr. Punch are panicked," she told him. "It's as if none of them wants to relinquish control, rendering all of them powerless."

Valian rubbed his chin. "The underguards can't realize he's Mr. Punch, or else there would be more of them here to apprehend him. No one else knows he's a Hob, do they?"

Ivy shook her head; as far as she knew, it was a secret.

"Look over there—" Valian nodded to one of the underguards who appeared stiffer and more robotic than the others. He seemed to be issuing commands and directing the others what to do. "I can't see any members of the Dirge anywhere, so where is that one getting his orders from?"

The underguard leader pointed at the Stone of Dreams and barked an instruction. Two of his men removed the copy of *King Arthur and His Knights of the Round Table* from the lectern and put there in its place a smaller book with a black leather cover, which they opened at the pages in the middle.

The ground rumbled. Up in the room in the tower, Ivy steadied herself against the stone wall. "What's happening?" The arrow-slit windows were expanding and filling with stained glass. Fiery torches were materializing on the walls, flooding the room with flickering orange light.

"They're changing the appearance of Lundinor," Valian realized.

He led Ivy back outside, onto the battlements. Lundinor was cloaked in darkness. The castle walls had grown higher, and a spiky black roof now covered the courtyard, obscuring Mr. Punch and the underguards. The jolly flags had transformed into tattered rags, and grotesque gargoyles loomed from the battlements.

Gazing into the distance, Ivy saw that Lundinor had turned into a decrepit medieval city. A black-as-night river ran through the center, crossed by arched bridges lined with nightmarish statues of winged creatures. The pointed spires of several Gothic cathedrals poked above the gloomy thatched houses on both banks. The stink of tar and sewage carried on the wind.

At the sounds of footsteps, Ivy turned. Four underguards were marching toward her and Valian, their faces immobile. One of them was holding Seb in an armlock. "Argh!" he yelped, gritting his teeth.

Ivy ran to help him, but the underguard leader strode out from behind them, stopping her in her tracks. The veins on his temple were purple and throbbing, as if he was straining with all his might against the Sword of Wills. When he opened his mouth, a familiar, deep voice spilled out.

"You couldn't resist joining me, I see."

Cold fingers traced the back of Ivy's neck. *Octavius Wrench . . . ?* He must be using the Sword of Wills to control the underguard's vocal cords.

"Welcome to my glorious New Dawn," he continued. "You lucky three will have front-row seats right here to watch Lundinor's resurrection using the Sword of Wills." He signaled to the other officers. "See that they are made comfortable."

Two underguards strode toward Ivy and Valian. Ivy considered trying to resist, but she was worried that she'd endanger Seb's life if she did. Her heart sank as uncommon paper clips were fastened around her wrists and ankles. The officer patted the pockets of her jeans and removed her magnifying glass and yo-yo before pushing her to the floor. Seb and Valian were secured in exactly the same manner and forced to their knees beside her.

One of the officers snapped Seb's drumsticks in half, making him cry out. Another untied Valian's boat shoes and removed everything from his pockets—he was carrying a considerable number of uncommon objects—and threw them, along with Ivy's yo-yo and magnifying glass, over the castle wall. Ivy heard a distant splash as they landed far below in the moat. With a loud scrape, three heavy iron fetters rose from the stone floor and were fixed to their ankle bindings.

The underguard leader lowered himself to Ivy's level, so his bloodshot eyes were at the same height as hers. "The sun is rising. In an hour's time, its light will cover this castle and I will meet you all again, face to face." He grinned malevolently. "Until then, enjoy the show."

The troop marched away, into the castle. A door slammed shut; the sound of their footsteps faded.

"What does he mean, 'its light will cover this castle'?" Valian asked. "We're miles underground. How can he get the sun to shine down here?"

Ivy remembered Mr. Punch's fragmented warning: *Great Gates . . . Blackheath . . . using the sword . . .*

"Blackheath is above us," she murmured. "*That's* how Octavius Wrench is planning to get natural light in here: the Sword of Wills can control the laws of physics. He's going to lift Lundinor to the surface!"

Seb's face went white as a sheet. "He can't possibly . . . Lundinor is gigantic. It would be like a massive earthquake; millions of people would die."

"*Billions* of people," Valian corrected, "if he repeats the process in other undermarts around the world. . . . Think of the Dirge's map."

Ivy's ears were suddenly bombarded by angry voices. She wriggled to her knees so she could see over the parapet walls. Selkies were slithering out of the river, over the banks and onto the Gauntlet, the main road heading toward the Great Gates. The hulking shapes of all kinds of dead races floated out under the portcullis of every castle and added themselves to the procession.

"The army of the dead," she said with a shiver. "They're moving."

# CHAPTER TWENTY-SIX

Seb scratched at the paper clip around his ankles. His wrists were joined so tightly he could only move his fingers a tiny bit apart. "How are we going to escape? These things are unbreakable."

"I freed Rosie with my uncommon boat shoes, but they'll be lying at the bottom of the moat by now," Valian said, tugging his bound feet away from the fetter embedded in the floor.

Ivy reached out with her whispering. Now that the dead were advancing toward the Great Gates, the castle was emptying of voices. She narrowed her field of sense to the curtain wall, concentrating carefully. "I think I can locate Mr. Punch. He's on the ground floor in a room with what feels like the Stone of Dreams."

"Can you ask the Stone to help us, like you did with the ship's wheel?" Valian asked.

Ivy got a sinking feeling, thinking of her failed attempt to communicate with the Sword of Wills. "I'll give it a go," she said bravely. She scrunched her nose up in concentration and searched for the broken soul inside the Stone of Dreams. Its solemn voice came into clarity for a few seconds before it became muffled again. She refocused over and over, but on each occasion she was only able to lock on to it for a brief moment. "It's no use," she said, shaking her head. "I'm not skilled enough."

"You have to try once more," Valian urged her firmly. "You couldn't detect Mr. Rife's pram when we were outside Forward & Rife's auction house yesterday. Now you can sense a room in the center of this castle. Your abilities have gotten stronger, Ivy, even in that short space of time. You *can* do it."

Valian was right. Even without the magnifying glass, she could perceive souls farther away than ever before. She took a deep breath and homed in on the Stone of Dreams again. This time, she told herself to be undaunted.

"*Questi sono tempi oscuri per Lundinor,*" the Stone uttered.

"I can hear it!" Ivy beamed at Seb and Valian. "It's talking in a different language. Italian, I think."

"Why can't it speak English?" Seb groaned. "I don't know any Italian."

"Me neither," Valian added, regretfully. "You'll have to make it understand you some other way."

Ivy considered the problem carefully. Mr. Punch had once told her that the Stone of Dreams was fond of books, which accounted for its extraordinary powers. Maybe her own love of reading might help her connect with it better.

She imagined some of the scenes from her favorite stories—a sword fight between a dastardly pirate and a flying boy, a water vole rowing along a river, a dragon's egg hatching in a boy's arms—and projected them at the Stone of Dreams.

*"Ciao, bambina con le storie,"* it said.

Ivy wasn't sure what that meant, but she'd certainly caught its attention. It didn't seem hostile. She refocused and tried something else. This time, she sent an image of herself, Seb and Valian imprisoned in chains on the castle battlements, followed by another image of three gallant heroes similarly detained: Athos, Porthos and Aramis from *The Three Musketeers* by Alexandre Dumas. She envisioned them in their striking blue capes and feathered hats, locked up in the Bastille—an infamous French prison.

Instead of responding with words, the Stone of Dreams sent her a vision of a dashing prince riding toward a terrible forest of black thorns. Ivy recognized the scene from *Sleeping Beauty* by Charles Perrault.

And thereupon the floor vibrated. With a loud *clang* the fetters fell apart.

"It's working!" Seb cried, shuffling away. "Whatever you're doing, keep doing it!"

A large crate appeared through the door of Mr. Punch's tower shop and dragged itself over the stones toward them with an ear-flinching scrape. It came to a stop at Valian's side; the lid flew open and Valian peered in. A grin spread across his face. He brought out a small red can of oil with a long steel spout and shook it close to his ear. Liquid splashed inside.

"Thank you, Stone of Dreams!" he cried. Squeezing the lever, Valian dispensed a few drops onto his ankle binding. The ultrathin wire unraveled like elastic and sprang back into a paper clip. Valian then passed the can to Ivy for her to pour it onto his wrists, as he couldn't do that for himself. "Uncommon oil cans change any fluid into what uncommoners call Quick Slick," he explained. "You can use it to loosen just about anything, including the cement between bricks. I've seen people demolish entire buildings with the stuff." Helping each other, the three of them used the Quick Slick to unfasten every paper clip. Valian tucked them inside the pocket of his leather jacket in case they might be useful later.

Once they were all back on their feet, they hurried into the castle and Ivy directed them to the great hall at the heart of the building. Ghoulish black banners hung from the vaulted ceiling, and a long table in the center was set for a feast, complete with spooky candelabra centerpieces.

They found Mr. Punch imprisoned in exactly the same way they had been. He had assumed the guise of the white-bearded store assistant that Ivy had met once before in Mr. Punch's Curiosity Shop. His spectacles were set off-kilter and his shirt and waistcoat had been torn—no doubt during the struggle with the underguards—but his appearance seemed to have stabilized.

"Thank you," he murmured as Valian used the Quick Slick to loosen his chains. Ivy persuaded the Stone of Dreams to open his fetter. "Hurry—we need to get to the gatehouse," he told them. He sounded weary but determined.

"Is everything all right with your . . . friends?" Ivy questioned. She wasn't sure how to refer to the other souls inside him without sounding rude, and she certainly didn't want to offend any of them.

"The others have finally realized the severity of the situation facing us all," he explained quickly. "I only hope it isn't too late. We have to unlock Lundinor's defenses *now,* if we want to stop the Dirge's army. This way!"

"What about the book on the Stone of Dreams?" Ivy asked as they strode toward the door. It was still lying open on top, but she couldn't read the spine.

"*Dracula* by Bram Stoker," Mr. Punch said, without stopping. "Octavius Wrench believes that if Lundinor looks frightening, commoners will be all the more intimidated when it rises to the surface. There isn't time to change it now. I don't know where they disposed of *King Arthur.*"

Ivy wanted to offer the Stone of Dreams a thank-you before they left the room, so she visualized Dorothy, the heroine in *The Wonderful Wizard of Oz,* saying farewell to her friends the Scarecrow, the Tin Woodman and Lion before she left Oz to return home.

As they rushed through the castle, Mr. Punch checked the walls and looked around every corner. He seemed to be searching for something. Ivy thought it likely he was finding the new layout of the building confusing. Just as they reached the gatehouse, he stopped to examine a tapestry hanging on the wall. It depicted a flock of red-beaked crows swooping down upon a burning village.

"Classic vampire décor," Seb muttered.

Mr. Punch pulled back the fabric to reveal a hidden staircase. Although the light only permeated a few feet down, Ivy could see the steps were thick with dust and covered with spiderwebs. "This passage only appears in versions of Lundinor when my shop has stone walls," Mr. Punch explained. "It leads to a spot outside the Great Gates. The underguards and I last used it during the Great Battle of Twelfth Night to evacuate many of Lundinor's citizens. I want you three to do the same now. Find the ladders in the arrivals chamber on the other side: they will lead you to safety on the surface."

"What about you?" Ivy asked. "You can't stop the Dirge's army on your own."

"I won't be on my own," Mr. Punch reassured her. "Come, you'll see."

He led them to the portcullis, which was still drawn up from when the underguards had left. The drawbridge beyond was flanked by wooden posts, each fitted with a rusty iron bracket that held a murky glass lamp. Flames flickered inside every lantern except one.

"Every undermart in the world has the same defense mechanism," he told them, approaching the cold lantern. "Only the highest-ranking quartermaster is ever told of it, so I doubt the Dirge know." He struck a match, opened the hinged glass panel in the lamp and lit the rope wick. A flame burst into life, sending a misty glow seeping through the sides of glass. The other streetlamps shuddered and, with a splintering *crack,* their wooden supports split in two. In unison they uprooted themselves from the bridge floor on their new legs and turned to face Mr. Punch. Their iron brackets unfurled to form arms, with which they lifted their lamps on top, giving them each a sort of large glowing head.

"Lamppost warriors . . . ," Seb murmured. "That's . . . cool."

"Stop the Dirge's forces from reaching the Great Gates," Mr. Punch commanded. "Ignore any instructions from the underguards: they are not themselves."

The soldiers saluted and turned in the direction of the

Gauntlet. Ivy remembered the different lampposts she'd seen in Nubrook and Strassa and guessed that they must have the same uncommon power. She bloomed with hope for a brief moment before remembering how vast the army of the dead was.

"Now you three get yourselves to safety," Mr. Punch ordered as he joined the rear of his battalion. "Good luck."

Ivy, Seb and Valian returned to the castle, descended the secret staircase and started down a long, straight tunnel. Uncommon lemon squeezers were fixed to the walls every ten paces, their pale-yellow glow muted by layers of cobweb. The cool air smelled musty and stale: it didn't surprise Ivy that nobody had been there for fifty-odd years. The place made her think of Judy and Scratch, alone inside the mountain at Strassa. She hoped they were OK.

After a few minutes of walking, they heard strange sounds overhead—high-pitched shrieks, thuds and bangs. They quickened their pace as the walls started to rumble. The conflict had begun.

"This path must run below the Gauntlet." Valian's mouth was drawn in a straight line, his forehead crinkled. "Everyone's right above us."

Ivy had a nauseous feeling in her stomach, and it was only growing worse. She pondered whether Valian felt as uncomfortable as she did about running away from a clash with the Dirge. After all, he'd spent his entire life fighting them and was bound to want to do so now. "I know we came here to help Mr. Punch—and we've done that," she said firmly, "but it feels wrong to leave when he's fighting to protect everyone we love."

"I know," Seb agreed. "But what can we really do?" He bared his arms, showing the empty space where his drumsticks used to be. "We've got no way to stop them. We wouldn't last a second up there."

"That doesn't mean we shouldn't try," Ivy told him.

"Hey—what's that up ahead?" Valian said.

A strange-shaped shadow lay across their path. As they got closer, they saw that it was actually several objects strewn over the floor, carpeted in decades of filth. Ivy brushed clean an underguard's tricorne hat, while Valian heaved a black bicycle upright. Seb found a small canvas pouch printed with the underguard logo—a five-pointed star surrounding a gloved fist.

"This must have been strapped to the bicycle," he said, examining the Velcro on one side. "Mr. Punch said that this tunnel was last used to evacuate people during the Great Battle of Twelfth Night. Perhaps an underguard officer left it here in all the commotion?"

Ivy put the hat down and ran her hands across the frame of the bicycle. It felt warm to the touch. "This is uncommon, but I've never seen an underguard riding one before. Do you know what it does, Valian?"

"No, sorry. The underguards must have used them before I was born."

Seb unzipped the canvas pouch and a silver thimble fell out.

"Now those, I do know a little about," Valian said, "although I've never seen one in action." He picked it up. "My parents told me that uncommon thimbles offer 'the heart's protection'—whatever that is."

Ivy knew buttons treated ailments, so perhaps all sewing-related objects had healing properties. "There might be other objects in the tunnel," she said, taking the bicycle by the handlebars and wheeling it forward. "Let's keep going and see what we can scavenge."

They quickly reached the end of the tunnel after collecting just one more item—a broken toilet brush that only worked when you gave the handle a good whack. As they climbed the steps toward the exit, Seb gazed despondently at the dying sparks between the bristles. With every step, the sounds of battle grew more ferocious. Ivy heard the crackling roar of fire and the splintering of wood. Perhaps the lampposts weren't faring too well. . . .

"It sounds like they're fighting right outside," she said. "If this tunnel opens on the other side of the Great Gates, then Mr. Punch must have failed to hold the Dirge's army back." Tears threatened at the corners of her eyes as she imagined what might have happened to him. "If Octavius Wrench raises Lundinor to the surface, the army will move into London."

"Then it's now or never if we want to help," Valian decided, gathering the uncommon paper clips from his pocket."

Ivy knew their chances were slim. She readied herself to mount the uncommon bike, her hands shaking on the handlebars. She had no idea what it could do, but if it had belonged to an underguard, then it must have some useful ability. Seb banged the faulty toilet brush against the tunnel wall to ignite the sparks, his knuckles white on the handle.

"Before we go out there," Valian said, his eyes watery, "I want to say thank you. I couldn't have found Rosie without your help—not just in the past few days, but before that too. Having friends like you gave me hope again."

Ivy smiled at him. She tried to think of something to say to make them all feel braver. "Let's do this for Rosie," she managed in a brittle voice. "And for Mum and Dad, and Scratch. Let's do this for them."

"And Judy," Seb added, "who I still may be able to see again—if by some miracle we survive this."

"And Mr. Rife," Valian said, "and Curtis and Johnny Hands and all our friends in Lundinor."

Ivy pictured the faces of all the uncommoners she and Seb had met in the last year who'd shown them kindness— Violet Eyelet, Ethel Dread, Mr. Littlefair, Miss Hoff and Miss Winkle. . . .

She clenched her jaw and felt her resolve stiffen.

The tunnel exit was hidden behind a large trader's information board, which swung aside to allow them through. A deafening roar hit Ivy in the chest as she caught sight of the battlefield ahead, filling the arrivals chamber. The wrought-iron gates of Lundinor were bent open as if they were made of nothing stronger than modeling clay, and a whirlwind of dead creatures poured through them, running on two legs or four, some slithering, others flying. There were beings immersed in flames; others that looked like huge spiders the size of elephants. Ivy spotted lampposts with burning legs and smashed lamp-heads parrying blows from three-armed ninjas with long swords. Wraithmoths swooped down upon them, turning the air noxious.

Adrenaline shot through Ivy's body. She leaped onto her bike, aiming for a group of grim-wolves who were swiping

at a lamppost warrior with their sharp claws. On the edge of her field of vision, she saw Valian run into the fray, throwing paper clips like Frisbees. Seb sprinted at his side, aiming charged flares at nearby enemies.

"*Gahhhh!*" Ivy cried, doing her best impression of the warrior queen Boudicca. She thrust her feet down on the pedals and shot forward, her bones shaking as the bike crossed the rocky cave floor.

Individual scuffles flashed past on either side—grimps pulverizing lampposts with clubs, green gobbles spearing wooden legs with their pincers. A series of dull thuds resonated by Ivy's knees. She almost laughed when she saw that the silver spokes of the bicycle wheel were detaching themselves from the rim and shooting like arrows toward oncoming aggressors. They seemed to have perfect aim. Ivy spotted one spoke pierce the tough, slimy hide of a selkie, who screeched in pain—*No wonder the underguards used them.* The spokes scattered toward the grim-wolf pack like porcupine quills. The wolves howled and fled to another part of the cave.

Knowing she was riding a weapon energized Ivy's muscles. She braked and, with one foot touching the floor, swiveled the bicycle around to face Valian and Seb. They were backed up against the cave wall, defending themselves against a pack of vicious-looking scarecrow creatures who attacked with flaming scythes. Ivy drove the pedals hard, rattling toward them at full speed. Enough spoke missiles remained on the wheels to defend against oncoming attackers without the wheels buckling, allowing Ivy to clear a path through the horde.

When she reached the boys, however, the bike collapsed. Ivy launched into the legs of one of the scarecrow creatures, stunning it before it could swipe its scythe at Valian's head. She grazed her hands and knees as she came to a skidding halt beside Seb.

A loud cracking noise sounded overhead. Everyone—on

both sides of the battle—looked up at the cave ceiling as dust fell in a number of places, clouding the air. Stalactites the size of refrigerators began dropping like giant daggers, shattering on the ground below. Entire swathes of the Dirge's army went flying, along with what was left of Mr. Punch's lamppost forces.

"This is it!" Valian grasped the torn sleeve of Ivy's coat and dragged her toward him. "Lundinor's moving to the surface; we need to take refuge."

Seb shuffled closer as Valian fetched the thimble from his pocket. "Here's hoping 'the heart's protection' can shelter us from those giant falling rocks."

Ivy held her breath, willing the thimble to save them. Valian pushed his finger inside, and a ring of ultrathin metal slid around the thimble's edge, about the width of Ivy's arm. Another ring formed, and another. They continued appearing—in increasing diameter—until they had formed a huge dome-like shield, with the thimble at the apex.

The ground tremored as rubble crashed down around them, but the thimble shield didn't even twitch. Valian's arm trembled, holding his finger in place. Ivy went to support his elbow, assuming the load was hard to bear.

"No, it's all right," he told her. "It's as light as paper."

It wasn't the weight of the thimble shield that caused him to shake, she realized; it was fright. Smoke crept under the edge of the shield and dust coated the inside of Ivy's mouth, making her cough. She tucked herself closer to the boys and closed her eyes, waiting for it all to be over.

# CHAPTER TWENTY-SEVEN

Sipping from a cup of tea, an old lady stared out the window of the number 89 bus as it rumbled along across the east corner of Blackheath Park. The heath was quiet and still, the dim, cloudless sky lit by the early morning sun. It made a pleasant change from the thunder and lightning of the last week during Storm Sarah.

The lady's gaze wandered around the ground floor of the double-decker. There were only two other passengers on board: a man in jogging shorts and a T-shirt, covered in sweat; and a teenage boy wearing a football shirt. The boy had a small Yorkshire terrier snoozing in his lap.

Just then a loud *boom!* sounded outside, rattling the windows. The old lady dropped her teacup and grabbed the nearest railing as the bus shook violently. There was a screech as it swerved off the road and mounted a bank, coming to a sharp halt. The impact launched her into the aisle, where she banged her head against another seat.

She blinked, rubbing a spot above her ear. Her head was sore, but she couldn't feel any injuries. Had there been an earthquake? She could hear a strange groaning sound outside, like the very bowels of the earth were moving.

"Everyone all right?" a man called.

"Yes, I'm OK!" The lady hoisted herself up. The door to the bus hung open, and the jogger was peering in.

"The driver's awake but dazed," he said. "I'd better stay with him."

The lady made her way over to the teenage boy with the dog. "Hello, son, are you injured?"

The boy was pale and speaking hurriedly in another language. The dog whimpered as she took the boy's shaking hand. "It's all right; you're going to be fine. Do you have any pain anywhere?" she asked him.

The boy rubbed the back of his head.

"There's smoke rising from the engine," the jogger cried. "We've got to get everyone out!" He pressed the emergency door button. A whiff of churned earth wafted in from outside. The old lady and the teenage boy helped each other down the step onto the grass, while the jogger attended to the driver.

"I checked upstairs: the top floor of the bus is empty," he added. "But I've got no reception on my phone. What's going on?"

The ground was still trembling—an aftershock maybe? Peering across the heath, the old lady noticed the crumbling outline of a tall structure that hadn't been there before: a gated archway with strangely shaped posts on either side. She rubbed her forehead, guessing she had a concussion and was seeing things. It was probably fallen trees or debris from damaged buildings.

Three figures were approaching from across the field. One wore a white lab coat. Another—who appeared to be *floating* over the grass—was dressed in a hooded robe. The tallest of the three sported a black suit and bowler hat and carried a cane.

"Hello? Excuse me!" the jogger shouted. "We need some help over here!"

The strangers murmured. As they drew closer, the old lady saw that two of them were wearing masks covering their faces. One had horns and tusks; the other featured a wide snake-like mouth and jutting fangs. But Halloween had come and gone. . . .

She glanced nervously at the jogger beside her, whose face was drawn wide in disbelief.

Sensing danger, she turned and ran.

# CHAPTER TWENTY-EIGHT

The tracks of Valian's tears were the only patches of his cheeks clean of dust. Blood trickled from a wound above his ear; his leather jacket was torn at the shoulder. He viewed Ivy and Seb nervously before pulling his finger out of the thimble. The rings of wafer-thin steel that formed the giant shield retracted, revealing a bright landscape beyond.

Ivy wiped her nose and forced herself to her feet. Pain throbbed in her hands and knees; her lungs burned as she heaved in fresh air smelling of mud and rain. The red and white lights of slowly moving traffic blinked in the distance. She recognized the vista: they were standing on a hill in Blackheath Park, overlooking London.

"This can't be happening," Seb croaked, staggering upright.

Brilliant sunlight illuminated the devastation of their

surroundings. The scythe-wielding scarecrows had vanished along with the rest of the Dirge's army. In their place was the empty floor of the arrivals cave, now fenced by a crumbling wall of soil, rock and debris, churned from the earth. The entire area had been dragged to the surface.

Ivy looked over her shoulder to where the Great Gates of Lundinor towered over them, twisted and damaged after being caught in the skirmish. Ten meters of rocky wall was still intact on either side, though wobbling ominously in the breeze. The path through the gates sloped downward into a giant chasm. "Lundinor hasn't resurfaced in its entirety yet," she remarked. "Maybe Octavius Wrench has to do it in phases because wielding the Sword of Wills takes so much energy." The thought gave her a sliver of hope. "We can't give up. Not yet."

Nearby, a bus had swerved onto the grass to avoid a large crevice in the road. Steam rose from the engine at the back; a few people—commoners—seemed to be sitting or lying in the field a safe distance away.

"Let's see if we can help those people," Ivy suggested. Adrenaline was still pumping through her veins; she couldn't stand still.

Seb nodded, though she could see that his hair was singed and his forehead puckered with red blisters.

"Can you sense the army of the dead?" Valian asked, looking left and right. "They can't have just vanished."

Ivy spread her senses across the park, but it was difficult to control her skill after the anguish she'd felt during the battle. Her mind and body felt shaken and weak. She managed to detect a prattle of fractured souls filling the gaping hole that dropped down into Lundinor. "They've stopped just under the surface," she said, "like they're waiting for something."

". . . or someone," Seb corrected, holding a shaky finger out toward the crashed bus.

Several shadowy figures were moving with calm purpose in their direction. Ivy caught the disturbing hiss of Octavius Wrench's wrecked soul among them. She angled her body defensively. "It's the Dirge. They're carrying the Sands of Change and the Sword of Wills."

Hemlock was easy to distinguish because of her white lab coat; the others were wearing dark clothes.

"They'll kill us if they see us," Valian said bleakly. "We can hide over there." He steered them behind a knoll of soil, where they all crouched down. Seb inspected his phone screen, being careful to shield the light so that it didn't give away their position. He spoke in a hushed voice: "I can't call the police. I've got no reception up here."

"It might have something to do with the Great Gates," Valian said. "Common technology doesn't work well in Lundinor. Perhaps the gates are interfering with the signal. We have to think of something else."

"With only the thimble, we won't be able to fight them," Ivy decided. "Maybe we can outwit them some other way?"

Murmured noises signaled that the group had drawn closer. Ivy's skin prickled as she heard a distressed voice. "Let me go!" a woman was crying. The sound was muffled, as if something was choking her.

Ivy peeked out from behind the mound. The Dirge stood in front of the Great Gates. Ivy could tell who they all were from the masks they were wearing. For the first time she saw Octavius Wrench's true face, in his Augrit form. His skin was transparent and, through it, she saw dark shapes shifting around like shadows under the surface. From the glint of silver in his hand, she could tell he was carrying the Sands of Change. The Sword of Wills hovered over his back, just as it had done when Monkshood had been wielding it to control Valian on top of Breath Falls. As long as Octavius Wrench possessed it, Ivy knew that the underguard would remain under his command.

Octavius Wrench was flanked on one side by Hemlock and on the other by Monkshood, who, as he floated, held an elderly woman up by her neck. The woman had graying hair and wore a periwinkle-blue scarf draped around her shoulders, the ends falling over the front of her long wool coat. Her slim legs dangled above the ground as she tried to wriggle free. The poor woman seemed as helpless as a rag doll in Monkshood's grasp. "Please," she croaked desperately. "What do you want with me?"

Fire burned within Ivy's belly. "She's a commoner," she muttered to Valian and Seb. "She's got no idea what's going on. We have to save her."

Ivy had no time to formulate a plan as Seb went racing out from behind their mound, shouting angrily. She supposed that was the only strategy he'd come up with—scream at the evil people until they went away. Her feet pounded on the cave floor as she hurried after him, considering their *real* options. They were unarmed and outnumbered; how could they possibly win?

"Leave her alone!" Seb yelled.

"Help me!" The old lady's voice trembled as she writhed around, longing to be free.

"You! *Again?*" Octavius Wrench snarled and turned a dark stare on Ivy and Seb. "What an unpleasant surprise." He lifted a gloved finger, and, at his command Monkshood hoisted the old lady higher. A small squeak escaped from her throat, yanking on Ivy's heart.

"Put her down!" Ivy cried, her nostrils flaring. "She hasn't done anything to you!"

Monkshood parted his robes with his free hand and, in a

streak of silver, withdrew his uncommon can opener. Hemlock lashed her electric cord and plug toward them, cracking the stone floor.

"Kill them all," Octavius Wrench commanded. With a flick of his fingers, a trio of grim-wolves came padding through the Great Gates and began sniffing around. "And search the area for any more."

Ivy and Seb started edging back. In her peripheral vision, Ivy noticed Valian run to join them. "Ivy, look out!" he yelled.

She moved away—just in time—as Hemlock's plug struck the ground by her feet. She knew it was only a matter of time before she was ripped apart—either by the plug's claw-like pins or a steel crab's pincers.

All at once a strange noise sounded overhead—a scream combined with creaking wheels and the high-pitched tune of a nursery mobile. Ivy looked up. Mr. Rife—feathered buccaneer's hat and all—came flailing through the sky, one hand gripped around the handlebar of a vintage pram. Squashed inside the carriage was a small girl with thick ice-blond hair.

"Rosie!" Valian cried happily.

The pram crushed Monkshood as it landed on top of him. Freed from his grasp, the old lady managed to jump aside in time to avoid being hit as well. She rolled and lay where she stopped, stirring only to rub her head. Rosie jumped lightly out of the pram.

Glaring at Mr. Rife, Hemlock charged—

But Mr. Rife was ready for her. "Right then." Tensing his jaw, Mr. Rife opened his jacket to reveal a battery of objects hastily strapped to the inside (Ivy had seen some of them displayed at the auction house). "Let's see how you deal with these." He grabbed a staple gun and fired it in Hemlock's direction. Although no staples shot out, Hemlock slowed. Her limbs jerked as if they were attached to strings being worked by a puppeteer. Then her feet cemented themselves to the ground, her neck went stiff, and with one arm sticking out at a right angle and her other hand stuck to her hip, she looked ready to perform the "I'm a Little Teapot" nursery rhyme.

"*Gah!*" she screeched, struggling to break free.

Meanwhile, as Octavius swooped toward the army of the dead and started barking orders at them to attack London, Monkshood activated his can opener, releasing a horde of razor-sharp crabs onto the cave floor. The slashing noises of their knifelike pincers sent tremors through Ivy's jaw as she stumbled back.

"Mr. Rife!" she screamed. "Help!"

Mr. Rife, catching sight of where Ivy, Seb and Valian stood defenseless, threw something at Rosie. Rosie bent her knees and leaped up to catch it. It was a long-stemmed wooden tobacco pipe—the very same one that her parents had scouted years ago in Bolivia. Ivy remembered having seen it on display at the auction house. But how it was going to help now, she couldn't imagine.

She stared as Rosie blew once into the pipe and then began talking . . .

. . . in *bird noises*? Ivy was still puzzled.

Trilling, tweeting and cooing, Rosie pointed at the surrounding trees as if she was giving instructions. For a second, Ivy had no idea what was going on, but then she remembered that the pipe allowed the user to speak any language on earth. She hadn't realized it included languages that weren't even human.

The treetops rustled as a noisy flock of pigeons shot out into the sky, and then dived toward the crabs. They attacked with precision—pecking at any weak spots in the crustaceans' shells or picking them up by their claws only to drop them from a great height. A whirling mass of dust, shell and feathers began to cover the cave floor.

Dodging around the brawl, Valian ran to meet Rosie. "You made it!" he declared, embracing her tightly. His laugh sounded free and happy, in spite of the chaos all about them.

Valian and Rosie's joy was still making Ivy smile—she couldn't help it—as she and Seb hurried toward the elderly lady lying on the ground. "Are you all right?" Ivy asked, kneeling beside her. Very gently, Seb helped the woman sit upright. She had a cut on her lip, and where her scarf had worked loose there were puffy red marks visible on her neck where Monkshood had been gripping her. She looked dazed, but managed to mumble, "There are others—by the bus . . . a young lad."

"We'll help them," Seb said. "Don't worry. You're safe now."

Above the squawk and clatter of pigeon versus crab, a deep, wicked voice resonated through the air—"Oh, I wouldn't say *that*."

Ivy's chest trembled as, a short distance away, Octavius Wrench stepped forward.

# CHAPTER TWENTY-NINE

"Your perseverance is pointless," Octavius Wrench told them blankly. "You can't possibly beat me: my power is unlimited."

Leaving the old lady with Seb, Ivy got to her feet. She noticed the Sands of Change still in Octavius Wrench's grasp and, steeling her nerves, she tried to assemble a plan. Octavius Wrench's weakness was his pride—he had boasted when he first met them how powerful he was, and again just now. She thought of how he had been the head of a rich and influential family, but how he had stood for election as quartermaster against Mr. Punch and lost. Maybe she could use their old rivalry to her advantage.

"You think you're invincible, but you're not!" she cried. "Mr. Punch is stronger than you'll ever be."

Octavius Wrench's laughter rumbled deep and low. "Mr.

Punch is currently cowering in an underguard prison under *my* control, soon to be tried by *my* new laws. His future is mine to decide. That is weakness, not power."

Ivy wondered if that was true. She didn't know what had happened to Mr. Punch during the battle. She hoped, wherever he was, that he was OK and that what she was about to say wouldn't put him in any more danger. Whatever her fears, she refused to let them show. Instead she took a deep breath: "But Hobs are far more formidable than *Augrits*," she argued, saying the name like it was a playground insult. "And Mr. Punch is a Hob."

Octavius Wrench's form shifted almost imperceptibly. The Sword of Wills twitched at his back. Ivy intuited that the information about Mr. Punch being a Hob had come as a shock. Hemlock's eyes flicked toward her leader; Monkshood slowly hovered upright.

Ivy continued quickly, before any of the Dirge could shut her up: "I don't know why that army bother following you," she said, pointing to the Great Gates. "You're not the most powerful race of the dead at all. *Everything* you say is a lie!"

The army became agitated. Ivy's insult had gotten a reaction. She just had to push Octavius Wrench a little bit further and her plan would work. She could see Seb's and Valian's anxious faces in the corner of her vision; they were bound to be wondering what she was up to. "The truth is," she resumed, "without natural light, you're feeble. You can't even step inside an undermart without using one of Alexander Brewster's potions. How can you be expected to locate anyone's soulmate?"

Some of the dead began poking through the shadows of the chasm, taking notice of what was going on.

Octavius Wrench's neck twitched, but his deep voice remained composed. "My power is unparalleled. As an Augrit, I can be whoever I want to be. I do not merely change my appearance but my whole constitution. I effectively become an entirely different race. Any race at all." He lifted away from the ground and expanded his arms, grinning malevolently. "Let me demonstrate." The ends of his jacket flared out as he spun. His strange, transparent face became a blur, and then, when he stopped, his skin looked fleshy and normal. "There. Now I am a Hob."

*Not quite,* Ivy thought, shuffling backward.

The air stirred. Monkshood wobbled and, along with several members of the Dirge's army, slid over the stone floor toward Octavius Wrench as if he was a magnet for the dead. The dead soldiers clawed at the ground, fighting against the invisible force pulling them in.

"What is the meaning of this?" Monkshood growled as they were all dragged closer. Splaying his arms for balance, he dropped his can opener, and the steel crabs disappeared.

"Something's wrong," Octavius snapped, throwing his arms out. "I can't change back."

Ivy could see the veins pulsing on his forehead from the effort of trying. "You can't transform again because you aren't yet a Hob," she explained. "You see, Hobs are formed from more than one broken soul. So in order to truly become one, you need first to amass other fragments of soul inside you."

Monkshood's can opener and Hemlock's electric cord both shot straight to Octavius Wrench and vanished in a tiny blink of light. He flinched as the broken souls trapped inside them were absorbed within him. His face flashed with panic. "NO!"

There was a loud *whoosh* as Monkshood and several of the dead finally flew the remaining distance to their so-called leader. As soon as they touched Octavius Wrench, their empty robes, and Monkshood's mask, fell to the floor with a soft *thud*. The other members of the Dirge's army retreated into the shadows.

"What have you done?" Hemlock asked in her quiet, calm voice. "Where is Blackclaw?"

Ivy didn't reply; she was too busy staring at Octavius Wrench, who was now the size of a telephone booth and getting bigger. The stitches of his black suit ripped apart as his limbs swelled like sausages. Ivy could see his features changing shape. She sensed the broken souls of Monkshood and the other races of the dead fighting within him, trying to wrestle control. Octavius Wrench's arms jerked, and Ivy saw the Sands of Change slip from his fingers and fly out of his reach into a patch of mud.

Her communications with Mr. Punch over the last few days had taught Ivy how problematic existing as a Hob really was. She thought about how often the souls within him had to compromise to allow one another an equal time in charge. Octavius Wrench was power-hungry with no desire to share anything. Ivy hoped he would find being a Hob a lot more difficult than he realized.

And she was right.

Beneath the rim of Octavius Wrench's burst bowler hat, his face altered. His skin speckled with liver spots; the shallows of his eyes grew deeper, darker. Monkshood's gaunt complexion, black lips and hollow nose socket appeared. "Leader, release me," he demanded gruffly.

Then his face changed as fast as a TV switching between channels. This time, it became the visage of a creature with cracked russet skin and tentacles writhing from its neck. "Let me out of here!" one of the dead soldiers demanded. They had a buzzing voice, like a frustrated insect's.

Then, for a moment, Octavius Wrench reclaimed control, his brow furrowed in a deep scowl. "Stop squabbling!" he bellowed. "Allow me to take power—" But as his concentration finally broke, the Sword of Wills went limp at his back and clattered to the ground.

Ivy's lungs emptied as she thought of all the underguard forces around the world who would be waking from a bad dream, slowly realizing what had happened. With any luck, they'd be able to jump into action as soon as possible. She looked around and saw the army of the dead begin spilling from the Great Gates. Ivy quickly assessed their body language to see if they meant her harm, but they were all focused on Octavius Wrench, curious to see what was happening.

Hemlock shook her only moving fist at Ivy and Seb. "You'll pay for this!" She tried to turn her head to address the army, but her neck was fixed. "Loyal supporters," she shouted instead, "attack everyone—now!"

The dead hesitated. Angry muttering flitted through their ranks. A few winged beasts bolted into the sky; a couple of scarecrows scarpered. The grim-wolves whom Octavius Wrench had ordered to search the area sniffed the air, snarled and scurried back into Lundinor.

A horn sounded in the morning air, like the rallying call of a mythical army.

"Is it just me, or does that sound familiar?" Seb asked Ivy.

She scanned the area and spotted people emerging from the surrounding fields and roads. They looked like commoners in regular winter clothing—gloves, thick coats and boots; some had handbags or backpacks. They were all carrying an empty lantern of one sort or another: some were made of glass and were highly decorated; others had been constructed from scrap metal. Ivy could sense they were all uncommon. Two women wearing puffy jackets and knitted scarves appeared from behind Ivy, and she spotted divergent arrow pins attached to the rims of their woolly hats. "They're Tidemongers . . . ," she told Seb as the women walked by. "That sound—it was the same alarm we heard at the Tidemongers' base in Nubrook." Hope burst within her like a firework.

They heard the flap of wings, rustle of bodies and stomp of feet as the dead scattered. A cry went up from one of the Tidemongers, and in unison they all opened the doors of their lanterns. Ivy stared as a group of selkies, who had been slithering away, suddenly changed direction against their will and sped toward a large railway lantern being lugged by two Tidemonger agents. A meter from the lantern, the selkies vanished in a slimy green flash and reappeared *inside* the lantern casing. Squashed behind the glass, they looked like strange green trifles with layers of seaweed limbs and jagged teeth. It couldn't be comfortable, Ivy thought. The two agents hastily shut the door of the lantern, trapping them within. And in fact all around, Ivy and Seb saw, the dead who hadn't managed to get away fast enough found themselves being sucked inside the Tidemongers' lanterns, as if they were formed of nothing more than gas. In a matter of moments, every lantern was filled.

A small group of agents had trapped Octavius Wrench in a

brass fuel-burning lantern and then used an uncommon chair to detain Hemlock. As soon as she sat down, the chair crossed its armrests over her lap like it was folding its arms, buckling her into place. Ivy ran over to where the Sands of Change was glinting in the mud. She picked it up, and, after checking that the clasp was safely unfastened, she wiped it clean on her sleeve and stuffed it in her pocket.

# CHAPTER THIRTY

When Ivy returned to the others, she saw a familiar figure in a long coat striding out of the Great Gates toward them. "So you're still alive," Curtis said, holding a hand to her chest, although she was scowling. "Your gloves were flagged at the gates of Strassa; I was about to come after you when Nubrook went into lockdown."

"Seb and I didn't want to get you into trouble," Ivy said honestly, "but we had to sneak away. It was a matter of life and death."

Curtis glared at them for a long moment, saying nothing. Over her shoulder, Ivy noticed the remaining army of the dead fleeing as officers from Lundinor's Special Branch—Ivy could tell because of their silver braid epaulettes—arrived and filed out into the surrounding area. Ivy knew it was their job to hide the uncommon world, although she wasn't sure how they were going to cover up the mess.

"This morning will be marked in uncommon history," Curtis told them, surveying the scene as, under heavy guard, a chair-strapped Hemlock and Octavius Wrench's lantern were returned to Lundinor. "The Tidemongers will see to it that the Hexroom is incinerated and those two are detained in ghoul holes until their trial. From this day forward there will be no remaining trace of the Dirge."

Ivy's nerves softened as the muscles in her body relaxed. The attack had been averted and the people of London were safe. She smiled at her brother. "Mum and Dad are going to be OK."

"About that . . ." Curtis pursed her lips. "Your parents were expecting you home five hours ago, and I've yet to devise an explanation for where the three of us have been or why we haven't contacted them."

"We'll think of something," Seb said dismissively. "We can always use the tea technique. It works every time whenever Ivy and I have to lie about uncommon stuff."

"The tea technique?" Curtis looked bemused.

"First you offer to make them a cup of tea," Ivy explained. "Then you put sugar in each of their cups. At least two teaspoons."

Curtis frowned. "How will a sweet beverage convince your parents that we're telling the truth?"

"It won't," Seb said. "What you've got to do is wait till they've taken their first sip before you start talking. They *hate* sugar in their tea. As soon as they taste it, they'll be so distracted they won't really listen to a word we say." He chuckled. "You know, you should feel privileged—we've never told any of our babysitters that tip before."

A faint smile traced Curtis's lips. "I see."

"Do you know what happened to everyone paralyzed by Alexander's Statue Salt?" Valian asked, his arm clamped around Rosie's shoulders. "Will they be OK?"

Curtis gave a respectful nod to Rosie and Mr. Rife. "After what you both did in Nubrook and Strassa—freeing the citizens with that music box—we have sent instructions to other underguard forces around the world. They now know what to do in order to reverse its effects."

Mr. Rife gave a brief smile of acknowledgment, but his gaze was focused on the old lady still sitting beside Seb. Her face glistened with tears as she stared up at them all. He bent down and offered her his polka-dot handkerchief. "Madam," he said graciously, "is there anything I can do to help?"

"Who are all these people?" she asked, dabbing at her cheeks.

"Why don't we get you to your feet and I'll explain," Mr. Rife reassured her. "Take my arm." He and Seb helped the woman up. She seemed weak and unsteady.

"You need to be seen by a doctor," Curtis said. "I'll show you the way." She escorted Mr. Rife and the old woman toward a couple of Special Branch officers. Ivy saw one of them fetch a whistle from his pocket. She had seen an underguard officer use one before, on her parents.

"They're going to clean her memory, aren't they?" Ivy said. "She won't have a clue what really happened here."

"That's the law," Seb reminded her. "It's either that or she has nightmares about Octavius Wrench for the rest of her life. I know which I'd rather have."

Three people, one of whom was floating, advanced across

the cave floor. As they passed Curtis, she bowed her head and muttered, "A rising tide lifts all boats."

Seb squinted. "Hey, is that *Judy*?"

"And *Mr. Punch*?" Ivy's skin cooled with relief as she recognized the fresh-faced quartermaster. His neatly trimmed auburn beard fell over the lapels of his red-tailed ringmaster's jacket, and his black top hat sat imperiously straight on his head. Judy skated next to him, her knee now free of the effects of the Statue Salt. Hovering beside them both was Johnny Hands, whose jester's hat wobbled as he came to a stop. Ivy spotted the long handle of the Sword of Wills poking above his shoulder blades.

"Don't worry, my dear, I know very well how to use it," he said, noticing the direction of her gaze. "I'll have the Great Gates buried and everything returned to normal before you can say 'Scaramouche, Scaramouche, can you do the fandango?'"

"Right . . . ," Seb commented.

Judy embraced Seb, Ivy, Valian and Rosie in turn. "Here you go," she said, returning Scratch and the satchel to Ivy. "Thanks for lending him to me. It would have been lonely back there without him."

Ivy closed her fingers around the little bell. "Good to see you again," she told him.

"You is too," Scratch replied. She could sense the broken soul inside him restless with energy now that they were back together.

"What happened to the Sands of Change?" Judy asked. "It's so powerful—did Octavius Wrench use it?"

Ivy slipped her free hand into her pocket, intending to pull out the Sands of Change, but then she hesitated. . . . No one knew that she had the necklace. . . . If she wanted to, she could use it on Scratch. . . .

"Not that we saw," Seb said to Judy. "Maybe Octavius didn't have the mental strength to wield the Sword of Wills *and* use the Sands of Change at the same time."

"I have the Sands of Change right here," Ivy said, quickly deciding it would be safer if she handed it over to Johnny Hands. She retrieved it from her pocket and held it up for all to see. The gem glittered in the morning sun. "I picked it up after Octavius Wrench dropped it. What will the Tidemongers do with it?"

Johnny Hands collected the jewel into a handkerchief and stuffed it into the pocket of his jeans. "We will keep it safe," he said firmly. "Judy has explained how it has changed her; there may be a way to utilize its powers to help any dead who wish to become Departed, and so end this soulmates crisis once and for all." Regarding Scratch in Ivy's grasp, Johnny Hands winked and lowered his voice: "I'm sure—for special cases—we may be able to loan it out."

"Agent Hands?" a voice called from the trees. "Sir, we need you."

Johnny Hands waved. "On my way!" He patted Ivy on the head as if she was a small puppy. "See you around, Ivy Sparrow. I hope our paths cross again."

After he'd left, Mr. Punch crouched to address them all. He peered into their faces one after the other—Rosie's, Valian's, Seb's and then Ivy's. "Thank you," he said simply.

"What happened?" Ivy asked him. "The army burst through the gates; we couldn't see you—"

"I got trapped inside Lundinor during the fighting," he

explained. "If it hadn't been for your quick thinking, the Dirge would have won." He bowed his head in respect. "Uncommoners everywhere are in your debt." From behind his back he brought out Amos Stirling's journal. Ivy noticed the pages were badly water-stained and crinkled, and she assumed the damage had occurred on top of Breath Falls.

"This was just recovered from Octavius Wrench," Mr. Punch said. "I wanted to return it to its rightful guardian."

"*Me?*" Ivy replied as Mr. Punch handed the notebook over. "Surely it would be safer if *you* kept hold of it from now on?"

He gave her a kind smile. "There is no secret among those pages greater than the one you have just protected. Because of your actions, the entire uncommon world remains hidden. I doubt there is anyone better qualified to watch over Amos's journal than you."

Ivy mumbled a bashful "thank you" as she slipped the journal back into her satchel. She looked at the old lady Mr. Rife was looking after. "Will commoners ever learn the truth about us, do you think?"

"Not all secrets can remain hidden," Mr. Punch pronounced, glancing at Rosie and Valian. "Maybe one day commoners will learn who we are, but until then we must continue to protect them from the dangers of our world and the dangerous people in it. . . ." He gestured toward Ivy's satchel. "Amos spent his life trying to do that. Perhaps, in time, you'll continue from where he left off."

# EPILOGUE

As Ivy placed her hand on the door knocker, she heard the *thud* of feet, and the door swung open.

"You're here!" Judy laughed as she ushered Ivy and Seb inside Hoff & Winkle's Hobsmatch Emporium. It was the winter trading season in Lundinor, and in fitting with the style of all the other shops, Hoff & Winkle's was situated on the ground floor of a rickety old Victorian house with a crooked black roof and dusty leaded windows.

"Sorry we couldn't come sooner," Ivy said with a smile. "We had school."

Judy was wearing faded jeans, a cropped leather jacket and one of Seb's long gray Ripz T-shirts. Now that they were dating, Judy occasionally borrowed his clothes.

In the hallway they bumped into Mr. Rife, hanging his cape over a hook on the wall. He was holding a bunch of pale lilac flowers. "These are for the birthday girl. Sky-blue sun orchids, all the way from Tasmania. I picked them myself."

"You're traveling again?" Ivy asked. Sasspirits like Mr. Rife, she'd learned, healed very slowly. After the injuries he'd sustained during the Thanksgiving Battle, she hadn't been sure he'd be able to operate his uncommon pram so soon by himself.

"Yes, I can't abide staying in one place for too long," he admitted. "Anyway, there's a new skymart opening in the Canadian Rockies next month, and Fred Farrow has been invited along for a preview. I can't miss it."

They crossed the shop floor, which was flanked by clothes racks stocked with everything from ball gowns to hazmat suits, and entered a small, sparsely furnished living room. The air smelled of vanilla and icing sugar.

"Valian's been baking," Judy whispered, "and decorating." Brightly colored bunting hung from the ceiling. Each pennant was printed with a different letter or number so that, all together, they read HAPPY 7TH, 8TH, 9TH, 10TH, 11TH, 12TH AND 13TH BIRTHDAYS, ROSIE! Ivy spotted the greeting cards she and Seb had sent propped up along with several others on the windowsill. A heap of torn wrapping paper lay in the middle of the floor, evidence of where Rosie had been opening some of her presents. On the mantelpiece over the fireplace was the Frozen Telescope of the North, gleaming like a Christmas bauble.

Rosie stood by the table in the adjoining dining room, snacking on mini sausage rolls. Her Hobsmatch—which Ivy had grown accustomed to over the past few weeks—combined a brightly colored flower-print dress with a tasseled brown suede jacket and an old green army helmet, which was far too big for her. "You made it!" She rushed over to give them all a hug. "Valian said it might be difficult for you to get here."

"Nothing we couldn't handle," Seb said. "Happy birthday!" He handed her a glittery gift bag stuffed full of presents. Beneath the wrapping paper were a selection of common items that had caught Rosie's interest after Ivy and Seb had spoken about them—wash-out hair mascara, six mini Bakewell tarts, a sheet of edible paper, a jewelry-making kit, the DVD boxed set of *Star Wars* and a packet of extra-strong mints.

Scratch vibrated in Ivy's pocket. "Happying of the birthdays!" he cried as she brought him out and placed him on the table.

Rosie giggled. "Thanks, Scratch."

Ivy wondered if the next birthday party they all attended would be Scratch's. After much thought he'd decided that it would be brilliant fun to be a human boy again, but he was happy to wait his turn to use the Sands of Change. The Tide-mongers were using the necklace to help those of the dead who were far more desperate than Scratch was, and, in any case, Ivy still needed to organize where Scratch would live when he became human again. He wouldn't be able to fit in her pocket anymore.

Valian peeped his head through the kitchen doorway. His dark brown hair was neatly combed and parted on one side; he'd replaced his usual leather jacket with a smarter cotton version. "Good," he said, "everyone's here. Judy—can you do the honors?"

Judy reached for the switch and dimmed the lights as Valian brought a cake through from the kitchen. It was designed like a world map, with green and blue royal icing. Little models of Rosie in different Hobsmatch outfits stood on each of the seven continents; a small gold candle burned on top.

"It's amazing!" Rosie squealed, taking a seat at the head of the table. "All the places Mr. Rife and I went to on our travels—" She signaled to the Frozen Telescope on the mantelpiece and added, "I've been learning all about our adventures."

Everyone gathered around her. In the candlelight, Ivy scanned their faces. Mr. Rife looked tired but happy. Judy and Seb were laughing. Valian locked eyes with Ivy, clamping his lips together as though he was trying to stop himself from bursting with joy. She wondered whether he had ever dared, during the last seven years, to dream about a moment like this—with Rosie back in his life, the Dirge gone, and his friends all around.

"All right, everyone!" he called. " 'Happy Birthday,' after three. One . . . two . . ."

There was a communal inhaling of breath.

" . . . three!"

And then the group began to sing. It was disjointed and out of tune, but full of vigor. Rosie grinned and rocked her head from side to side in time with the melody; her army helmet wobbled. A murmur fluttered into Ivy's ear, the voice of a broken soul. It stood out from all the others in the room because it was singing "Happy Birthday" with them. She scanned the dining room carefully and tensed as she realized what it was. "Rosie, wait! The candle—"

Her warning came too late: Rosie puffed her cheeks and blew. The flame flickered and died, leaving behind minute glowing embers. Judy turned the lights up and everyone clapped. Ivy hurried around the table, surprised that Rosie was still visible. "That candle was uncommon," she said. "How can I still see you?" She knew that extinguishing the flame of an uncommon candle turned you invisible—she'd used one before.

"That wasn't just any old candle," Valian explained, leaning closer. "It was a birthday candle. They have an additional uncommon power . . . they grant small wishes. Our parents always gave us one every birthday when we were little." He stared at Rosie. "What did you wish for?"

She wound a strand of blond hair around her finger. "I just wished for a birthday like this every year, with all of you here."

"Well, I don't see why that won't come true," Mr. Rife commented. "I'll certainly travel back from wherever I am to celebrate with you."

"Us too," Ivy said. "We're a family now . . . we're uncommoners."

# ACKNOWLEDGMENTS

There are several people I wish to thank for their help while I was writing *The Deadly Omens*. Huge appreciation goes to my editors Phoebe Yeh, Naomi Colthurst and Elizabeth Stranahan for all their advice and guidance while I reshaped and polished the story.

Karl James Mountford, thank you once again for lending your brilliant talents to another title in the Uncommoners series. It's been so thrilling to see places in Nubrook, Strassa and Lundinor brought to life by your rich and detailed illustrations.

Polly Nolan, Sarah Davies and everyone at Rights People, thank you for continuing to represent me and my writing. The Uncommoners books are now translated into many different languages because of your hard work, and I am very grateful.

A special thank-you to Mr. B. and his students at St. John's Church of England Primary School in Canterbury for sharing their ideas about uncommon ties and for coming up with the name for the Tierrific Ties shop. I hope that designing an uncommon object inspired you to find the creative potential in even the most mundane things.

My gratitude goes to my friends Tara, Nichol, Beks, Nat, Charlotte and Sarah for their excellent listening skills, encouragement and good humor. Mum and Beth, I appreciate all the patience and understanding you've given me since I became a writer, during this last year especially. When I don't believe in myself, you're the two people that convince me otherwise.

Peter, thank you for everything you do to inspire and support me. Here's to all of our adventures to come. . . .

# ABOUT THE AUTHOR

Londoner Jennifer Bell began working in children's books as a specialist bookseller at Foyles—one of the world's most famous bookshops—in Charing Cross Road. There she looked after the shop's five not-so-deadly piranha fish as well as recommending children's books to celebrities, royalty, and even astronauts. After having the privilege of listening to children talk about their favorite books for many years, she started writing a book of her own. Jennifer came up with the idea of *The Crooked Sixpence* while packing for a holiday and wishing she could just disappear inside her suitcase and be there already. The world of Lundinor is inspired by sayings from traditional English nursery rhymes as well as the stories Jennifer grew up with about the cockney markets her grandparents used to visit.

jennifer-bell-author.com

# ABOUT THE ILLUSTRATOR

Karl James Mountford was born in Germany and brought up around the UK. He now lives in Wales, where his sketchbooks rarely get a day off. Karl works in both traditional and digital mediums to create his illustrative work. He graduated with a master's degree in illustration and visual communication from Swansea College of Art.

# Nothing is quite as it seems. . . .

Discover a world of wonder and whimsy.
Catch up on the whole series!